317038/
BRANCH i2/14

FIRSTBORN

FIRSTBORN

LORIE ANN GROVER

BLINK

BLINK

Firstborn
Copyright © 2014 by Lorie Ann Grover

This title is also available as a Blink ebook.
Visit www.zondervan.com/ebooks.

Requests for information should be addressed to:

Blink, 3900 *Sparks Drive, Grand Rapids, Michigan 49546*

Library of Congress Cataloging-in-Publication Data

Grover, Lorie Ann.
     Firstborn / Lorie Ann Grover.
       pages   cm
     "This title is also available as a Blink ebook."
     Summary: "Tiadone has been forced to live her entire life as a female
accepted as male in her community in order to survive as a firstborn child. But
when she needs to pass the rites of manhood, she finds the Creator may have
use for her feminine traits after all." — Provided by publisher.
     ISBN 978-0-310-73930-2 (hardcover)
     1. Sex role — Fiction. 2. First-born children — Fiction. 3. Faith — Fiction. 4.
Love — Fiction. 5. Fathers and daughters — Fiction] I. Title.
 PZ7.G9305Fir 2014
 [Fic] —
 dc23

Cover design: Mike Heath/Magnus Creative
Interior design and composition: Greg Johnson/Textbook Perfect

Printed in the United States of America

14 15 16 17 18 19 /DCI/ 20 19 18 17 16 15 14 13 12 11 10 9 8 7 6 5 4 3 2 1

To firstborn females—
may they all be allowed to live.

With thanks to those women who circled
and sang over these bones:

Agent Elizabeth Harding and Editor Jacque Alberta

Family:
Emily Grover, Elle Fricks,
Karine Leary, and Martha Grover

Friends:
Joan Holub, Dia Calhoun,
Laura Kvasnosky, and Justina Chen

and two men:
Wayne Godby,
and David W. Grover, my soul's portion

At first dawn, the condor woke, flew over his dream realized, and dipped the tips of his wings into the great river. The golden droplets flicked from his feathers, and a second set of wings bloomed from his back, wings of divinity. The Four-Winged Condor circled the earth and in his glorious daybreak annihilated all other gods raising their heads from their dreams.

You shall worship the Four-Winged Condor and none besides.

—THE MADRONIAN CONFESSION

The Creator Spirit moved through the empty. His whisper twirled into being desert, waters, and sky. With a soft sigh, he made man and rapion to glorify Him through their days.

You shall worship the Creator Spirit and no other.

—THE R'TAN ORACLES OF FAITH ·

CHAPTER 1

TAKEN

In the dim market alley, I gulp from the dipper. A beetle struggles across the silvery water in the communal rain urn until I flick him free.

That has to be enough bartering and haggling for a day. I hitch up my pack, bulging with mutton and herbs. Father must be ready to head home—if only I could find him.

Behind the adjacent door, bells clink against bones. The priest! I sputter and drop the ladle, leaving it swinging on its twine.

I lurch past the butcher's clay pots to disappear in the market throng, but Priest Sleene crashes open the alley door. *Bang!* Ducking behind a refuse basin, my boots squish in rancid meat scraps.

The priest pauses on the threshold. His black robes clot the doorway, and his attached wings arch stiffly from his shoulders. "Your firstborn female is worthless!" he hisses to the couple inside.

A tiny babe thrashes and starts to cry in the blue scrap of linen dangling from Sleene's clutch. The material is taut across the infant's open mouth and little jerking fists.

Despite the baby's outrage, I can't get past the door without the priest's notice. No one wants to draw his eye, least of all me. "Boy," he sneers whenever he sees me, making my skin pimple.

Sleene sweeps out into the alley. His oiled, bald head glints.

I shudder when the young father stops on the doorstep and bars his pale wife from leaving. She thrusts her thin arms beyond his, and her pleading fingers spread wide. "Our daughter! Don't take her and leave her out there. She'll die!"

Sleene spins and glares at her. He raises his voice above the wail streaming from the cloth. "You and your husband would declare her a male then?" He swings the squirming bundle before her, just out of her reach.

Yes, I beg silently.

"We will!" the woman promises and grasps at the air, but her husband shoves her behind him.

"No! Take the babe." He elbows her back.

"Filthy R'tans," Sleene mutters, as if even the name of my people dirties his tongue.

I grip my knees and duck my head lower, while anger flames my skin.

The woman lunges past, but the man grabs her around the waist and spreads his hand over her mouth.

Sleene glowers. "Tame your woman, Hangrot, or I will."

Crying and flailing in her husband's hold, the woman's shirt slides off her shoulder, and I notice two wet circles spread into the bodice as her body leaks milk for her babe. Hangrot whispers into her ear.

Finally, Sleene shifts the wriggling bundle and stomps past my hiding place. A newborn fist tears through the cloth. To keep from reaching out to it, I jerk back against the butcher's wall and cross my arms.

As the priest turns the corner, his robe whips about his ankles, rattling the attached bells and bones sewn along the hem. The end points of his wings drag through the dirt. Trailing jangles haunt the passageway, and a long black feather sticks in the mucky ground.

Why, why did that man let Sleene take his daughter?

The mother wrests her mouth free. "She'll die, Hangrot! We can't let him leave her out there. Our baby deserves to live! Declare her male!"

Please, so you can keep her! I want to shout.

"Do you believe she could provide for us when we are aged?" Hangrot's voice rises. "A female charaded as a male her entire life?"

The woman starts to answer, but Hangrot wrestles her inside the dwelling and slams the door.

Slowly, I stand. "Yes, she could have taken care of you," I whisper.

Like a mother goat's keen over her stillborn, the woman's cry rises.

I scramble out of the alley, into the market.

CHAPTER 2

RATHO

The square overflows with people. Fourteen years after the conquest, we R'tan villagers still give a wide berth to the ruling Madronians. Clad in roughspun trousers, ponchos, and layered dresses, R'tan sidestep the Madronians in their ornate robes, and we continue to avert our eyes from their kohl-dotted ones.

I scan the temporary stalls leaning against the stone shops and homes, and the boisterous crowds of R'tan clumped before them. Everyone is focused on their business, their desires, their needs. Flatteries and cajoling swoop like birds around the market square. In small clusters, Madronians ring the plaza, attending to their own business.

In the throng, I twist around, frantically searching for Father. Boots splat in puddles cupped in the cobblestones. Three whining children tug their mothers' skirts at the nearby sweet stall. The jelly-coated prickle pear draws water to my quivering mouth.

A woman suckling her babe nudges past me, his tasseled cap marking him as a boy. White-blue milk dribbles down his plump, chapped cheek.

In the mayhem, I turn and find my best friend, Ratho, reaching out and steadying me. He flips his black hair coils behind his shoulder as his thick brows arch over his eyes. "Tiadone! Are you all right?" Concern flows through the touch of his strong fingers.

I pretend I stumble so that I can lean into his shoulder for just a moment and breathe in the scent in his tightly woven poncho. Sunshine and lavender from his father's fields overpower my panic.

The village leatherworker hurries by clenching an armload of belts. He jostles Ratho and me closer, and I don't resist.

"Are you well?" Ratho repeats. Even though he is R'tan like me, he makes the Madronian gesture to ward off evil.

I still his hand, nod, and then wipe my nose on my sleeve. "I just saw Sleene—"

Father grips my arm and spins me around. "Tiadone! There you are." In warning, he rolls his full lips inward and tilts his head to the Madronian acolyte at the edge of the crowd. One of Sleene's private guard adjusts his whip, looped on his belt, and overlooks the market. Father's gray-streaked beard twitches.

I stifle my whimper, which sounds more like a babe than a male youth. "Sleene took a new—"

Father interrupts. "And Ratho!" He smiles but jerks me close against him, his arm resting on the top of my pack. "Nice to see you. Having a good day then?"

Ratho gestures respect and nods. "We'll be harvesting the lavender and tuber fields by the end of the week, Goat Tender."

"Wonderful," Father says.

"What were you telling me, Tiadone?" Ratho asks, his eyes looking straight into mine.

But a woman counting finger squash in her basket cuts between us. "Six, seven, eight ..."

A tall man carrying a honking goose shoves through as well. "Haste, haste! Out of my way," he puffs. Brown droppings are smattered down his sleeve. Once he blusters by, the three of us tighten our circle.

Father pats my best friend's shoulder. "You and Tiadone can talk another time, Ratho. We finished our shopping, but we still need to tend an ailing goat."

"But, Father, I want to—"

"Say hello to your parents for us, Ratho." Lacing his fingers and presenting his palms to my friend, Father indicates we are truly departing. Ratho mimics him.

"I'll see you after the harvest then, Tiadone," he says.

I nod, and he steps away but pauses. His look lingers on me until the crowd shifts, and then he's gone. Immediately, panic burns into my centerself.

"Father." I squeeze his clenched forearm. "There was a baby girl and a mother in the alley." He gives me a strong shake. I stop speaking and sputter as he pulls me to his rigid chest. Heavy goat scent weights his clothes.

It's true. Finally, I've seen it for myself. Sleene murders firstborn girls. My tears dampen Father's poncho.

"It's all right, my son," he says loudly. He nods at the staring acolyte and maneuvers me to an empty space in front of the butcher shop. The priest's guard follows us as Father clasps my shoulders. "Four pork and cheese pies will make you ill in the stomach."

The acolyte rolls his eyes and moves on. From his shoulder cape, heavy incense puffs and lingers over the butcher's fresh slaughter. The headless goose dangling above me drips a splat of warm blood onto my cheek.

With the inside edge of his soft sleeve, Father swipes my face clean. "Have mercy, Creator Spirit," he mouths. He leads us around the dingy building and away from town.

Trudging up our steep hill, the quickly setting sun barely brushes our backs. My pack sits heavily between my shoulder blades. I kick a stone loose in the sandy soil, and it comes to a stop by a shriveled rock rose plant. Father's step crushes the flower beneath his boot. I avoid trampling the small bit that still may survive. The pale pink blossom lies crimped in the dirt.

According to Madronian law, I would have been taken like that newborn. Sleene would have stolen me if Father hadn't declared me male. I was a firstborn girl.

CHAPTER 3

CANDLELIGHT

Father treated the ailing goat at the Bersbad's farm by holding a warm mustard poultice to its blocked teat until it opened, and the milk flowed for its bleating kid. All the while, he shushed the goat's moans exactly like he shushed me.

Now we are home, and night has settled atop our shrub-speckled hill. The coals in the center pit in our pebbled floor barely glow. A couple of stars glitter through the ceiling hole, while a flame flickers in the clay oil lamp on the table.

Father tugs the edge of one window curtain over the other. He sits down on the bench across from me, rubs his hands on his squat thighs. His body is hunched with tension, but he straightens and braces his elbows on our stone table.

"Now, Tiadone, we are safe from Madronian ears. You may question."

The words rush from my centerself, the place of belief and hope in my gut. "You've always told me what the Madronians do to first-born girls when their parents don't declare them males, but today, Father, today, I saw for myself! Sleene's truly going to leave a girl on the Scree to die in that wasteland?"

He frowns, reinforcing the shallow wrinkles between his brown eyes. "It's as I've said, Tiadone—"

"But it never seemed so real before. I saw Sleene and the parents. The mother ..."

He presses his temples and looks to the rafters, intoning the enemy's dribble once again for me. "Madronian priests in all quarters of R'tania dispose of firstborn girls. They limit our race and add necessary males to their soldiering. You know it is the same in every village and kingdom the Madronians conquer. Only girls born within their native lands are always granted life."

I can merely stare at him.

"At least it is only our firstborn females under the scourge, Tiadone." He lowers his gaze to me. "It is a gift that after a male is established, all daughters are accepted."

A gift?

"Tiadone, remember the Madronians believe the first living child carries the greatest strength. Can you imagine them permitting a girl to have that power in a conquered village, or that they'd allow a family to offer only females to society?" He holds his hand up to keep me from cutting into his speech. "And we can be thankful they offer us the chance to declare our firstborn girls male to avoid ekthesis on the Scree."

"But ekthesis is murder!" I clench the table edge like lichen grips a rock. "There's no way a babe can survive if she's left alone in that shale wilderness. And what of those parents? That father? He didn't want to risk his future on a female?" My fear claws up and hisses, *firstborn females are worthless.* "Do you doubt I will provide for you in your old age?"

He reaches over and pats my hand. "I have no doubt in your strength, Tiadone. But yours is the first generation to reach maturity. Our village hasn't seen a declared male proven. All are waiting on you, Tiadone." He squeezes my curled fingers. "They worry about your bird. When your rapion hatches, they wonder if it will join you."

With a jerk, I cover the large egg beneath the gauze wrapped round my waist. My mouth parts hearing these doubts tip from my father. Will this bird reject me?

The rapion gifted me the egg at my birth in exchange for my

placenta to nourish their elderly. I've carried their treasure my entire life, and it will hatch soon. Everything will change, but not as Father hints. "I will guard the land with my rapion on my shoulder and then by my side, as well as any other boy. It will work with me to protect the border of R'tania. Everyone believes it."

My father averts his eyes. "People doubt, Tiadone. The declared are not truly male to some. Think. This is why there are no other declared males, at least in our village."

"That's foolish!" I smack the table and lift the fist-sized, red amulet hanging from the sinew tied about my hips. "How can that be when the Madronians mandate the declared carry a desert cat's heart in his father's hair coils?"

I squeeze the soft mass in my fist, and the dry tissue compresses inside the leather pouch. Together, the heart and hair suppress the femininity I was born with and imbue me with the power of the fiercest, most dreaded in our desert, the cat. The amulet makes me male in my mind and in society. As a declared male, I'll wear the amulet for life and contribute as any other male in our village.

I can't believe any would doubt the fierce power. The Madronians trust their ritual and only watch to be certain I am not too weak as a R'tan for the amulet to be effective. As if that would be possible.

"I have the strength of man and feline, Father. My peers accept me as male. In fights, I am as strong as any."

"There are still some R'tan in our village who privately doubt, Tiadone. Over the years, I've seen the look on adults and children, but it is their fear of the Madronians that protects you. They are forced to respect the ritual. I'm glad you never noticed their secret doubts." His sigh deflates his chest like a violet curls beneath a fingertip. "I've trained you hard to prove your equality and value. To prove declaration is effective so that other firstborn girls might be saved as well."

The table jars as I kick, kick, kick the leg. Father finds my foot and holds it still beneath his own boot. The uneven pebbles press through my sole.

"Well, why don't we just rebel against the Madronians?" I blurt.

"Tiadone," he sighs. "I know I'm the one who has fueled your hatred and anger for the Madronians—"

"As is right, Father."

"But now it is time to accept our situation. It's time as you ready for Perimeter service."

"But what of rebellion?"

He snorts. "What sort of rebellion could you expect from high-desert goat herders, spinners, and farmers?"

"But you—"

"I have done what I can by raising you. You suggest military revolt now? It takes all we have to meet Madronian taxes and bend to their false religion. Everyone lying under the sweeping skirt of these people is drained."

My exasperation wobbles the oil flame. "But we have the rapion, birds that work with us for survival."

"And the Madronians don't. And because the birds have always refused to join them, plain jealousy makes for further oppression." He rubs the rim of the lamp. "Jealousy."

I swear beneath my breath.

Father glances at his javelin by the door. "And then there's still the danger along the border of the Triumverate: cat, sandstorm, or further invasion. There's the C'shah to the east, the Porites to the north, or the—"

"I know," I snip.

He grasps the back of his neck. "Eventually, Tiadone, you will understand our oppression and know there is nothing more R'tanians can do."

I prop my forehead in my hands. Priest Sleene flits through my mind: his pasty skin, his scent of decay, and his musty wings. Fear slices up my back like chipped obsidian.

Father covers the table's shallow fissures with his palms. His square jaw ripples. "There's no more, Tiadone. Just bow and worship as the Madronians dictate, and we will continue to live on our ancestors' land as they did."

What? How are false religion and murder life for the R'tan? Why does our Creator Spirit permit this? "How am I living like our ancestors, Father? I'm made to live as a male when I was born a fe—"

He cuts through my prohibited words with his gravelly, deep voice. "There's nothing new here, Tiadone. It's time to acquiesce, to survive. We'll focus on the upcoming change with peaceful thoughts. Your rapion will accept you, and together you will serve well." He glances at the glimmer of my turquoise egg beneath my wrap. "Still your mind, now, and ready for bed."

Father pinches his tongue between his thumb and forefinger and kills the flame. Darkness grabs me from all sides.

CHAPTER 4

NIGHTMARE

*S*eeing the babe taken has brought my nightmare back. I untwist the sheet, and my egg presses my hip. I scoop up the large, leathery shell. The warmth radiates into my cold palms.

In my dream, I was running from Sleene on the Scree. My amulet was gone. Nothing marked me male as my feet clattered on the flat rocks layered over skeletal baby girls. Open jaws and brittle fingers snapped and crumbled under my boots.

When Sleene's knobby fingers reached out and tore my wrap, my rapion egg fell. It smashed open, and the sticky baby bird stiffened on the gray stones as I woke gasping.

I press my lips to my whole, precious egg.

Like a hoarse goose, Father snores behind the thick bed curtain that divides us. I kick my sheet straight. Now it will be even harder to get back to sleep. And if I do, will my nightmare wisp close again? It stalks me like the fiercest desert cat, trotting over sand.

But I have its heart.

Cupping my egg in one hand and my amulet in the other, I chant, grasping at peace. "I am male, worthy of life."

Strangely, following my horrid dream, I wake in the morning to something tickling my side. I swallow, and jerk back the covers.

Scattered over my sheet are pieces of broken turquoise shell. A thick, sweet scent weaves up from the wet, red stains.

"Chamber of Verities!" I swear by our lost place of worship. The damp, brown bird stirs its slick head on its thin neck.

How did I not hear it hatch? Thank the Creator Spirit I did not crush it!

"Father, my rapion!" I yell, sitting up and whipping open the heavy bed curtain. Our main room is empty. Breakfast dishes clutter the table. Father's slippers crouch beneath his rocking chair waiting for his return. In the center pit, a small fire releases a tongue of smoke that rises to the lip of the ceiling hole.

Father's already left for laboring.

Fright burbles my centerself, because even though I've carried this egg from my birth, the rapion may still reject me. In just moments I will know. I pull the collar of my sleeping shirt up over my chin.

The bird's umber head rolls left then right. The moist, feathered shoulders hump and fall.

My collar slips from my weak hands. If this rapion rejects me, we will not serve together, and my bird will die without uniting with me, without twining. I will be sent off alone as a novitiate to one of Sleene's acolytes.

"Father, there's too much at risk!"

I wipe my forehead on my sleeve, draw my sluggish legs under me, and kneel before the hatchling. The bits of jagged shell bite into my palms. "I have to try."

When the bird fully raises its face, I take a deep breath and release it toward the blue noseplate. A male! *Wooooooo,* my air rushes out and teases the damp feather tuffs ringing his neck. The bird's bulging eyes stay closed like a tight secret.

"Creator, twine us!" I frantically beg. "Please, please!" Another shaky breath in, and the rapion's double lids slide open, one set and then the next. I exhale once more.

The round black lenses focus. The hooked beak separates.

Wooooooo, the rapion breathes into my face. Warm, sweet cinnamon wafts over my brow.

As the sun moves higher, light pools through the open window, making our home glow like my centerself. In the soft breeze, the lavender bush grazes the front of the house, and the scent wafts on the warmth.

Now that the rapion's birth moistness has dried, his feathers are light and puffed. About the size of a rat, he squats on the table, plucking the sand lizard from my hand. He shreds the meat with his talons and beak before swallowing the morsels.

Awe settles over me again like the warm honey sinking into my hunk of hot bread. The bird is twining with me, a declared male! He will understand words and eventually anticipate even my thoughts.

With meat dangling from his beak, I have to fight off my giggle. He cocks his head in question to my snort.

"It's just that you eat like a desert cat tearing through prey." He waggles his eye ridge and returns to his breakfast with even more gusto, causing my chuckles to freely escape. He only pauses to belch.

Finally finished, my bird cleans his beak with his foot and ruffles his feathers, now glinting gold. His wings stretch open for the first time, and thin bones splay beneath the feathers. He teeters at the edge of the table then steps onto my outstretched hand. His talons gently grip, but I'm not fooled; he's taking care not to pierce me. Taking cautious, shallow breaths, I hold my hand steady.

He tilts his head, blinks slowly, and fills his chest with air. His beak opens and a tremolo note slips free. More follow, and more, skittering after each other like a row of weaving quail. A soft melody forms, and his whole body sways.

"Song?" I croak. My rapion sings? Rapion are silent birds, must be silent birds! My fear thrums against his music. I fight the urge to fling this aberration from my hand. I stiffen and pant. What will the Madronians say? Sleene? What kind of evil will they imagine?

The song pulses to an end, and my breathing slows. My rapion draws the folds around his beak up into a proud smile and lowers his head. Exasperated, I try to mimic him. Apprehension has walked nimbly up my back, and shame sits heavily on my neck.

Of course there is something terribly wrong with my bird. Of course there is.

CHAPTER 5

INTRODUCTIONS

At midmeal, I hear Father drop his gear outside on our little front porch. I pick at the rocking chair's woven seat while waiting for him to come in. My strange rapion sleeps on my lap, his belly distended nearly as round as my amulet.

A few nuzzles with the curve of his beak in the crook of my elbow abated my pulsing panic after his song. His mesmerizing hum folded peace into my centerself. I couldn't fight off the tranquility or reason it away.

When I moved with him over to the chair, he plopped down in my lap and tucked his head to sleep. The twining felt complete. Already, I can't imagine being apart. Did I actually think to throw him from my hands earlier? He sings, and I can't change that. I have more troubles ahead than thorns in a chasm full of prickle plants, but I am his bearer.

"It's been a complete morning of bloodsuckers and fly bots," Father complains to himself. Water splashes, and I know he's scrubbing his hands in the outside basin. "One herd left," he says, as his boots scuff across the dry stones.

Finally, he steps into the house, running his wet fingers through his hair twists. Sunlight skims his bulky shoulder and sets me aglow anew. "Tiadone!" he gasps. "Your rapion!" He rushes to my side.

"We've twined, Father, the male and I! We've twined! But shhh!" My smile slips. "He, he sleeps now."

"You've honestly twined?"

I roll my lips and nod. "And I've named him Mirko. Fierce strength."

"Excellent choice!" he says eagerly yet softly. "I knew the rapion would accept you! I knew it." He touches my cheek with the calloused heel of his hand. "You see? We are blessed! Haven't I always said there would be a twine?"

I sniff and smile. "More times than bells have rung on Sleene's robes."

He huffs at my tease then hums a chord of praise to the Creator Spirit.

I shift in the chair. I have to tell him, but he goes on.

"Oh, he's a beauty," he says. "The deep brown with flecks of gold, and the broad crown. I can't wait for him to wake to see his wingspan and compare him to the bird I tended!" Father gazes at Mirko with his hands behind his back. One never touches another's rapion. Even the Madronians honor this out of fear of our mysterious link. Although I know Father must be dying to pet Mirko. His bird was released after their service together so long ago.

"Yes, but—" I try to swallow, except my mouth is too parched. "Father . . . Mirko . . . he has song."

"What?" He snaps upright.

I look down. "Mirko sang. He sang as we do in worship. Well, notes, I mean."

"No! No, Tiadone!" Worry skitters across his broad forehead. He clutches his belly. "You're certain?"

"I'm not jesting," I whisper.

He covers his mouth. Mirko's side rises and falls in sleep.

Father rubs his face. "Well . . ." He drags his fingers through his beard. "We have read of Rapion Singers in the *Oracles*."

"Can it be good that Singers are mentioned in forbidden R'tan writings?" I rip off a loose straw from the seat. "I know it's my fault, Father. Being declared male—"

"Shh, Tiadone!" He drops with a thud onto the bench by the table.

Mirko burrows his beak beneath his wing and hums a tune. Father's face washes pale and his silent mouth hangs wide open.

CHAPTER 6

RETURN

Go forward. You'll both be fine." Father nudges me, and instead I lean back into his pressing hand. Aside from special ceremonies, the Madronians prohibit R'tan from the Rapion Cliff Dwellings, where all released birds return. Without the other villagers, the sheer red sandstone walls surrounding us seem to squeeze me like a sidewinder swallows a rat. Above, only a fracture of cobalt sky arches between the rocks. Six days old, Mirko peeks from my blue poncho pouch. He is shaking worse than I am.

"Perform your offering, Tiadone. The rapion must gather Mirko's scent to welcome him back to their clan when he is mature." Father knocks my slim shoulder and whispers, "Try ... try to keep Mirko quiet."

I roll my eyes. As if I can silence my rapion. He has sung erratically since hatching. Nothing I say or do stops him. I worry the edge of my poncho, weave the corner tightly under and over my trembling fingers.

Father speaks his prayer to thwart rejection or attack and backs away from my outstretched hand. His eyes dart to the high, purple rock fissures. I know he longs to stay and possibly catch a glimpse of his formerly twined rapion, Nuncia, but this is a lone bearer's offering.

Forcing himself to leave, the edge of his brown tasseled poncho slips out of sight. Between my teeth, my lip pops. I lick the blood droplet away.

There is a real reason to be anxious. Will my offering suit the Cliff Rapion and guarantee the safety of a home for Mirko when grown? Will they reject me now as a declared male and attack us? Or instantly try to destroy my bird because he's a Singer?

I hitch up my loose trousers, grip the basket handle, and inch over to the Stone of Offering. Barely breathing, I lift out each of Mirko's shell pieces and line them along the obsidian shelf. The turquoise bits make a mosaic against the black sheen. The last piece sticks to my sweaty fingers, but I pull it free and tip it gently onto the edge.

"There," I whisper, and hold Mirko as close as possible. He snuggles into a smaller ball, making it look as if I'm still wearing my egg wrap. Thank the Creator Spirit that fear at least keeps my rapion quiet.

The soft red sand shifts under my fingers as I squat. Though the cool air is tinged with the acrid odor of rapion droppings, I take a big breath anyway, then lean back and shout the liturgy my people have recited for every Return. "The rapion has hatched. I am his bearer! Accept my return of your offspring's shell!" My voice pings up the porous red and pink walls. Then silence. Even the wind stops nudging the gray, thorny weed wedged in the rock base.

With one hand, I palm my amulet, and with the other, I hold Mirko tightly. "Please, stay quiet."

Sweat dribbles down my side.

I rock on my tight haunches.

Whoosh! The air is sliced by brown wings. Creamy undersides rush over my head. Rapion dive down the cliff and encompass me. Bird after bird rips past. Signicos the size of goats, raised by boys, and Miniatae smaller than field mice, raised by girls, beat and flap. Male and female of both kinds clip by us.

My throat clogs while I stand below the sweeping talons and hooked beaks. I press Mirko closer yet. The rapion race along the ground, then shoot high, only to skim down the sides of the curved walls again and again. More and more thrust their heads from the dark crevices and pour out. Some fly with legs lowered and talons outstretched. Others drop fast with tucked feet and folded wings before snapping them open and climbing upward again. I hunker, but there is no attack.

The whirling sand pings my face. Lifting my hair twists, an energy spins through the canyon. Clean hope swirls down inside me. Mirko, however, cowers and soils my poncho pouch.

"I am Signico Mirko's bearer!" I shout.

The shell is gathered from the stone, piece by piece, by different rapion, until there's nothing left. Mirko is accepted!

Slowly, the air empties. The birds fly back into the shafts, and the last gold-spotted female Signico beats her great black-tipped wings over the top of the tallest rock face while the tiniest male Miniata zips past my nose into a nearby fissure.

Sand dribbles from my clenched fists. Wobbly, I stand and beat the knees of my trousers clean.

Mirko is a stiff ball when I pull him from my pouch. His eyes blink fast, and he tries to scurry back into the pocket. "It's all right." I gulp to steady my voice. "We're safe, Mirko, and you will be welcomed to your clan when you return!"

He stills and peeks about us. Using the material, I swipe him clean, pull the poncho off, and shake my hair twists free.

Mirko rubs his head against my stomach. I cup a hand to my mouth. "My thanks!" I shout against the rock, returning the power the rapion have poured into me. I kick the sand in celebration, and raise Mirko above my head.

With a shrill, joyful note, he ruffles, leaps, and takes his first flight. He flaps his weak wings hard to circle me. His bold whistle runs high, intricately turns back to a lower register, then rises higher than before.

I hold my breath until it's obvious — no rapion are returning. They've accepted a Singer or have flown beyond hearing, I don't know which, but my worry is gone. By his song, Mirko pulses his ecstasy through me instead.

"You are a brave Signico!" I proclaim. He chortles and heaves himself to my left shoulder, then grips the leather pad and clicks his beak as his breath rushes in and out. I stroke his back. "You are fantastic, Mirko."

He trills agreement, and the walls stretch to the beautiful sound. The warm stone and purple shadows twirl his song to the sky. I turn from the cliffs. Proudly, we hike home.

CHAPTER 7

BESPELLED

Having graduated two months ago from Madronian male secondary school, following my five years in their elemental level, it's a relief to no longer daily drill their catechism, study their oppressive military history, and pretend to believe and understand their complicated superstitions. I'm free of the endless chants and recitations. Now I wait in isolation with Mirko for the call to serve. I'm even excused from Weekly Worship since rapion are a distraction to the Madronian service.

Until we leave, the days are stuffed with household chores. At least with Mirko, his joy and discoveries make even the dullest routine pass quickly. Even now, with a prideful grin, he chortles and drags a crooked pine branch to my kindling stacked behind our round house. "Good work!" I say, and lay my armful of sticks on the pile. He ruffles and noses his wood closer.

A chilled gust whisks a windweed against my leg then carries it off. Mirko flies up into a willow bush. He watches the weed roll past our home and bump down the steep hill toward the village, bumbling along like an old woman with a mouthful of gossip.

I pause, taking in the view I won't have soon. The town's busy market square before the marble temple pointing to the sky. Beyond, stone houses dot the combed flat land ready to yield crops along the river Sineck. Farther out, farms with clustered pens squat in isolation.

I know behind the morning haze, three mesas roost about the great valley, circling R'tania along with the Chendon mountain range to our north. Our own mighty Eastern Mesa rises beyond my village, south of the Rapion Cliffs and Scree. Across the village and high desert is the Southern Mesa. I shade my eyes and see it, tucked under a ridge of dark clouds. The Western Mesa is completely hidden right now.

When school ended, Ratho and I rolled the Madronian knuckle bones and found we will work the East. The other boys' rolls placed them in the two more distant mesas.

Soon, Ratho, with his twined, and Mirko and I will be patrolling this edge of our land against the Triumverate. We will join Perimeter Defense to raise alarm for cat, sand, or invasion in our portion of R'tania.

"Tiadone!" The call breaks my thoughts. It's Ratho! My center-self hiccups.

"In back!" I answer. We haven't seen each other in weeks because of the harvest. He hasn't even met Mirko. I need my best friend's approval.

Ratho runs past the curve of our house. His trousers are a little short and brush about his goat boots at the ankle. He's grown again. Have I as well? When he spots me, a huge smile opens his face until a dimple sits deeply in his right cheek.

My hands raise in an informal greeting though I long to hug him as I would Father. "There's no better friend," I chant under my breath. "He will accept Mirko."

A faithful follower of the Madronian beliefs, he gives me the formal salutation for reunion after long separation. His hand passes over his forehead, his chest—which seems broader all of the sudden—and his stomach. I return the greeting to escape his chide. My eyes linger on his lips, holding a secret.

"Tiadone, look!" he shouts and turns. Perched on his pack, his hatched Signico flaps open its wings. The nose plate is yellow. A female! Her brown tail feathers are extra long, and her feather tufts framing her thighs are thick. She hops to his shoulder as Ratho spins back around. He laughs. "Isn't Thae perfect?"

"She's beautiful, Ratho! And look at Mirko!"

"Mirko?"

"Yes!" My rapion bounds from the bush to my shoulder. He turns to the side and beats his wings. "Mirko!" I announce, flinging my arms wide.

Ratho's admiration gleams as he reaches out and seizes my arm. "You are blessed as well, Tiadone! Mirko is a perfect companion to my Thae. Look at his deep color and fierce beak!"

I curl my hand over Ratho's and draw in his warmth. My other hand brushes my amulet, which is so obvious without my egg wrap. Does it remind Ratho more strongly that I was female? Or maybe with it in plain sight, it reminds him of my greater strength, especially now that I have a twined Signico.

All is perfect until Mirko bugles his joy. Ratho jerks from my palm and stumbles backward. Thae burrows under his hair until only her thin face peers at me through his black hair coils.

"You, you said Mirko's perfect," I plead.

"But he is with sound?"

"It's song. He has song like in … R'tan history. It makes him even more special." Mirko poses. He's magnificent, grown to nearly two feet in length from head to tail in a month.

I jump so that Mirko might meet Thae in the air. My rapion crouches and soars as my boots thud back on the ground. Dust rises about my feet. Thae only tracks Mirko, barely moving her eyes.

"What's wrong?" I ask, already knowing but not wanting to believe it.

Ratho pets Thae's foot. "Nothing," he mutters, looking away.

I lift my arm, and Mirko floats down to me. "Do you want to practice the javelin?" I try. "All my chores are nearly done."

"Uh. No." Ratho kicks at a dirt clump.

"Come on," I needle. "It will be even more fun with Thae and Mirko. We only have a couple weeks left before Perimeter." I step forward and grip Ratho's shoulder. He jerks back, Thae arches out of his hair, and with a whistle, Mirko shoots above my head to defend me.

"Stop it, Mirko," I say. With an angry, shrill note, he turns and alights next to the kindling. He pecks at the patch of red sand. "What's wrong, Ratho?"

He stalls by pulling Thae into his arms, where she buries her head under his arm. Frowning, he finally admits, "Your rapion is bespelled with sound like the Featherless Crow."

I gulp. "Ratho, that's ridiculous. The Madronian Four-Winged Condor has sound, and there are many other types of birds with song."

"Yes, but the Four-Winged Condor has the voice of man, and song birds do not twine with men." Ratho inches back and lowers his voice. "The Featherless Crow calls men to the grave for the Condor. He's the one without any strength but his song, and that is what he uses to capture souls."

"I know of their Featherless Crow, Ratho." I stamp my foot, and Mirko chortles a rebuke as well. "But my rapion sings like others have in R'tania. If you knew anything about our own history, you'd know that. He is strong. Just look!"

Ratho and Thae barely dart a glance at Mirko, who hisses. "Stop it," I say to my bird, but he only darts his tongue out in mockery.

"See!" says Ratho. "A singing tongue of evil," he whispers.

I raise my voice. "You undo those words!" Mirko pierces the air with a screech. I shout, "He's not evil, and you know strength has nothing to do with song!"

Ratho argues, "All worthy rapion are silent." And as Mirko's sound ends, Ratho's words snip the quiet into my centerself. "That Signico should have been left on the Scree!"

I'm stunned, and Mirko snaps at the air. Holding Thae tightly, Ratho crosses his chest for protection and walks away from me.

"You, you . . . coward!" I pick up a stone and hurl it at his back, but it flies past his shoulder. "Why don't you just say it, Ratho? Say I shouldn't have been declared male. That I should have been left on the Scree and never gotten Mirko in the first place. Maybe he sings because of me, and that scares you!"

His shoulders hunch, but he doesn't even look back. He turns past my house and is gone.

"What do you know about anything? Stupid Madronian myth." At the same time my anger bursts out, dread rushes in to take its place.

"Left on the Scree" rings though my mind.

I wipe my nose on my sleeve. "It's not true," I whisper. Mirko leans against my leg and hums. "You are worthy to serve," I tell him, and he blinks up at me. "And so am I."

And then some part of me pathetically wants my friend. "Please, come back," I whisper. "Please, Ratho. I need you to believe we can do this."

Mirko flies into my arms. Chortling, his talons pluck my poncho and snag yarn bits. I ruffle his head feathers. Will we patrol the Perimeter alone? Chamber of Verities! I at least hoped for Ratho's acceptance.

Mirko nudges his face against mine. My jagged breathing evens out against his soft feathers.

"Ratho will come around, Mirko. He's just rigid sometimes." Mirko cocks his head.

I go ahead and give in to the looming hopelessness. "Anyway, for all we know, the Mesa will collapse the second I walk into it to serve since I'm declared." He chitters and stares incredulously at me.

"Well, it could." I kick my kindling pile and send the sticks twirling in the dust cloud I've raised.

CHAPTER 8

ANY OTHER GIRL

The night wind rustles along our thatched roof and down through the smoke hole. I shiver, scoop the juniper shavings off the table, and squat beside our firepit. Empty, it is like a yawning mouth. Carefully, I stuff the fresh-scented curls between kindling. My pile collapses. "Chamber of—" I start to say under my breath.

"Don't swear by the name of our R'tan holy place." Father wipes our plates dry. He carefully stacks the dishes on the shelf over the clay sink basin.

"Even though the Chamber's been lost for centuries in the Mesa, I can't swear by it?" I mutter.

"Not the holy place where the Creator Spirit whispered his *Oracles* into the rock, Tiadone."

"I know, I know." I cut him off before his lecture drones on.

"If reverence doesn't hold your tongue, how about fear? Just last week Priest Sleene put old Solumo in the box for only mentioning the R'tan Creator Spirit."

I crumble a brittle twig. "No! Is he all right?"

"I stopped by his farm yesterday, and his daughter told me he's been released. For his first offense, he only received five lashes. He's expected to recover."

My skin pimples.

"Now, stack the kindling again," Father says, nudging his hair twists out of his eyes. The steam from washing the dishes has freed a few short, wiry gray hairs to rim his head like a faint crown.

I lean the twigs against one another. This time the wood stands in a cone, mimicking the flare of a girl's dress. Mirko chitters his approval from the rafters and puffs up. I clatter our fire stones together until the wood catches the sparks.

Flames spurt through the kindling while Father settles behind the changing canvas. It is the only place we are safe to worship our Creator Spirit. He lifts his palms in prayer.

Do other R'tan worship privately like us? Do they have sacred R'tan writings hidden in their homes? Or do they all bow to the Madronian Four-Winged Condor like Ratho's family?

Does anyone hoard any other books? Something to read beyond Madronian history and catechism? If so, I wish I knew them.

I can't imagine what it was like for Father to grow up with books in reach. And yet he had to watch the Madronians destroy them all. The thought cuts my centerself.

Mirko drops onto the braided rug beside the fire and waddles into a squat. He stares into the light, making his golden-brown face shimmer. I smile and rub his eye ridge until his pale lids slide shut.

Restless, I get up and pace, ending in front of the metal gazing plate hanging on the wall above our shelves of bottled goat remedies. If I were still a girl, I'd be preparing to move into the temple as a visionaire, to be secluded for a year. There, with the help of a tiny Miniata rapion, I'd have foreshadowings of dangers so that I could alert the village. I'd live far from Perimeter, in safety. Well, as safe as one can be near Sleene.

Father has twitched the canvas closed. Rocks clatter as he removes our *Oracles* from behind the shallow stones.

In one motion, I spin my amulet until the pouch hangs behind me. I pull my brown hair back like Father's friend, Frana, wears hers. My cheekbones are sharp beneath my light brown skin. What would it be like to be known as a girl? To dress and work as a female? To whisper with friends in tight circles like other girls do?

Before Mirko's hatching, I used to stand with the villagers in the square during Weekly Ritual and watch the visionaires in service, poised on the roof of the temple. Their long white robes contrasted with the tiny brown rapion flitting around them. I'd ignore Sleene's sermon and the acolytes' chants to the Four-Winged Condor while I coveted a Miniata like the visionaries had, even though Mirko's big Signico egg filled my wrap.

What would Ratho think of me if I hadn't been declared male and still been allowed to live? Blushing, I trace my arched brow. I've seen him relieving himself, his dangling male parts.

Well, it doesn't matter what he would have thought. All that's important is that I carry equal or greater power than Ratho in my amulet now; I know in my centerself that the male desert cat's heart is fierce enough to have frightened away all of my former feminine traits while even now manhood spirals into me through my father's hair coils. It is at least one thing the Madronians have right. If it wasn't true, they wouldn't let me live.

When Father first explained I was formed differently than other males, I denied it. I threw a tantrum and shouted that I was never a female. But even I could look at a goat and see I was lacking. It was then Father began his mantra: Don't dwell on your past. Live now as any boy and appreciate life.

I try to live without shame that I was a female. I push and press it down when it sneaks in. But there are times when reality snaps and frees it completely, and I tumble. Like when I'm near Sleene at Weekly Ritual. With his wings dragging along behind him, sometimes he stops and sniffs me as if he can smell my former, weaker sex. My centerself pounds until he moves past.

If I were a second-born girl, I do know Ratho would never have said such things about my rapion. Comparing Mirko to the stupid Featherless Crow is ludicrous. That thing supposedly reeks of garlic, for Verities' sake.

But then, as a second-born girl, Ratho would not be permitted to even speak to me—and I would not have Mirko. I let my hair twists swing free and cover much of my face. Turning away, I spin my amulet so the pouch hangs correctly.

"Father, what does the Creator Spirit say of my male declaration?"

The canvas twitches. "The *Oracles* say living is the greatest honor."

"I want my life to be honorable," I whisper.

Mirko yawns and tucks his head beneath his wing. The fire snaps at my hopes.

CHAPTER 9

THE FEAST

My father and I approach the village square in the sunset's pink blush. Torches flame along the sandy path, and sandalwood incense curls in the air. On my shoulder, Mirko shifts his weight from one foot to the other, anticipating our Initiation Ceremony. This quarter's secondary school graduates enjoy a celebration tonight with their families. Boys vow their next day's departure for Perimeter, and girls pledge their dedication to the temple. All will be able to see Mirko and I have twined. Maybe as Father wishes, others might declare their firstborn girls now.

Jitters run down my own legs as noisy chatter knocks against the sandstone buildings. We come round the corner and see the crowd in their most festive tasseled and striped clothes. I straighten my own zigzagged poncho, and Mirko ruffles his feathers into place.

Father boldly leads us into the party. He smiles at a group of married ladies with little hats cocked on their foreheads. The styles mimic the larger brimmed hats of their husbands. Hesitantly, the ladies nod back.

A couple of children run past in their Weekly Ritual finest, ponchos and bows flouncing. Yet, when they spot Mirko, they zip off like nervous Miniatae.

The acolytes stand apart in green robes trimmed in gold. Nearby, the few Madronian military are rigid in their helmets and vests, crossbows at hand. They remind us of our subjugation, even now.

A better sight is the food! Covering the tables are roasted geese, brown flat breads, and sweetened tubers. Warm oil rings the platters of meat. The desserts are honeyed pastries and edible flowers.

Making our way to an open table, conversations stream past. Parents brag about their daughters' dainty Miniatae or discuss the wingspan of their sons' Signicos. I spot a few girls across the courtyard whose rapion preen and flutter about them. The birdlets are adorable, but none seem as perfect as Mirko, I think, and he nuzzles my ear.

A quartet raises a tune on pipes and drums in front of the butcher shop. How is the grieving mother who lives next door? The one whose baby girl was taken?

Finally, we do have to inch past a group of Initiate Males with their beautiful Signicos, and they instantly quiet. Each bird is just a little different than the other. One deeper brown, another more golden. One larger, another bigger beaked. All staring. Is each boy and rapion relieved not to have to serve with me? Even though I've known Dwino, Col, Klane, and the others all their lives, and they know me almost as well as Ratho does?

Rippling outward, silence whooshes through the crowd. Even the musicians' ditty peters. Obviously, Ratho has spread rumors of Mirko. I tighten my muscles to still the trembles.

As we expected, Mirko gathers himself up and belts out a greeting to all the other rapion. Most duck and hide in their bearers' hair coils, but Father straightens his shoulders, and I try to do the same. We slice through the whispers licking our ears like sidewinder tongues and sit down at an empty table.

"The one who sings!" Sleene darts close. My throat pinches as I lean away from the leering priest whose eyes flit between my amulet and bird. The murderer's wings graze my face.

When Mirko hunkers and growls a line of deep notes, Sleene gawks; his blue-lined lips move silently in prayer. Does he, too, think of the Featherless Crow? It doesn't seem so. He looks more enamored, actually. I shiver. Finally, he steps away to an acolyte gesturing for his attention.

Sleene's lust for a rapion is obvious. In the midst of the commotion and clatter, his eyes linger on Mirko, and occasionally slip to the other birds. The corners of his mouth glisten as he strokes his black wings.

The musicians resume their tune, and the noise in the square climbs again. Benches scrape the stone, and friends call to one another from table to table. The villagers take turns staring at me and Mirko, but he can't be their only interest. There's so much to speak of because the harvest has kept them from their regular gossip, and tonight is a celebration. Or could a few R'tan actually respect the memory of the Rapion Singer?

I sit in the whirl of sound while the birds flutter the air around me. Awe overpowers fear, and I absorb the moment, not dwelling on how the priest's acolytes form a barricade around the seating area.

I grip Mirko's scaly foot. Humming, he nuzzles my fingers with his smooth beak, and I nestle my nose in his neck feathers. This is our Initiation. Finally! It's not as if Madronian law makes us serve; R'tan youth have performed this service for centuries. The Madronians just make the conditions harsher, and the soldiers we aid are theirs.

Mirko quiets as Ratho's father enters the plaza, his heavy ram boots clomping. He knocks back his hat and looks for a table for his family.

Ratho's little sister, Tleana, grasps their mother's checkered skirts. Hanging from the girl's neck, a red Miniata egg nests in a tiny crocheted pouch. She peeks at me and hides her face before she sees my greeting gesture.

Ratho pulls his eyes from mine, and my hope that his opinion of Mirko has changed drops with a thump. The family scans the square. Only our table has space for them.

"Greetings," Ratho's father finally says to mine after approaching. Father offers an open palm welcome.

They join us, but Ratho chooses a seat at the opposite end of the table. His damp hair drapes around Thae, who is settled on his shoulder. His hair is always so curly and soft right after he washes it. He catches me staring and a regretful look passes over his face. He misses me too.

With amazing forgiveness, Mirko sings a greeting to Thae, but Ratho and his Signico turn their backs.

I cover my pain and anger for Mirko's sake. "They will come to know your worth," I whisper to him. "We can wait out their foolery." He chortles agreement and waddles. I wish I could believe myself and forgive as quickly.

Father's friend Frana bustles over and slides in next to me. Her fleshy arm squeezes my waist. Mirko leans forward to see her and chitters. "Congratulations, Tiadone!" she exclaims. "Oh, he is the beauty among them all!"

I hold my hands in a cup shape to receive her shocking praise. "Thank you, Mistress." Her enthusiastic nod bounces her short hair coils all over her head.

Sleene climbs the winding stairs to the podium clinging to the Monast above the great locked doors. The square quiets again except for Mirko's simple song. A few people nearby turn and glare or steal another peek at him.

Sleene clinks his garment bells and bones, then leads a collective prayer to the Four-Winged Condor. "Let these initiates serve the country well, alerting all of danger. Let the females have visions and the males identify threat of the Triumverate. By your power, Four-Winged Condor."

As if their god empowers R'tan youth! I restrain from spitting over my shoulder as Sleene's acolytes return the responses many R'tan only mutter softly.

Finally, the prayers conclude, and we feast! I cram every worry and irritation aside. We are in public with Mirko. None have been rude, aside from staring. There have been no threats against us or seeming rejection. Soon, maybe even Mirko will seem as normal as the other rapion, like tonight, how a declared male is counted among the male initiates.

I eat my fill of roasted roots and mashed nuts over sidewinder. Mirko munches in my trencher, making his tail sweep happily in my lap. Father and Frana talk, occasionally including me, as all our bellies round with food.

When Frana turns and speaks with Ratho's mother, Father reminds me, "There will be nothing like this spread at Perimeter."

"For certain." I wipe my mouth on my linen napkin. With that thought and just a bit of time left, I notice that no one is at the dessert table but one Initiate Female. I excuse myself and Mirko for seconds of currant pudding.

"Hello," says the blond girl hovering by the sweets. Her gauzy pink dress floats just above her ankle boots. A newly hatched Miniata sits atop her head. The birdlet is as small as a sour cherry! I blush at the girl's boldness. "I am Jenae." When her brown eyes flit over my amulet, she doesn't shrink back. She does glance about to see no one is nearby. "This is Zoae." The birdlet bobs and swings down into one of Jenae's elaborate hair loops.

"I am Tiadone," I whisper. Mirko nips my ear. "And this is Mirko." He twitters.

Jenae giggles and rocks on her heels. "He is amazing. Even more so with his song." Mirko grins and chortles.

"Zoae is beautiful also," I add.

"Thank you!" She hands me a bowl of pudding. "I envy you going to Perimeter!" she whispers in a rush, her breath damp with vanilla. "Be extra careful." Jenae winks and hurries away from the approaching acolyte.

The priest's guard stops before me. "Ready yourself for Initiation," he says with a thick Madronian accent.

I bow and weave my way back through the tables. The villagers look when I pass, but I'd rather think on Jenae's voice, so kind, like Frana's. And she liked Mirko. See, Ratho! My rapion is worthy to serve. Others believe it. Can't you? And she envies me going to Perimeter! Imagine!

I give up my pudding to Father. He and Frana wish me well, and I join the line of initiates. The families cheer while Sleene dabs his lips with his draping sleeve and leads us from the square.

CHAPTER 10

INITIATION

In the deep twilight, we follow the priest. Ratho leads the males, whereas I am last before the females. Jenae is the last of all. The cool air whisks about my face and charges my nerves until my scalp tingles.

Our winding row stops behind the Monast Temple, beneath the huge sculpture of the Four-Winged Condor; its broad wings arch above us. Everyone stands apart from Mirko and me.

Sleene glides before the condor's jutting, lowered head. "Our subservience to you," he chants. "I am your spokesman." Then he strokes the wood and kisses the idol's open red beak, first the upper and then the lower half. His hand reaches in and slowly caresses the black tongue.

Like a wet goat skin clinging to my back, the Madronian religion weights me. I shrug to be rid of it, but it holds fast. How similar their god looks to our rapion, but without a speck of life.

Mirko flaps his wings and resettles, which causes a chain reaction down our line. "Be still," I whisper to him, but it doesn't stop him from rocking from one foot to the other.

Against our backs, the beautiful Monast releases warmth from the sunlight it has absorbed through the day. The white marble shimmers pink now. This was the R'tan holy place of worship before the Madronians claimed it. Aside from our visionaires serving with their Miniatae, R'tan are restricted from the building. It's hard to believe that once Father and Mother worshiped the Creator Spirit, inside, whenever they chose.

"Proceed into the Holy Garden," commands Sleene. He motions the Initiate Females to long swings newly hung from the out-stretched necks of tall condor sculptures scattered throughout the area. Each bird is frozen in a classic war position, with feet ringed by rock rose and pale green succulents. The girls sit nervously on the slats; their dresses wave below the teetering seats, above small clay pots in the greenery.

Father says this was once a beautiful Meditation Garden where one could contemplate the Creator Spirit. Now it's lost in this maze of statues.

"Defend as men," Sleene intones, and draws each boy by the arm to stand behind a girl. My forearm throbs beneath his crushing thumb. Mirko flaps above us until Sleene releases me beside a girl with a chubby face and a Miniata on her shoulder. Her rapion ducks its head to Mirko, who sings in return. The girl and I exchange timid grins. Another who doesn't fear my rapion overmuch!

Across the garden, Ratho is teamed with Jenae, who coyly smiles. When Ratho beams and his dark eyes loiter on her, my face grows hot. I should be his partner ... if I wasn't declared male, of course. Mirko clicks his beak in my ear. I relax my fists before anyone reads my irritation.

Jenae reaches out and brazenly straightens Ratho's sleeve, which doesn't meet his wrist. He has grown again, for certain. Will he end up being the handsome man Frana always predicted? I force myself to look away from Jenae's fingers lingering on his hand. She will be whipped if she is caught.

Sleene lifts a long taper and lights the candles clustered atop the tall column in the garden center. The flames twist and jerk. With a whistling breath, he kills the taper blaze. "Swing," Sleene shouts, and spins, throwing his arms wide.

With Miniatae clinging tightly to the inside of their hair loops, the girls pump their legs hard. A few don't clasp their dresses between their knees and ankles, and the forward motion exposes their leggings. The opposing swing backward covers their immodesty, but still, I spot several boys leering. Ratho looks away from Jenae exposing even her thighs!

Who is this overly friendly girl at ease with both me and Ratho? At least he isn't completely taken by her.

"Ignite the pots, Initiate Males!" Sleene dances between us.

Hearing his command, Mirko flies to the column and retrieves a candle. He drops it into the pot below our swinging girl. Other Signicos retrieve candles and deliver their fire. The ancestral stones within the pots ignite and fling icy green rays into the air while the girls' skirts caress the chilly radiance.

The fires extinguish and smoke puffs high. To check our efforts, Sleene whips through the garden, making his hooked toes, cluttered with rings, slide forward in his sandals. He leans down, and the tip of his clammy nose chills my ear while he sniffs my scent and straightens my amulet. I stiffen to keep from jerking from him and showing my fear.

"I am watching," he murmurs, making my spine crackle. He steps away and throws out another command. "Males, claim the pots for the Four-Winged Condor! Bear your new roles for the village, country, and Madronian Empire!"

For the R'tan! I counter. After the girl I'm with swings forward, I lunge at the pot and feel for the stiff wire handle. I grasp it and stumble to the side when the girl flies back through the air.

"Circle the visionaires, Initiate Males of Perimeter Defense."

I hurry around the swinging girl with Mirko on my shoulder. I can no longer see the others through the hovering sweet smoke. Only the head of this condor peers down at me.

The Miniata buzzes his wings, and the girl swings higher. Invisible drummers strike a rhythm on the Monast roof, and the acolytes' chant drifts from the Vestuary. The smoke absorbs the sound but bells it out again. Rattling his robes, Sleene's face looms close then shrinks away.

I fall to my knees in the raked sand, and Mirko lands beside me.

My face drops to the ground. When my grip on the handle loosens, the pot rolls, pouring smoke over my face. Mirko sidles to me.

I breathe with the Madronian beat and creaking swings. The females should be having their first visions while power infuses the males. I close my eyes and inhale. From the smoke comes pulsing strength, and—a vision of my past.

I burst from a bubble of warm blood,
my wet cheek pressed
against my mother's inner thigh.
Reaching,
she pulls me upward, kisses my slippery lips,
and passes.
Father howls.
In anguish and shaking panic,
he lops at our birth cord,
and then hacks coils of hair from his head
with his black knife.

Sleene scowls
but extracts a pink drained heart
from a bag at his waist.
He slides it
into a crimson amulet pouch
along with Father's hair.
My flushed body thrashes
against the sinew
Sleene ties to my small, bare hips.
While I scream against the act,
he glares
at the amulet lying
atop my shame,
and my father begging
at his feet.
Mother's blood

stretches in strands
between Sleene's steepled fingers.

At the Cliff,
rapion accept my placenta
to feed their ancient.
They fly the bloody mass
up into a high crack
in the circling cavern wall.
An egg, clutched in talons,
is flown in return to Father
and dropped into his palms.
A turquoise egg.
Mirko!

CHAPTER 11

SECRETS

Despite the cold night, sweat pastes my clothes to my skin. Sleene said nothing to me after Initiation. He only picked a scab from his scalp, flicked it into the air, and watched me leave the garden.

Father and I hike up our hill. Mirko rides my shoulder, chittering to himself.

"Initiation went well, Tiadone?"

"Yes."

"I understand the ceremony hasn't changed much despite the Madronian presence."

"I guess."

"And as the other males, did you feel the strength imparted to you from the Smoke of Sending?"

"I did." But do I also say: I saw a vision; or, Like a female, I had a vision; or, I saw my mother for the first time, saw her brown hair curling along her jaw, her full lips, and fierce blue eyes?

Should I say: I saw, while in your deepest grief, you didn't hesitate to save me no matter the cost to your future? Questions I've always pondered flap about my head. You loved me, Father, but why didn't you consider leaving R'tania so I wouldn't have to be declared? Of course there are benefits to being male, but it would have been less complicated to remain female. So, why didn't you merely leave?

I tug my poncho away from my neck. Does my father suspect

my vision but is too afraid to ask? Or does he think Mirko, a Signico, would inhibit visions within me? Is my twine with Mirko
the reason my vision was strangely of the past, unlike visionaires
who see the future? Maybe Father fears to ask at all as I fear to say
anything of it.

My drying sweat chills me despite how I hug myself. This was
probably just one vision from the Creator Spirit, brought on by the
ancestral stones.

Mirko rubs his head against mine. I reach up and ruffle the
feathers on his breast.

Father grips my free hand. "I will miss you, Tiadone," he says
into the darkness.

"And I you." I squeeze his palm.

"You are my soul's portion."

I brush away frightened, confused tears. Mirko leaps from my
back and leads us through the dark.

Back home, I stare at the fig-shaped sponge. It is inside a loosely
woven bag with a long string dangling from the end. The sponge is
actually the root of the prickle plant, romnis. Its little purple flowers
are common across our high desert. When I need more, they will
be easy to find. I cannot believe what Father expects me to do with
this thing.

"The flow will occur only once a month."

I look at the rafters. Frana has hung clumps of rosemary to dry
about the smoke hole. Mirko nibbles a sprig and dangles his tail
above my head.

"It is like the estrus of goats so they might bear kids after mating."

My whole body flames with the thought of men and women acting as animals. But then how else are children conceived? I wipe my
forehead on the back of my hand. Ratho and the other boys joked
and hinted such things, but I never believed them.

Well, mating is not my worry. Declared males remain single after
Perimeter, never to have a spouse to live and work alongside. Never

to have children of their own, firstborn girls or boys. Father chose solitude for me the day I was born.

"I should have taught you this sooner. But"—Father rubs his hands on his knees—"it is hard to speak of, and your body has been slow to change. Regardless," he sighs, "I tell you now. It is the way of women, even those declared male, we presume." He tentatively pats my hand.

I draw back.

"Frana, your mother, the visionaires," he adds.

I pick at my thumbnail. This seems a betrayal. Doesn't my body know I am declared male? Won't my amulet restrict this flow as it thwarts every other feminine reflection, thought, and desire?

"Tiadone, at Perimeter this will remain unnoticed." He looks at the rafters now, purses his lips as if not wanting to go on, but he does. "If your estrus time has begun, go to the latrine periodically to remove the sponge by the string, squeeze it free of your flow, and reinsert it. And remember, you'll have private steam pockets for regular cleansing."

I grind my heel against the floorboard. He nudges the thing toward me.

"The sponge will hold several days blood if you are on patrol. Look, I have sewn a pouch to the underside of your pack." He lifts my bag from the floor and peels back a hidden flap. "Keep the sponge concealed here until your first bleeding." He quickly slips the strange object inside. "I have placed the sap of the grintso plant along the edge of the flap. You can open and close it repeatedly." His shaking fingers press it closed, hiding this thing from our sight.

I sit on my weak hands.

He coughs and nods, maybe gathering his gumption to finish this horror. "Some women line their undergarments with the fluid from pinoni stems to prevent any escaped flow from absorbing into their skirts. It's a soft repellant."

I stare along the curved edge of the ceiling. A spider dangles from a thread until Mirko flies over and eats it.

"I'm told chewing the pinoni leaves also quiets the thrumming pain many women feel."

The pause is so long I nod to fill the queer space.

"Now then, do you understand, Tiadone, what to expect eventually?"

"Yes, Father."

"And you see it is imperative to keep your estrus hidden? You need nothing more to draw attention to your difference at Perimeter."

"Yes."

"And you will of course bind your breasts when they grow."

I nod but bury my chin in my clavicle.

"Tiadone." He lifts my face with two fingers. "You are declared male. There is no true shame in your body."

I close my eyes. There must be. Look at all I must do to hide it.

CHAPTER 12

WHY

Mirko resettles in my hair coils spread over my kidskin pillow. He shovels his beak into the twists and hums. Still, my breastbone feels as if a boulder balances upon it.

I kick at my covers. Mirko clicks his beak, climbs out of my hair, and perches beside me. He nips my shoulder. "Ow!" I whisper. Already he has grown to sense I want to speak and pushes me to do so. His round eyes catch the moonlight. He blinks.

"Fine!" I yank my sleeping tunic and amulet straight. There are only a few hours left for questions that I have secreted away for years.

I sit up, stirring my sleeping curtain. My bed rests next to Father's higher one. With mine pulled out from under his, we fill nearly half of our home. At least the arrangement puts me close to the firepit for the last flickers of warmth. I slide apart the bed curtain a sliver.

"Yes, Tiadone."

"Why didn't you and Mama just leave R'tania when she carried me? She could have birthed in a foreign land, free from the Madronians, their male declarations, and their ekthesis."

"Madronian law forbids emigration."

"But it's rumored people have left. Certainly if you wanted—"

"We didn't know whether you would be a boy or girl."

Mirko leans into my leg. "But it was possible I'd be a girl. And it's not as if you already had a boy and my sex wouldn't have mattered. Like how Ratho's parents got to keep his little sister."

"We prayed you wouldn't be a girl."

Shame hollows my centerself like a sand-filled wind carves a grotto. My parents prayed against my first identity. And they chanced an unanswered prayer.

Mirko squawks.

"Well" — I force strength into my wavering voice — "wouldn't everything have been easier is we had just fled after my birth, after — "

"This is our home, Tiadone."

"Yes, but we could have crossed the desert and gone to Randan, or escaped to C'shah even. There you could have read the *Oracles of the Creator* in open air. And found other books — who knows, maybe whole libraries free to every person, not just the priesthood." I drop my voice. "If you had, I wouldn't be leaving for Perimeter in the morning." Because truthfully, who really knows if declared males can serve? Perimeter is so different than the work of a visionaire.

Mirko hums and rubs his eye ridge on my knee. I stroke his feathered back and try to breathe evenly. In the moon shaft, Father throws his arm across his eyes.

"Why don't we just run now? Couldn't we try? The Madronian Empire doesn't reach everywhere," I beg.

"Now, Tiadone? When Mirko must be returned to the Cliffs after your patrol? It is impossible. His life would be endangered if we left before then."

I bite the inside of my cheek.

"You must raise him and then return him to his clan. This is your duty for his service. Think of it! What greater dangers would we have without rapion assisting our boys in Patrol and enabling visions in our girls? And you know if he was returned to the Cliffs now, he would be attacked by the grown males."

"Then why didn't you go before I even received Mirko?"

He rubs his beard into his shoulder. "Tiadone, I will try to explain." His voice catches. "The Madronians took so much when they conquered: our religion, our books and libraries, most of our customs, our firstborn daughters. But they did leave us our language and ancestral homes. It was their way to gain our submission and trust." His sigh is sour. I turn my head for a fresh breath. "Aside from speech, my home and wife were all I had left. You know both sets of your grandparents were killed in the Madronian invasion. And then by your birth, I lost your mother."

I completely turn away. Mirko moans.

With a jagged breath, Father continues. "I could not face a wasteland alone with a newborn babe." He chokes. "And still today, I am not able to separate from the Cliffs of the Rapion. Nor will I be able to after Mirko's return."

I sit up quickly, and Mirko flaps to stay on my bed. "But apart from ceremonies, the Cliffs are prohibited anyway, Father!" At the thought, my head aches, but I smash down my fear to stay in the argument. "And since the Madronians ban all grown rapion from the village, you most likely won't ever see your bird again!"

"But I am still close to her," he whispers. "Even though I haven't seen her, I almost feel my Nuncia at times."

I want to yell: nothing will come of it! And: I am your child! My face burns. Because you didn't want to leave a place, or because of a feeling that Nuncia may be close, you kept us here and plan to stay?

The sharp words cling with talons on my tongue. I ball my sheet in my fists. Your twining was over, Father! It is a crooked excuse that you couldn't and won't leave the Cliffs. There might be other lands that twine, where rapion and people coexist their entire lives. We could travel and find one!

Father breaks my thoughts. "This is the best I can do," he says. "Your mother would approve." He slides the bed curtain closed between us.

Mirko brushes his head against my cheek. My father places the Cliffs and his ancestral home before me?

The next morning, the village drumbeat rolls up from the valley, instructing the Initiates to report to service. The distant drummer's mallet clods my temple. *Thump, thump, thump.*

On the front porch, I squint at the early sun and breathe in the sharp pine scent. Father's gear by the wash basin, the lavender bush, the yellow straw flowers lining the front path, our small home—they'll all be here when I return.

Right now, it's as if our disagreement the night before never happened. Father closes the door behind us and hands me the javelin he has carved, the first weapon for young men on patrol. Among the curves and coils he has cut, a Signico flies above a house like ours. Father has trained me for years with a simple shaft. I am honored to receive this embellished weapon. "It is beautiful," I whisper.

He smiles and pinches my poncho closed at the neck. Then he pats my pack slung over my shoulders, tightens the hip knot of my amulet.

My anger still simmers, but I can't leave my father with bitterness between us. Like I'm banking a fire, I push the heat down and cover it.

I'll report to Perimeter and try. Just as I tried when Mirko was born, and the Creator Spirit twined us. What else can I do? Who knows how I will be enabled? Doubt slurps the words right out of my mind.

"Keep the *Oracles* within, Tiadone."

"Yes, Father." It will be a year before I can read our sacred book. It is one more loss.

"Play the Madronian game. They will make everything harsh and hard, but you are strong," he reminds me, or maybe himself. Distracted, he searches the sky. My rapion leaps among the encrusted branches of our twisted pinyon pine. "Come down, Mirko," Father calls.

"Mirko," I scold. He releases his hold and dives to my shoulder.

"That is not usual," Father says under his breath, "that he moves so far from you. Keep him close at all times. Others will notice if you don't. There is enough to draw attention already, and we don't want them to have cause to doubt you further." His eyes graze my amulet one more time.

"I will try." I rub my cheek on Mirko's feathered leg while he plucks my hair.

Father clears his throat. "So, I believe you're ready. Keep the watch well, Tiadone. I have no doubt that you will succeed."

Really? The vibrations in my stomach shake out to my hands and feet. I clutch my javelin to still the ground tremor within me. "Yes, I will succeed."

"There you and Mirko are, Tiadone!" Frana bustles over the crest of our hill, her layered skirts gathered in her plump fists, her flushed cheeks puffing. "I didn't want to miss your Sending, dear. I heard the drums."

"Yes, it's time," I manage to eke out.

"Let's take a look at you then." Shielding her eyes, she walks past Father and around me. Her hare bracelet jangles her nervousness while her goatskin shoes scuff over the porch. "Very fine," she announces. A false grin slides on and off my face. "Now here's a medicinal sack for you," she says. "I'll just tuck it in." She reaches around and slips her gift into my pack.

"Thank you for your kindness, Mistress," I manage.

"Oh, it's nothing. You know the herbs and ointments." I nod. Her voice wavers. "All right. I just saw Ratho making his way out. You'll be sure to catch him in no time. Well, then. There you are." She winks at Mirko, who grins back at her. "You'll be back and receiving your Labor Assignment before you know, dear. What is it that interests you again? Leather working, butchering, goat tending?"

I wrinkle my nose, Father raises his brow, and Frana goes on quickly. "Well, we'll see what the priest assigns when you return. Let all forbid a soldiering position." We thumb our chins and spit to the left.

Frana adds, "For now, may Patrol fly fast and protection hover its wings over you and Mirko. Your father and your ancestral home will be waiting for your return." She squeezes his hand.

"Yes, we'll be right here," Father says.

"I'll come back after my service passes." My voice cracks.

"Of course you will," says Frana.

Thump, thump, thump. None of us moves. With slanted eye ridge, Mirko whimpers. A small cloud whisks over the sun, and I shiver.

"Go well," Father says.

"Go well," repeats Frana.

"Stay well," I whisper. Mirko clambers to the top of my pack as Frana smothers me in a hug. Her cries stop her words, and finally she lets me go.

Father steps close. He drags his fingers down his cheeks and makes the blessing hand gesture on my forehead. His fingers mark the pattern with his tears. "Go, Tiadone. Grow to manhood. Protect the village, and thereby our people." He wraps me in his arms. I squeeze him tightly. "I'm sorry," he whispers. "This is my best effort." He pries me off and steps back. "Go. You have a day's journey ahead."

My feet refuse.

To help me one last time, he takes Frana's hand, and leads her inside our home. "Go, Tiadone," he says, and slowly shuts the door.

Mirko nudges my neck and hums. I inch backward one small step at a time.

CHAPTER 13

THE TREK

Along the copper ridge, my boots kick up orange dust. It coats the inside of my mouth and nose, after half a day's walk. Mirko flies a distance over the sand and scrub, then returns, only to fly ahead again. By the far copse of rintell trees, Ratho hurriedly walks, and Thae is only a smudge.

Even though we've imagined reporting together our entire lives, Ratho's refused to wait for me. Fine. I'll report to Perimeter by myself. Stepping around a prickle plant, I lean into the gust.

Would the other boys going to serve at the other Mesas be as prejudiced against Mirko as Ratho? Who knows? But it sure wouldn't ache as much.

A rattling sidewinder and the occasional wind whirl fill the quiet. Ahead, the enormous Eastern Mesa sweeps up from the sand. I aim for the northeast craggy corner.

With each lonesome step in the wide wilderness, anger bubbles free in my centerself. This is my father's choice. Not mine. Would my mother have chosen this for me? Would she have stood by while I was declared male? Or would she have convinced Father that the three of us should run before the amulet took full effect?

My vexing empties me further. Maybe my mother, too, would not have wanted to leave our home and the Cliffs just to provide an easier life for me. I kick a rock and send it spinning. "Maybe, as a newborn, I should have been left to die on the Scree," I mumble.

Flapping to my shoulder, Mirko hisses a rebuke then hums in my ear. I touch my head to his breast.

My glance skitters over the open vista. Beyond the rocky desert and the distant humped dunes are other lands. Countries we could have run to, free from the Madronians. We might have found a haven.

I squint at the hazy horizon. Like Father said, I can't run now and endanger Mirko, but could I ever hope to journey and find my way on my own? What would another society think of a declared male?

A grain of sand flings into my eye. "Ouch!"

Mirko chitters concern. I tear up and rub at the granule, which blurs everything. My stumble over a clump of scrub makes Mirko fly upward. "Verities!" I hiss but regain my footing, and my rapion alights on me again. The sand washes out of my eye with one more swipe.

I'm a fool! Who am I to even consider traveling alone? If my father couldn't, certainly I can't. It is enough to try to live successfully here. And right now that means facing the Mesa. Enough. I straighten my poncho and amulet.

Mirko hums and nudges peace into me. I take a deep breath. Peace even if Ratho speeds ahead faster whenever I gain on him. The festering flea bot. He will miss me, eventually. I know it.

The sun passes out of its zenith. The wind whisks my eyes dry.

Creator Spirit, protect me in the Mesa as possibly the first declared male to patrol. My mind turns. *Do you hear me?*

CHAPTER 14

WELCOME

After hiking all day, through dusk and an hour or more of darkness, finally I reach the glow of the fire that teased me for so long. I nudge my heavy feet toward a group of boys gathered around the warmth, and they turn to look at me.

Coming into the firelight, I don't recognize any of them from my village. All seem just a tad older than me; a few with chin stubble, one with broad shoulders. Each wears the dull issue clothing of Perimeter Defense, the color of sand. Signicos, looking so large compared to Mirko, peck and preen at their sides, barely glancing at us. Most of the rapion are as tall as a goat already, the females slightly smaller, even with their spotted crests. Full-grown, they are too large to ride on their partners' shoulders now.

While gawking at the height of the shadowed sandstone looming behind them, I bump into a light-skinned boy. "Watch it!" he growls.

"Sorry," I rasp.

Mirko rumbles, and everyone freezes. Throughout my life, I have been nervous before new people as I waited to see how they reacted to my amulet, my declaration. Now, Mirko's song draws at least half of the attention. Whispers weave behind dirty hands.

Bugling, Mirko stretches his wings and then flaps above my head. The other rapion hunker beside their bearers. Thankfully, no rapion challenge us. At least physically. Only the fire cracks and snaps a response. Sparks glint upward.

I clear my tight throat. "Hello." I squirm my heels in the sandy dirt but make a greeting hand gesture by placing my thumbs together. No one returns it to me as Mirko lands on my pack.

Finally, a female rapion bursts through the air and circles me and Mirko. My rapion dives off and joins the fully grown beauty above the fire. Her bronze feathers glisten in the light as Mirko's song pulses with the flames.

"Hello." A tall boy with a face of freckles steps into the circle. He assesses me and counts me a male, as his eyes don't narrow in the least nor does he step back, thank the Verities. "Welcome to Perimeter Patrol," he begins, but is quickly sidetracked. "He is amazing!" He tilts back his head to watch Mirko.

"Thanks," I manage to say. Everyone silently watches the two rapion dive and roll. They twirl above the sparks. Alone.

Mirko's joy brims between his notes. His rush of happiness nudges back my anxiety.

The youth grins, showing crossed front teeth, and points. "That's Els. My name's Lalo." He swings his matted hair twists behind his shoulders.

"Tiadone and Mirko," I answer.

He nods and pages through a roster. "I was notified you were reporting with a Song Rapion. What a specialty for the Carterea division. They are out patrolling, but on return I'm sure they'll be eager to welcome you."

My hope uncrinkles. Maybe I will be welcomed to my own division better than these boys seem to receive me. I straighten my poncho and pack.

"Two things about Perimeter, Tiadone. Youth are always coming and going." Lalo raises his voice. "And the second is the Carterea are always stronger than this lazy Baltang division!"

The boys pretend anger while their rapion flap. Lalo laughs and rolls the roster closed. "Follow me." He clicks his tongue, and his rapion drops to walk beside him. In height, her head nears his hip.

Mirko glides to my pack, and I sidestep a couple of boys. "Spawn of an acolyte," a Baltang mutters and leans away.

I grip hold of Mirko's leg. "Don't rise to it!" I whisper. It is not worth one boy who matters nothing to us. Mirko gives in to my plea.

Beyond the fire circle, the darkness skims us. I stop beside Lalo. Three curved entries are cut into the Mesa stone. Lalo points to the first. "Eating Pit, Govern Quarters, and Clinic. The second holds the Armory and Briefing Ring, and the final contains Shelves and Steam Pockets." The holes are lit by glowing lichen strands clustered on the sand.

Lalo notes my stare. "No lanterns or candles at the Mesa; the caves are full of lichen. It's harvested when these dull." I nod. "The two other mesas don't compare to ours. You are lucky to join us." Els claws the sand and bobs her head. "Shift change is every evening, but initiates receive a day for equipment issue and briefing."

"That's good," I blurt.

"Glad you approve," he teases and knocks my shoulder. "You'll bunk in the Ninth Alcove."

"Yes, patroller," I reply.

Els leaps into Lalo's long arms. "Oof." He pulls the great bird close. "He's just a big birdlet," he teases. Els nips at the boy's poncho. "Mercy," Lalo says. A nervous snort escapes me, and Mirko bugles.

"Okay, enough." Lalo grins and pets Els. "We need to finish up."

I poke Mirko to pay attention. Quickly, he ruffles and settles down.

"Let's see. Your shelfmate is the other initiate, Ratho."

I ignore the heat creeping up my face. To sleep so near Ratho before his rejection would have been comforting, even exciting. Now it may only cause him to push me away more. Still, my stomach flutters at the thought of being shelfmates. I fiddle with my amulet.

"The spring is at the edge of the Common; latrines are twenty paces beyond. And what else?" He scratches Els' head. "I guess only that evening meal's past. If you head in and get some sleep, you might not miss breakfast."

"Thanks for your help, patroller."

Els jumps to the ground as Lalo tucks the roster under his arm and makes the gesture for welcome with both hands. I offer the return.

Lalo lopes back to the fire. "Off you go then," he calls to me. My legs stiffen. "Check out your bunk!"

With Mirko on my pack, I find I'm ducking through the hole into the great Eastern Mesa before I can think twice.

On the sand path, lichen strands glow and illuminate the tunnel twists and turns. A chilly breeze lunges through the irregularly arched passage, joining Mirko's warbles. The Mesa's inside is cool as Father warned, but my hands still sweat. I try to drag them dry along the rough walls.

I am the first declared male to ever step here for patrol! My feet tingle. *Father, are you out of your mind? Will the walls collapse for this heresy?*

I squat and still my centerself. A full breath in and out clears my eyes. I wait for the rumble. Wait.

Lifting my face, I see the truth. There's no disaster; the Mesa stands firm around me. "It is well!" I whisper to Mirko, but he is distracted, hissing at the lead figurines in the narrow wall niches. I shrink from the statues of the Four-Winged Condor, stand, and edge forward.

I count the sleeping alcoves we pass. Another hairpin turn and I've found mine. A nine is carved into the gritty orange wall. I lean against the steady rock and rub my tired face. Thank the Creator Spirit for his protection!

In the room, Ratho sits on the top shelf. He's faced away and hunched over Thae. Neither turns to us. I inch farther in. Our quarters are small, rectangular, and Ratho will lie directly above me. Every night.

I slide my javelin next to Ratho's in the rack opposite the doorway then climb quietly onto the empty lower rock shelf. The cold eats through my trousers as Mirko explores the carved circle inlaid to one side of the head of the ledge. He pecks at it and settles in a heap.

Ratho sniffs. My reflex is to reach out to him. I stop myself in time, pull everything from my pack, and hang it on the hook above Mirko. I hold my kidskin to my nose and inhale the scent from home. Before my tears begin, Mirko tugs it from my grip, curls up on it, and raises his eye ridge.

I smile. His levity brings a glow to my centerself. So far, we're all right.

Adjusted to the Mesa temperature, I peel off my poncho and place it in the small alcove shelf beside the hook. There's also a hole carved beneath my bed, perfect for my socks and boots. I flex the aches from my feet.

A key sits in the wooden door at the foot of my ledge. I pull it open and find it is a place to keep things safely. I set aside a hunk of goat cheese and a hard biscuit and stash the rest of my food and Frana's medicinal bag inside. The key turns easily, and I tie it on my trouser thong.

Bits of biscuit stick in my throat, but I have to eat. Earlier, it was impossible, yet now we are here. The Mesa hasn't crushed us, and no one stopped me from entering as a declared male. Madronian fear does protect me, as Father said. What's a bit of name calling? Even the coarsest and most vulgar do me no harm.

Mirko's song raised suspicion, but we'll prove ourselves soon enough. Even to Ratho, and I'll have my friend again. I cling to the thought, take a swig of water, and gulp the biscuit down.

Mirko waddles to my side and begs with big, round eyes. I share a chunk of cheese. "Ratho, do you want some food?" I whisper.

"No."

At least he answered. I snuggle Mirko to my cheek, but he leans away and rips a hunk from my bread. There's a shred of normalcy.

CHAPTER 15

STEAM POCKETS

Three boys file past with their rapion and towels. Their shadows shift along the tunnel while their jibes and laughter ping off the walls.

I trace the grooves in my shelf carved long ago by the R'tan. The lines flow through the broad, smooth swaths of color. Seeing this makes it easier to imagine the small villas our people once carved within the top of the Mesas.

A Madronian of some sort whisks past our doorway. I huff and cross my arms. How ironic that this great rock was our ancestors' protection from enemies and now they are here with us.

Father says when our people forgot the Creator Spirit, they settled in the valley between the monuments and forgot the Mesas' secrets too. Without habitation and care, tunnels near the surface collapsed. Pocked openings eventually let in the elements. Waters flooded and drained, leaving stagnant pools behind. Our villas clogged and collapsed; our history rotted. Even the Chamber of Verities was lost, and the line of prophets died. More than that, when the Madronians attacked, we couldn't escape to our Mesas. We lost our freedom.

I stroke the edge of my shelf. At least our people always cared for the corners of the Mesas for patrol. Even the Madronians understood and continued the work.

"Save a pocket for me!" a patroller yells and runs by, kicking up sand. I roll onto my side and scratch Mirko's head. He licks his beak and closes his eyes.

It's probably good the Madronians never could map what was left of our villas or find our ancient Chamber of Verities. They claimed the Four-Winged Condor swirled it to oblivion with their conquest.

I sit up. Did the holy Chamber of Verities ever really exist? Did it speak to the prophets? Record our history in image? Pulse and strengthen R'tan boys on patrol? I press my hand to the porous rock.

Nothing.

Since Mirko now snores on my shelf, I grab my threadbare towel and climb out quietly. The sand is gritty under my bare feet. I have no clean clothes until my uniform is issued tomorrow, but it will feel good to be cleansed as I am so grubby. Father said the area was private, but that doesn't stop my centerself from lurching. Being naked, with only my amulet on, leaves me vulnerable, shamed as my body reflects my former state. I hate it.

I follow well behind a group of boys ahead, memorizing the turns, as they joke and roughhouse. Their rapion flutters remind me that I should have brought Mirko. But he is so tired from our day's journey, and if I return for him I might not find my way back. I'll bring him next time.

Finally, one last bend ends in a dim narrow hall. Each boy and Signico squirms under the layered skins covering individual steam holes.

I move into the empty hall and choose a pocket for myself. "Hello?" I say. With no answer, I lift the heavy goat skins and stumble down three stairs. *Crack* goes my shin against a shelf. But for a cluster of coals and rocks in the corner, the room is black, and now my bruise will be also. I rub the spot. I am sure the pockets are darkened to support the Madronian obsession with modesty, but wouldn't a few strands of lichen add a bit of safety? At least I do not have to look at myself, I suppose.

Behind the shelf is a stagnant puddle, smelling of rust. In a moment, I'm out of my tunic, trousers, and underclothes and giving them a good beating to remove the dust and sand, the whole time feeling my amulet tapping my thighs.

Discovering a pair of tongs by the coals, I pluck hot stones off the red heat and drop them into the water. Steam sizzles hot mist against my cool face.

My muscles relax as the moist air presses through the tiny room and sweats my anxieties away. Crouched on my haunches, my long march eases. The steam soothes and assures all is well.

Eventually, the air cools and I stand, toweling off my sweat and grime. After plucking the rocks from the water and dropping them back on the coals, I dress and emerge from the skins into the hallway.

The sounds of rapion and boys relaxing in their pockets float into the hall. I'm sure Mirko will love the steam too.

The way to my shelf comes with only a couple of missed turns in empty passages. Lalo meets me at my alcove with Els behind him. "Tiadone, you've found your space?"

"Yes. Thank you."

He grins. "And your skin must be reddened from the Steam Pockets. You found them as well?"

"Yes."

Lalo's gaze settles on my amulet, and he immediately blushes. Quickly, he looks away, around, and behind me. "But your rapion? Where is Mirko?"

"Oh." I rub my towel through my twists to stall. I really should have returned for him! I inch into the alcove. "He's just there, waiting on my shelf."

A question hovers on Lalo's forehead. "That's odd. I don't remember seeing him come down the passage."

I snap my fingers behind my back. Yawning, a sleepy Mirko flaps to my shoulder.

Lalo shakes his head once. "Huh. I must have just missed him. At any rate, rest quickly now, as you'll be called for morning meal before you like."

"Certainly. We'll get to sleep." To show submission, I pull my first two fingers of my right hand past my forehead.

Lalo shakes his head. "No need, Tiadone. The Madronians don't give R'tan any authority here." He lowers his voice. "They keep us equal and fighting."

"Oh," I say.

"I hope your beginning's a little easier than mine was. But then, no matter how tough the start is, the end is worse," he says. Els rubs her head against his trouser knee as Lalo stretches his back and looks at the ceiling.

Of course! He'll release his rapion shortly. My throat coats with bile, and I swallow the nastiness back down.

Lalo runs his fingers through Els's crest. She leans her entire body into him when he pats her side. Sniffling, he wipes his eyes on his shoulder. "Sorry about that." He smiles weakly.

I nod and Mirko gently clucks. That brings a grin to Lalo. Rubbing his face, which now likely rivals my own in redness, he says, "After six days at the Lookout Tower, I'm ready for sleep. Good night." He moves down the passage with Els close at his side.

"Night," I call. Inside our alcove, I crawl onto our shelf.

Ratho leans over and eyes Mirko. "You were unnaturally separated," he says in that superior tone he knows I hate. I roll my eyes until he pulls from sight. Thae whisks her tail up and away.

Fool, I rebuke myself. I must keep Mirko close. It's not like I need more to fuel doubt in our abilities.

I climb onto my bed and dust off my feet. "You have to stay at my side, Mirko," I whisper. He chortles and pads around in a circle before squatting in a lump. We don't need any more difficulty. Our pack is full!

I curl on my side. Of course Lalo's right, though. Nothing will be as bad as the end of Perimeter.

CHAPTER 16

FIRST DAY

A drum sounds, mimicking the beat for Weekly Ritual. I open my eyes to dimness and stone. Mirko scratches his tiny ear hole beneath his feathers with a talon while I groan and sit up. Patrol! I inhale. My centerself beats double time to the drum.

I leap from bed, toss my poncho over my head, then cram on my gritty socks and boots. Ratho jumps down with Thae as Mirko swings to my shoulder. We grab our packs and hustle into the empty passage, my stomach grumbling loudest. "Did you miss evening meal also, Ratho?" My question flies free before I can censure it.

"Yes," he answers, maybe out of habit only, but it is good to hear his voice first thing this morning.

We run headlong into the misty dawn. Before us, the scrub desert stretches out to the dunes that roll to the horizon. The other boys are going through their packs at the edge of the Common, beside a shimmering spring bubbling from a Four-Winged Condor statue. The water spills out of the curved creature's mouth and splashes into a runnel down its tail.

I don't spot Lalo to ask for direction. "If I'm remembering, the far entrance is for meals," I say, pointing. Ratho barges past, and I run after. Our rapion cling tightly.

We bend and enter but come to a halt. In the immense room, fire pits glow behind an empty, sunken eating area. The Madronian cook's gnarled black beard rests on his stained apron. Into a great pot, he pares a tuber while a lanky R'tan sweeps the eating ring. His bald head sprouts a little tuft from the crown, the mark of apprenticeship.

"Excuse me," I say. The two look over at us, my amulet stopping them in place. "We are the initiates, and we were told this is where we'd find our morning meal."

The bearded cook recovers and smacks the side of his knife on the cutting board. The apprentice laughs outright.

"Where might we find food?" Ratho asks.

"There is none until tonight," the cook says, licking a bit of something pulpy from the back of his hairy hand.

"But the drum just sounded," I say. "We came quickly." Mirko adds a low grumble that leaves the cook and apprentice gaping.

A towering Madronian ducks into the cave from an opening to the right. "So here are the initiates." His long braid is fed by a full head of slick brown hair. First, he flips the tight coil round his neck and over his shoulder, then he crosses his thin arms. "I am Govern Droslump."

Ratho and I make a gesture of respect. What will this man do for us? His delicate eyebrows point down to his long, thin nose. As he saunters closer, his floor-length tan cloak drags about his feet, making the embroidered condors along the edge dart and withdraw. The cook and apprentice sidestep from the room.

"You've missed the meal generously offered," Drosump murmurs. I lift my chin, but my stomach groans its hunger loudly.

Ratho bows his head. "We came at the drum, Govern."

The Madronian narrows his eyes. "And that means you are tardy." He stops in front of us, flicks my amulet with a long fingernail, and then slaps Ratho's face. My fists curl, though I don't even have a second more to react before the govern strikes my cheek next.

Ratho and I jerk our heads straight. Mirko growls, and Thae writhes. This man is a brute! A Madronian no better than Sleene. *Play the game* flits to my mind—Father's reminder.

"So this is the Singer," he grumbles.

"Mirko," I say, and refuse to take a step backward.

"Interesting." He clicks the tips of his nails together. Pulling his gaze from my rapion, he says, "The meal is over, and you are bound to be late for your briefing. Report for clothing issue before I administer serious correction. This is a poor beginning, initiates."

We salute the govern and back out of the cave. His stare remains on us until we turn into the open air.

I curse. "How unfair was that?" I ask Ratho, who rubs his cheek.

"Completely," he mutters.

Across the Common, Lalo washes his face at the spring. A few boys fill their water sacks along the curved tail while others scrub their teeth with tooth sticks.

"Tiadone and Ratho." Lalo waves while Els preens at his feet. We jog to him. "So you've found meals are early and correction quick?" The other boys at the spring huff.

"Who cares about early? The food is tasteless," a weed of a boy adds.

"True," another partroller agrees, one much stockier.

"But I'm starving," Ratho tells Lalo.

He grasps Ratho's chin and examines his cheek. The redness is now a welt. What does my face look like? I dip my hand in the water and draw it to the sting.

Lalo squeezes Ratho's shoulder. "Get used to being hungry. On Lookout we get no food from the Madronians, besides wafers." Ratho pulls away, and Lalo swings his pack to his shoulder. "Sorry I couldn't warn you more specifically. The Madronians keep our meals lean so we fight, hunt for ourselves, and gain strength."

"What?" I can't follow the garbled logic.

He doesn't answer and instead points to the middle cave. "That's where you report next. You have time to use the latrine, but I would still hurry." He pats my shoulder and runs off with Els flying above him. "Your evening meal will arrive before you know," he calls back.

With Thae clinging to his pack, Ratho races for the line of latrines in the distance as the rest of the boys disperse as well. Once alone, Mirko leaps from my shoulder. He faces the sun sliding above the ground and bugles a welcome.

My stomach gurgles. *Creator Spirit, give me patience with this Madronian lunacy!*

Mirko dives and snatches a lizard from between two boulders. He waddles over and lifts his catch to me.

"No. You go ahead," I say and turn to the spring to fully wash the throb from my face.

CHAPTER 17

CLOTHING ISSUE

Rows and rows of wooden shelves stuffed with clothing fill the room behind the plump R'tan woman, the Clothier. She bobs about like a potato in a boiling stew pot. So, there are females serving at the Mesa, simply not as patrollers. She reaches across the counter. From her pudgy hands, I take the rough, sand-colored trousers, leather shoulder guard, tunic, and poncho.

"Change in the far cubicle, birdlet," she says.

I return the smile sunk in her flushed cheeks, bow, and carry the bundle the few feet to the small, open changing room. Newly dressed, Ratho steps with confidence from the first cubicle. He glances to see if I am looking and then saunters back to the woman. In his uniform, with Thae perched on his shoulder guard, he looks like a true patroller!

A little sigh slips from my lips, and Mirko lets out a soft whistle. I hurriedly duck us behind the canvas. "Mirko!" I hiss, but he just grins back at me.

I overlap the curtain, check to be sure no one can see in, then exchange my clothes for the assigned set. The material is a coarse spin, but the pockets down the legs will be useful. The waist thong pulls the trousers to fit beneath my amulet. I transfer my cupboard key then pull on the tunic, which hangs comfortably loose over my pants but is short enough to still show my pouch. The poncho, too, doesn't cover it completely. My declaration will remain in view, but otherwise, I'm dressed as a twin to Ratho. I tug my own boots on and strap on the shoulder guard.

I walk from the room with as much swagger as Ratho, but he is gone. Mirko continues to explore the changing cubicle further and nips at a tunnel spider.

"Come here now," the woman calls, and takes my old clothes. She hands me another set, plus two undergarments, two pairs of socks, and wood goggles with only a slit to peer through. On each clothing piece she has marked through a former number and added *9 L*—meaning ninth lower bunk? She dumps my old clothing into a sack.

"When will I get mine back?"

She winks. "You won't." She ties the top of the bag and rolls it behind the counter. "You'll outgrow them before you leave here."

"Oh, but couldn't I keep them for now?" To just remember the smell of home? My father bought me that poncho, and Frana wove the shirt herself. I, I want my clothes back. "Please?"

"Sorry," she says and pouts. "Madronian rules."

I swallow. "Oh."

"You'll return at winter season for warm gear. By then you'll need new boots as well."

"All right," I manage to say, playing the game.

She adds a square head covering cloth to my stack, reads over her list, and squirms between the shelves. "Here we are." She labors back out with a huff. "One rain slick for the downpour that will visit. Believe me." The material is wrinkly boar intestine. The woman plops it on top of everything else. "Outside the Steam Pockets is a laundry hole. Drop your dirty clothes in the chute upon return from Perimeter. Your set will be cleaned and returned to your shelf." She reaches over and pats my hair coils as if I'm a wee babe. "Never seen a declared male before. You're still a pretty one, aren't you?"

My pulse quickens, and I hold my breath. I've never heard such words! Surely my amulet blocks these kinds of thoughts in others. But why not now?

"Well, go along to the next room, birdlet."

Mirko bounces on my pack still resting on the ground. Ignoring my centerself flummoxing, I bend down and cram everything inside my bag.

"Hurry then," calls the woman, using her apron to fan her dewy face.

Mirko and I duck through the opening. Does something still linger, some outward reflection of femininity that she sensed? The Madronians will be furious, if so. It's certainly not what I want. *Creator Spirit, make my amulet effective. Bear out my malehood!*

Across the curved armory, Ratho is just leaving through the opposite arch. Javelins and bolas crowd the red and orange walls, rising to a high-domed ceiling. A sweating R'tan Armorer with an eye patch hardens a javelin point in a wall oven while a gangly R'tan apprentice equips me with a bola, a ball of twine, and two water sacks. Both men have trouble pulling their eyes from my amulet, as well as Mirko, who quietly chitters in this new place. Neither speaks ill of us though.

"You've come with a javelin?" the apprentice asks.

"Yes, it's back at my shelf."

The Armorer flings a knife into the thick, wood table between us. I jump backward. "That should do then." He grins.

I chuckle to hide my embarrassment, step forward, and pry the obsidian blade free. It slips into the leather sheath the apprentice holds out to me in his long fingers. I gather the two fire rocks he offers and drop them into my pack. The men nod me on, but I pause to scan the walls a last time. There is none of the equipment I've seen Madronian soldiers carry. No crossbows, helmets, or vests. No accolade whips even.

At least R'tan patrollers are not called to soldier here. We only stand to raise alarm. Of course when we return to the village, any of us could be assigned to enter the ranks of the Madronian army, a possible future that chills my centerself whenever I think of it. But for now, I will work as my ancestors did, patrolling, and I'll do it well. By the Chamber of Verities, I swear I will!

I push back my shoulders, and Mirko flaps to gain his balance. As both men whisper, I walk through the arch.

CHAPTER 18

BRIEFING

Ratho and I, the only initiates present, have sat in the tiered Briefing Cavern so long my backside sleeps on this stone ledge. There wasn't even a midmeal break! My anger at Droslump's earlier slap is what keeps me alert. He won't catch me off guard again. Mirko and Thae squat at our feet, still giving their full attention too.

Govern Droslump drones on about schedules and regulations. We have nothing to write with or on but are expected to remember it all. He fingers his braid then scrapes a pointy fingernail across his sharp chin. A pale white line lingers.

"Patrol lasts one night and day." Droslump paces, making the stitched condors swish and slide past each other. "At the multiple outposts, shifts are taken, and the Perimeter is walked. This being the very edge of our kingdom, all are forbidden to go beyond into the wasteland." He stops before us and leers. "It is from there, the Triumvirate, your nightmares rise: sandstorms, foreign invaders, and desert cats. For these dangers, raise alert."

Ratho shifts on the stone. "Could you explain the alert, Sir?"

Droslump releases an impatient breath. "Rapion fly torches into the sky and swirl patterns to communicate danger. Observe." He takes several steps back then itemizes the calls. His hand sweeps through the shapes as if he begins a sacred dance to the Four-Winged Condor. Mirko and Thae mimic and memorize each progression by moving only a talon over the stone. I have already forgotten the first pattern.

Droslump finishes, and with his fluted sleeve dabs the sweat above his taut lips. "Rapion signals are received by the Madronian Lookout in his tower atop the Mesa. The lookout sends another fire message to the Receiving Posts throughout the villages. Patrollers and rapion are the first and weakest in our line of defense."

Mirko hisses, and Thae sits upright. Ratho and I place a restraining hand on our birds. In response, Droslump smooths the hair leading into his braid as if he hasn't noticed he's given offense. His open prejudice is as ugly as an infected boil on the backside of a rutting ram.

"Plus, declared males have not been tested in the Eastern Mesa," he adds.

I jump to my feet. "I will perform as any other initiate!" Mirko swoops the cavern and returns to my shoulder while Ratho and Thae inch away from us.

"Yes, well, we'll see." Droslump continues. "Patrollers return to the Mesa for a day of drilling with javelins and bolas before hiking to Perimeter again. The cycle turns without stop."

Now Ratho stands. "But what of the Seventh Day, to worship the Four-Winged Condor?"

"There is no time for full genuflections at Perimeter," says Droslump. Ratho lowers his head and hands in submission. He's always embraced Madronian worship unswervingly. There's no straighter cactus spine than Ratho, Father used to say. I just thought the quality made him a faithful and true friend.

To me, it's a blessing not to spend a day in their worship. I can honor the Creator Spirit silently during patrol.

"You will learn by doing," the govern concludes. "You face the desert tomorrow." I keep my face passive. "Questions?"

Ratho asks immediately, "Who will we each be teamed with?"

The govern raises a brow. "Each other, of course."

CHAPTER 19

EVENING MEAL

Lalo was wrong. Our division, the Carterea, return toward the end of the day and avoid me the minute Mirko bugles a welcome beside the spring. These boys are no different than the Baltang. They are just as dirty, shaggy, and prejudiced as ever, even though a few are from our village.

"What is that abomination, Jilbon?" a blond boy with thin twists asks his partner, who's washing his hands in the trough.

"No telling," Jilbon answers. Dirt covers his face, except for around his eyes where his goggles have been. He squints at me and flings the water from his hands.

I look to Ratho and Thae lingering by the Sleeping Cavern entrance, but they turn away. Not a speck of support from my own partners.

"No telling," Jilbon repeats, drying his hands on the back of his enormous rapion, who stands beside him. "But it is perfect for a declared male weakling. Both worthless bits." All the boys laugh. "Condor, protect us as these patrol."

Mirko shoots into the air, flaps above the spray slipping from the condor's mouth, and screeches his anger. My hands curl closed, but there's nothing to be done.

"Come, Mirko!" I call, but he disregards me.

Jilbon's rapion flies upward and hovers before Mirko.

"Attack the scraun," Jilbon shouts, and everyone cheers.

What? That is insane! "No, Mirko!"

The two birds beat the air, circling each other, their talons wide, but it's Mirko who flings forward and draws blood from the other rapion's breast first.

"Enough!" I shout. I raise my hand, and Mirko retreats to my shoulder. He puffs his feathers and caws his victory.

Jilbon reaches up and draws his rapion into his arms, despite the huge bird's flapping wings and its writhing head trying to keep an eye on Mirko.

"You barbarian," Jilbon hisses, kicking sand at me. "Rapion don't turn on each other."

"You are the one who called attack! What were you thinking?" I yell back.

He curses me and heads to the infirmary, his palm over the shallow swipes on his bird's breast. If it was worse, the bird would be weaker for certain. His nervous partner and rapion quickly follow.

The division skirts like a skittish dog into the Eating Cavern. Even Ratho runs.

I pick up a rock and heave it out onto the empty scrub desert. "He asked for it, Mirko. Calling me weak and you scraun. Bird offal." I spit.

Mirko hisses and cleans the blood from his talons with his tongue. "You showed them. Showed them all. You were magnificent. And we'll do it again if we have to." Mirko bobs his head. "So, there's been no rapion conflict before. Well, there's been no Singer and declared male, either."

Mirko leans forward and grins at me.

"At least none mentioned the stupid Featherless Crow!" Mirko chirps his agreement.

Since no govern appears to correct me for the conflict, I cross the Commons and enter the Eating Cavern, taking a seat on the lower ledge of the circle by Ratho. Everyone else and their rapion shift away from us. Pretending they don't bother me at all, I pet Mirko.

If the governs hear what happened, it may please them. Or maybe the boys are tight-lipped about such things because they've learned better. Perhaps even Jilbon invented a tale for his rapion's wounds.

The cook and apprentice clatter pots along the back wall. Glowing fires make their caldrons spit. I'm so hungry I could eat anything they might serve!

With Thae on his shoulder, Ratho keeps his back to me. I scratch Mirko's neck. You'd think Ratho would support us, be proud since we are partners. He should have felt the slight as much as me and my rapion. And then taken pride in Mirko's win. Why can't we be united?

Mirko hums and nibbles a talon. His tail warms my back.

I scan the now quiet group. There's the boy whose father teaches at the elemental school, and I definitely recognize the other with scars along his jaw from his brush with a desert cat. His father and eldest brother killed the beast before this boy was dragged off. It may even be that feline's heart in my own amulet. I adjust my pouch so it's in full sight.

The apprentice strolls over with a stack of clay bowls. He clatters one before each patroller.

From a great pot clenched at his side, the bearded cook ladles gray slop into each bowl. He leaves one empty—and a fight erupts. "Give me yours!" a boy with a deep voice says to the surprised patroller on his right.

"No!" The boy covers his food with his arms moments before the first throws a punch. While his victim is doubled over, he spoons the boy's food into his own mouth. Rapion flap in the chaos. Mirko and I quickly eat our own tasteless paste.

The cook sneezes into his beard then heaves three loaves of bread into the circle. It is shredded and eaten by boys and rapion before I can turn and grab a mouthful. Govern Droslump walks through the cave without a glance at the wildness in the Eating Pit. He departs through the right arch.

So this is the Madronian way to make us hate, fight, and grow stronger? Obviously, we'll have to forage with the food so lean. But aren't there better ways to learn?

The circle clears and Ratho remains, staring into his bowl. Is he the one who emptied it?

CHAPTER 20

THEFT

I guess I shouldn't be amazed I'm still hungry after evening meal. Why expect more? After using the latrine, I head to my bunk. Mirko swoops above, gathering tunnel spiders from the crevices as we turn into our alcove. "Ratho's not here," I mutter. "Maybe he's out scrounging for more food already."

Mirko flaps along the wall as I dump my pack, fold my change of clothes, and repack my gear. I can't believe how the governs rule this place! Does Father know how crazy their game really is?

My rapion flies down to our shelf and peers at me. "You have a spider's leg hanging out of your beak," I say as his tongue curls it in. "Oh, you turn my stomach." I shudder. "How about food from home?"

He bounces on his toes. I slide my key into the lock, and the door opens on an empty cubby. "Someone stole everything!" I seethe.

Mirko hisses and rakes his talons on the stone. I shove my hand into the vacant space. Frana's bag, my food, and the few sweets I brought are gone. "Unbelievable!" Mirko struts back and forth.

I rip the key off the thong of my pants and fling it onto the shelf. "I know I left it locked," I say. "Ratho would never steal from me, right? No. It is against Madronian law." I shake my head at my doubts. Already this place is affecting my mind.

"Wait! Was it Jilbon, while we were eating?" He never appeared at mealtime. "Let's find Lalo, and he can tell me how to report it."

Not wanting to lose anything else, I shrug on my pack, and Mirko jumps to my shoulder. I stomp into the hall past a couple boys. "Gruntlothian," one utters, insulting me with the name of a distant hill tribe rumored to intermarry. Does everyone have to be so hostile? My rapion drew the first blood in conflict. Doesn't that mean anything to them? I glare while Mirko grumbles, but the boys have already disappeared down a side passage.

Outside in the dusk, Lalo is by the fire working over his bola. Maybe retying a rock into a pouch? Els circles on a draft above like a reoccurring thought. This appears to be the only way other rapion separate from their bearers. So Mirko has a horizontal advantage as well. It's ridiculous we have to hide it; it could be an asset someday.

I glance at the few patrollers sitting around the firepit. Jilbon and his partner are there with their birds. All four look away from me, although Jilbon's mouth quirks in a sly smile. It's the only proof I need.

"Lalo," I call from the cave opening as Mirko jumps to the ground and bugles. My friend looks up. Setting his weapon aside, we meet halfway. Els drifts with him in the evening's blue glow.

"Tiadone, I heard about your conflict." He tips his head at the boys and frowns. "That was risky."

I blush and Mirko cleans his beak beneath his wing. "I tried . . ." I stop my defense. It likely looks worse that I can't control my own rapion.

Lalo shakes his head. "Let's hope the harm was small, and that it doesn't happen again."

"Right," I agree, but Mirko only stares at the horizon.

"So, how was the briefing?" he asks.

I ignore his question and rush on with my own concern. "Someone stole the belongings I locked in my cupboard, Lalo, and I'm pretty sure it was Jilbon. After he went to the infirmary, while I was at dinner." We glance at him. His rapion lies curled on a medic cloth at his feet while Jilbon smirks, picking his teeth.

"See, Lalo?"

"I'm sorry." He shakes his head.

I cross my arms. "So tell me how I report it. I'll go to the governs this time and not tempt my rapion further." Now Mirko struts back and forth between us.

While rocking his javelin in its holder, Lalo whistles Els down from the sky. She lands next to his worn boots and rakes the sand for bugs. It's obvious Lalo's stalling. Finally, he answers. "You shouldn't report it, Tiadone."

Mirko squawks. Els stares until my rapion quiets.

"Why?"

"It would only please the Madronians." He checks over his shoulder, and weaves a hair twist behind his big ear. "I told you they believe controversy makes soldiers stronger. Same reason no one told about your conflict. Yes, they'd take the report. But then they'd make things more difficult for everyone else — and you for complaining."

"That's ridiculous!" I kick a weed clear out of the soil. Its roots lie upturned like a withered claw.

Lalo reaches out and squeezes my arm. "I am sorry about your cupboard theft, but if someone hadn't lifted your things today, it would have happened tomorrow. For all we know, it could have even been a Madronian. So forget it, and go forward. Oh, and keep everything in your pack. It's the only thing respected between patrollers."

I huff, and Mirko clicks his beak.

"Lalo!" a boy at the fountain calls. "How many days until your service ends?"

"Two!" Lalo calls.

The boy raises an encouraging fist, but Els leans heavily against Lalo's ankle. Sorrow sticks to their faces like that dinner slop stuck to my spoon.

Lalo sighs. "Well, I have duties to finish, Tiadone." Els jumps into his arms. "I return to Lookout tonight. Be strong this year," he says. He pats my free shoulder and walks back to the fire.

Refusing to make eye contact with Jilbon again, I drag myself toward the spring. Els's and Lalo's grief follows me. His loss will go so far beyond what I've just had stolen that it can't be compared.

Creator Spirit, comfort them; and then I add despite myself, *and make Jilbon sick to his stomach!*

I hitch my pants up over my complaining stomach and walk out of the Common. *This is such a stupid game, Father!* My mind rages anew. We are here to do a good, important work—defending our village from threat—and the Madronians make everything so difficult. Thieving results, and no one cares. Well, in this case, it was retaliation, but still, there's no justice.

I wipe my eyes, kneel in the dirt, and tear a bulbous nob off a nearby prickle plant. Mirko peels away the tough, ridged skin with his beak and talons, and we share juicy bites.

The sky is now a deep purple, stretching over our heads. Long finger clouds thrust to the east. I lean back and squint at the tiptop of the Mesa. Like a pointed nose on a broad face, the Lookout Tower juts darkly into the air out of the rippled rock. From the rotunda, the lookout can see in all directions in case rapion signal danger.

Sour juice spills down my throat. I wince at the tang and lick my lips clean. Shivers cross my skin, as I try to take in this beautiful mesa, even more imposing at night. This is the place of my R'tan people. I'm going to work Perimeter as my ancestors did, despite the danger. And I will be the first declared male bearing a Singer to succeed.

"We are going to serve, Mirko. Not for the Madronians, but for the R'tan. We'll raise alert for the Triumvirate, and we'll find our own food when we have to. Tonight's loss is nothing. I can even replace Frana's herbs."

Ratho comes out of the latrine, and he and Thae head to the spring. Sticky juice drips off Mirko's talons and beak onto the back of my hand. "Hey, that was my bite," I say, and smile for the first time today.

CHAPTER 21

BOLA

*S*omeone nudges my arm. "Psst. I only wake you because I must patrol with you." I open my eyes to Ratho's trousers. He's bent over and adjusting his boots. At least he speaks to me this morning. And it's not a bad sight, his backside. Though he means it so. A blush warms my face. I roll off of my amulet so it is not smothered and dulled.

We have a breakfast much like dinner, although no food is withheld this morning. We are in training immediately.

"Chamber of Verities," I swear. Mirko scratches at the dirt and looks up at me.

"You shouldn't swear," says Ratho. "Especially by R'tan mythology." I narrow my eyes. Mythology? "If a govern heard you, we would be severely penalized."

As if I don't know? "Well, this ridiculous bola just rapped my knuckles again." I lift my hand. The swelling bulges red at the base of my fingers.

Ratho shrugs. "That's no excuse. You offend the Four-Winged Condor."

A snort escapes me. Mirko crouches and waits for my next attempt with the accursed weapon. His fierce expression compresses his eyeridge. I squint in the bright light and yank off my poncho.

Even though the sun is barely clear of the edge of the desert, a bead of sweat already rims my brow. What has happened to autumn?

I drop the material to the ground and gaze at the boys practicing well beyond Ratho and me. Their bolas whip through the air and encircle the drill posts planted in the sandy dirt, winding faster and faster, until the balls slam the wood. *Crack!*

Jilbon's partner seems most adept. My jealousy brews, and I immediately vow to ignore the two, or at least notice them no more than anyone else. They aren't worth my thoughts.

I turn back to Ratho. The Drill Govern assigned us here, far to the side, to practice by aiming at the dead pine only a short distance away. The burly govern adjusted his head cloth, pulled the back tail of his robe through his hefty legs, and looped the material under his waist thong. We followed him in his makeshift trousers to this removed spot. He said we'd be a danger to everyone until we grew familiar with the weapon. Here we would only maim each other.

"You'd better progress quickly," he said after teaching us how to throw. He tugged his robe free and it fell again to cover his squat boots. He fingered his bola ropes and said, "Your life depends on it. This will feed you on Perimeter and bring down a desert cat."

"Watch this, Thae," Ratho now says. He grips the handle, from which hang three ropes, and raises the weapon in a whirl above his head. The three rocks within their sacks at the ropes' ends blur and wiz. Ratho leans forward and lets the bola loose while Thae flies behind it out of danger. Whipping through the air, the rocks lose speed and twirl into the red soil. A cloud of dust rises as the balls drag the ropes to a stop. "Closer that time," says Ratho.

Thae dives and drags the bola back the short distance to him. Ratho takes it from her talons, and drinks from his water sack.

I shake out my hand and adjust my grasp. "All right. Another try." Mirko sits up straight. "Revenge on the tree!" I yell, and circle my head. The round force tugs the rocks in opposite directions. I spin them faster, aim, lean forward, and let go. *Whoo, whoo, whoo*, they fling. The collision with the pine rings across the air. "Yes!" I yell, raising my fist.

Mirko speeds to the tree and works at freeing my bola. He pretends to peck the eyes of the desert cat we have just downed in our imagination.

"Did you see that?" I shout at Ratho.

He and Thae turn. "No. I was looking the other direction."

I humph as Mirko flies back, dragging the bola. The rocks bounce over the ground. He isn't strong enough to lift the weapon higher. Yet. When he reaches my feet, he drops the bola handle. Breathing heavily, he smiles up at me and chortles before he cleans the dust from his face with his wing. Ratho and Thae shrink from him.

"You should be happy for my success, Ratho. We are a team. We are going to need each other."

"Thae and I will work to cover the partnering."

Mirko and I both gape at their audacity. Ratho assumes the throwing stance and hurls his bola. It bounces to the ground short of the tree.

I smirk. "Maybe *we* will work to cover the partnering," I say, and Mirko chirps. Ratho's ears tinge red as Thae flies to retrieve the weapon.

I untangle my bola and prepare for another throw. I'll master this before Ratho!

The twirl above my head breaks rhythm, and the rocks clack against my elbow. "Chamber of—" I drop my bola and fling my arm to hurry out the pain as the bruise spreads.

"Don't swear," says Ratho.

Step to the right, lunge, straighten, twirl, lunge. The pattern repeats, making my javelin feel as if it was cast in lead. *Step to the right.* I squeeze the shaft until Father's carved patterns press marks into my palms. *Twirl, lunge.*

Madronian javelin routines supposedly strengthen the mind and body and mimic the flight of the Four-Winged Condor. R'tan used to do similar drills to mimic the glory of creation by the Creator Spirit.

My foot wobbles on a pebble, which causes Mirko to dig his talons into my shoulder cover. He chitters encouragement as I watch the boy before me and hurriedly mimic the right move. *Thrust, thrust, thrust.* We jab the weapons forward and arc the wood over our heads in the closing victory sweep.

I stretch out the tight kinks in my back before the Javelin Govern calls for the pattern repeat. You'd think, given the hard rays of the sun, they'd let us practice in the shade of the Mesa or near those few cottonwoods in the dip across the way. No, that would make sense.

The long-limbed instructor with a dangling mustache inspects a patroller's javelin in the front row. Mirko's chitters cause the govern to look over, but he doesn't approach us.

Next to me, Ratho assumes the ready stance, as if eager to begin again. I can't catch his eye. Is he so prejudiced because Mirko's song reflects back to the *Oracles*? Whatever the case, in hours we leave for Perimeter, and we really will need each other.

I shake my head and rub my tired calf muscles. One thing at a time, Frana always says. One furrow in the garden, one seed planted, and, before you realize, one tomato bursting between your teeth. One thing at a time, and right now, it's one more javelin pattern.

Ratho and I move into formation once we reach the Commons. Offering a prayer to the Four-Winged Condor with the Mesa at his back, Droslump spreads his arms wide. At the same time, Ratho rubs the back of his head where a lump is raising. He was struck hard for stepping aside at the spring for the Bola Govern instead of Droslump. Not as if they bothered to tell us rank earlier.

"It is so," Droslump concludes. "Come forward for Oblation and assignments."

We gather by twos into straight lines. Each patroller is given a wafer and a sip from a black clay goblet. It is a Madronian ritual meant to cleanse away our supposed unworthy service.

A dark-skinned apprentice hands an animal-hide map to each pair of boys. "Front point one. Front point two," he assigns Jilbon and his partner. The spring trickles in the background as the appointments continue. After each location is given, rapion study the maps and fly slightly forward at a pace the boys can follow.

"And last, the initiates." Droslump grimaces. His crowded teeth nibble a wafer, and he places a thin disk in each of our mouths. I try not to move. His curved, pointed nails hover a moment above my tongue.

Next, he slurps a swallow of wine then holds the cup to my lips. I barely brush the edge of the goblet. A drop of hot redness slips onto my tongue, and the spiced bitterness fills the wafer. I swallow the mush while Ratho receives his portion.

Droslump steps aside. The apprentice, who is not much older than we are, hands us a map. "Wide point eleven and twelve, one of the farthest positions." He shakes his head, making his hair tuft sway.

Mirko and Thae attempt to see the ragged leather map Ratho and I tug. Drosump glares. Instantly, Ratho gives up the struggle. I clutch the map, and we start walking, not even sure where to go.

"Peace of the Four-Winged Condor on you, Govern," Ratho calls back. Droslump ignores him and tips back the goblet. A line of libation leaks from the cup and dribbles down his sharp cheek.

I sign a farewell to the apprentice, and he returns one to me. We pass the spring, and the latrines, until eventually the mesa we have just settled into starts to diminish over my shoulder. We walk out onto the high desert, where no one but patrollers are permitted. All the other boys and rapion are tiny spots splayed over the huge expanse. Mirko studies the map and leads us south.

CHAPTER 22

FIRST NIGHT

"Finally," the patrol calls to us. They stand beside a dying fire with their hands on their hips and their packs already on. The clearing is empty but for one rintell tree and a couple stacks of rocks.

"Good greeting," I yell back. It's wonderful to have arrived! Ratho was slow to believe Mirko was reading the map correctly, but eventually he conceded.

"You always had to lead when we were little too," he mumbled.

"And I was good at it." He didn't argue with that.

For several miles we topped knolls and hiked the empty valleys until all the other patrols were out of sight, and the mesa faded. It's amazing the Lookout will still be able to see rapion signal flame from here.

Mirko flies to the tree's lowest branch while we come to a stop beside the cairns, one tall and one short. "Go on; move a stone, left to right," says a boy with pimples all over his face.

"Does it count the days then?" Ratho asks.

"Brilliant, these two, Pensot," the other answers.

I lift the top rock and set it on the shorter pile. Ratho straightens it.

"We knew you'd be the initiates," Pensot jibes. "Later than ever. Now we have to hike back with poor light." Under his breath, he curses.

Ratho rolls his eyes, and I huff. It's not as if we are so late.

The other patroller wipes his upturned nose on the back of his hand. "With a declared male and Singer, this lot is worth a pile of goat pellets."

"For certain, Finden," Pensot jeers.

Mirko pierces the air with a shrill note.

Gesturing for protection from evil, the boys duck and cross their chests. Ratho glances at me, and I smile in return. Side by side, we've fought off enough bullies in the village. The look says we can take these braggarts as well.

Keeping an eye on Mirko, the Baltang patrollers recover their bravado. "Dung clods. Thanks for reporting!" Pensot goes to shove me, but Ratho knocks him off balance by driving his elbow under the patroller's raised arm.

I drop into a fight stance, my javelin stripped from its holder and balanced in my grip. The point is aimed at Finden's meager chest and does not waver. Thae and Mirko flap about our heads while the Baltangs' larger rapion stay aflight, with extended talons.

Please, don't attack, I beg Mirko silently, glancing between him and the Baltang. "Want to rethink your welcome?" I ask.

Finden nods, but Pensot has to take a step forward and spit at me. Within a second, Ratho grabs and twists his arm, throwing him completely off his feet. Thae circles in celebration while Mirko trumpets.

Scrambling to help his partner up, Finden says, "Let's just go, Pensot."

Brushing off his trousers, Pensot shrugs. "Sure. Why waste our time?"

Mirko shoots high above and dives at their rapion, who race to their partners' shoulders for safety. The boys block their faces as Mirko screeches past the four of them.

When he returns to rest on my shoulder, the Baltang quickly inch backward, away from camp. Yet, they still dare to call out slurs in the dusk.

"Plumdogits," Ratho shouts back. I can think of worse. Mirko crows, and Thae flaps to the taller cairn. We stare at the boys until they disappear beyond the slope. The air seems to slowly cool at the same rate as Ratho withdraws. But maybe, I'm only imagining it.

"Thanks," I finally say.

Ratho pets Thae without acknowledging me. Definitely, I'm not imagining it.

I can't decide if I'm flattered he protected me or offended he thought he had to. "I could have taken him."

No answer.

Well, as least we acted as if we were a team. "I'll gather brush for the fire," I say. "You two want to search for food?"

He shrugs.

Silently, we walk off in opposite directions.

I stoke the fire against the darkness. Ratho rubs sand through the bowls and pot I found earlier in the crevice of the tree. They were lodged beside a large hourglass hanging from a branch. The only other notable part of our position is a latrine trench behind dense shrubs over the ridge to the south.

"The lizard and bluben soup wasn't bad," I say.

"I've always hated blubens," Ratho complains. What's not to like about blue lichen? It has a gentle tang.

Mirko stretches on the cairn. It's officially my guard, so he is watching the starlit, flat sand speckled with shrubs that hunker before the distant dunes. Thae naps on Ratho's pack, and will assume Mirko's position when the hourglass has emptied. I'm thankful Droslump's briefing at least explained regular shift changes.

"It's amazing how a little lizard really has a lot of flavor when it's boiled." I pick at a bit stuck in my back teeth. Ratho places everything back in the tree, then hands me my spoon and stashes his own in his pocket.

We both move closer to the flames. The warmth the land was shimmering earlier is completely gone, but for now, the fire beats back the chill.

Mirko crows that all is safe. When I raise my hand in salute, he waddles with pride, settles, and glares into the night. His rapion eyes are perfect for such a task.

"Our shift is almost over," I say. Ratho glances at the hourglass and nods. "Mirko and I will walk the paces to the Perimeter." Only the crackling fire offers a response, and my run-on mouth tries to fill the quiet. "After we get back, I'm guessing it will be time to switch. I'm looking forward to crawling into the sleeping hole. It was funny when I fell right into it, wasn't it?"

Ratho's head barely moves in agreement.

"Whatever then." If he wants to be as boring as a stick insect, let him. Whistling Mirko to the air, I snatch my javelin and dig a dry signal branch out of the brush stack we made. I stomp out the paces while leaving Ratho, Thae, and our fire behind.

The night is incredibly dark. Noises snicker and shadows dart over the sand. Each time my foot pounds the ground, a bit of irritation sloughs off and fear crawls in to replace it. I could be walking into one of the Triumvirate right now. My breathing speeds.

Stop it! I straighten my weapons. "I can do this," I whisper, and fling my arms to be rid of the fear.

Mirko's shimmery underbelly winks pale against the black sky. We'll be fine. My ears rise as I listen for danger.

Nothing. Just the *whump, whump* of Mirko's wings and the scuttle of little creatures. There are no large animal tracks in sight. I walk toward the piles of rocks marking our edge of the desert.

After returning, I curled up in the sleeping hole, but now I struggle to roll over. The sand covering my body from the waist down resists my turning, pressing against my movement as if the Four-Winged Condor has landed on me. I finally manage to rotate, and squirm on my hip to resettle. As I tug my tunic to my chin, Mirko recurls in my hair. His warmth radiates around my neck.

Hunched by the snapping fire, Ratho watches the darkness. Thae crouches alert on a cairn and faces the horizon to the east. I close my eyes. Sleep has to come because it will be my shift soon, and then Ratho will be filling this pit.

The wind changes direction, and the smoke from the fire wafts by. It's pungent. Drifting off to sleep, I wonder, did Ratho find lavender branches for fuel?

Father twirls.
The firepit flickers.
His arms wrap someone
and meld gently with the curves.
A face flits past.
Frana!

"Tiadone." A boot jiggles my shoulder. "Tiadone, it's your shift."
I gasp in grains of sand and struggle to sit up in the pit.

CHAPTER 23

THE VISION

I flip the hourglass. Mirko flies a short sweep over our position through the heavy mist and lands back on the rock pile as the sky glows pale pink along the distant curves of sand. The wet air is heavy and musty. I shiver.

Thank the Creator Spirit, we've survived our first night!

Ratho snores softly in the sleeping hole. He refused to let me help cover him with sand, so Thae had to work hard to rake in a mound.

I drop roots into the boiling water and use a stick to lift the pot off the coals. Licorice steam rises. It will be good and sweet after the twigs steep. I get to my feet and use my javelin to stretch out my kinks.

My dream returns. Was that all it was? I dreamed Father was dancing with Frana. But I felt the heat of the fire, the touch of spun cloth, and I smelled the pine burning in the fire pit.

I've had another vision.

Was it the near-past this time, the present, or future? I'm guessing it was at least the present. Father would be burning ash if it was future, say winter. And none of my clothes hung on the wall pegs, so it wasn't the past.

I shake my amulet to fight off this lingering female trait. What could be wrong? I need all the power of the male and none of this weakness leeching through.

I plunge my javelin into the sand and rub my face. With clasped hands, I drop to my knees, and mere seconds later Mirko flaps to my side and steps up onto my lap. I look into his pupils as the black circles grow wider. Shifting in their darkness, colorful shapes expand. Father and Frana twirl in a dance in our home beside our firepit. Mirko hums, and the vision vibrates apart. He blinks slowly.

I let out my held breath. We both saw the vision.

At midday, I sit by the fire and pinch stingers off the dead scorpions Mirko caught. The heat of the sun bores down on my neck, and the desert wavers in the distance.

If visions come as I sleep, that poses no danger to my position, right? And none need know of this strange, lingering femininity. I've examined my amulet, but there are no tears or holes. And couldn't it be a blessing to see my past or what is happening now? I did get to see Father, and Mirko did too.

But what of Father dancing with Frana? A jealousy gnaws my centerself, and I battle it down. Father is lonely, and Frana is his friend. And mine too. They only pass time together like they often do. I twist the scorpion stinger and rip it from the body.

I need to stop fretting. Think of here, the work, winning Ratho over. I glance over as he stokes our fire. The light brightens his strong profile further, and now my centerself warms. I catch his eye a quick second and say, "Seems like what we'll do out here for the most part is find food and survive the weather." Mirko bobs his head. Ratho gives the barest nod.

Thae flaps out of the nearby shrub and drops a small dead rabbit at Ratho's feet. He glances at me to see if I have seen his rapion's catch.

I focus on the scorpion I'm working on and toss the removed stinger into the flames. Mirko grasps another scorpion from our pile then carefully sets it in my palms. When we are done, I'll skewer and roast them.

"Between that rabbit and the scorpions, we'll have a great midmeal."

Ratho grunts. "I guess I'll share my rapion's catch." He flips the rabbit and begins to disembowel it.

I add the scorpion to the pile without stingers and stir the prickle plant brewing in the pot. Another few minutes and the spines will fall off, leaving only the tender green flesh.

"Time for patrol sweep," Ratho says. "The hourglass says so. Look." He points.

Are we going to go through this every time? What a nagger he is! He always complained about his mama badgering him; how quickly he forgets those calls of, "Ratho, retie your egg wrap. Ratho, it's time to haul water. Ratho, come back and finish your prickle plant." I smile. So he acts like her now, but will he eat his greens out here?

I pull the pot off the fire and snap the stinger from the final scorpion Mirko passes to me.

"It's time," Ratho says firmly.

"I'm going!" I grab my javelin and a branch, then stomp out toward the Perimeter. The paces practically echo from my feet. Mirko catches an air current and hovers while waiting for me to catch up.

CHAPTER 24

FORGIVENESS

Help! I'm caught!"

Stepping from the latrine trench, I hear Ratho's faint yell. "Tia-done!" he calls. I tie the waist of my trousers on the run, my amulet bumbling against my thighs.

Mirko shoots ahead then circles back.

"Where is he?" I cry. My rapion bugles and streaks beyond our post with me racing after him.

"Help me, Tiadone! Sidewinders!"

Far beyond the scrub patch, in the open desert, I catch a glimpse of Ratho and Thae rolling in the sand, and I stumble over a shrub in my panic. *Oof*! Striking the ground knocks the breath out of me.

I scramble up and suck air into my flattened lungs. Running furiously, I finally reach them and hurl into the fray.

Ratho is surrounded by sidewinders, most as long as my legs. His boot is stuck in a nest hole, and the winders writhe around his ankle. Two sink their fangs into his boot even as he beats at them with his javelin. Thae clamps her teeth through the back of one hissing head at a time and flings the diamond-patterned, ropey bodies to the side.

"Help me!" Ratho yells again.

Mirko dives into the thick of the nest with a loud growl and pierces the base of a huge winder's head. I club my way toward the hole, throw aside my javelin, and link my arms under Ratho's as

I pull with all my strength. Winder pits tend to collapse and trap intruders, but thankfully, this one releases Ratho. Relief jars through me as we stumble onto our backsides. He lands on top of me and rolls off. Before I can get up, Ratho is on his feet and attacking the nest.

"Augh!" I yell as a fang pierces my leg. The slick winder flaps about. I grasp it tightly, and twist the head. The fang breaks from the mouth, but the body still thrashes. I fling it through the air. Its head hits a boulder, and the winder flops to the sand. I tug up my trouser leg and pry the fang from my skin; while I do so, the burn shoots across my calf as the hole seeps red. I stuff my sleeve against the wound.

"I'll finish them!" Ratho yells. Thae and Mirko continue to attack the winders that haven't retreated while Ratho stabs his javelin down the opening.

"With care!" I call and put more pressure on my bubbling lesion.

The rapion are quick to sink the death bite and flap into the air before another serpent can strike. Winders drop lifeless to the sand. Blood sprinkles from the sky.

Soon every sidewinder above ground lies motionless. Ratho collapses beside me as Mirko and Thae swoop over the carnage. "Come down," Ratho and I call. We need to check them for wounds, but they ignore us in their celebration. Thae appears to have no fear of Mirko now!

"Well, are you all right, Tiadone?" Ratho asks.

"I don't know." I lift the material away from my leg. The blood has slowed, but best of all there's no blackness rimming the hole.

"No poison," he says, and wipes winder splatter from his cheek. "I need to check my ankle."

"I'll do it." He doesn't jerk from me and instead leans back on his elbows. I pull off his boot and sock. There isn't any blood, and there aren't prick marks anywhere. The hide has held.

My hands linger on his muscled calf, now covered with hairs like Father's. When did he grow such hair on his legs? I bite my lip and scramble for words. "So, don't tell me your mama made these boots from Old Goatgrinder," I say.

Ratho sits up. "Nothing tougher than that plumdogit goat." We both start laughing. "That goat would try to mate with anything!" Ratho hoots.

"My father's leg!" I cackle.

"A fence post!" he shouts. We both howl and roll in the sand.

As our giggles pass, Ratho sits up and slowly pulls on his sock and boot. Mirko sings of victory and Thae lifts a dead winder and shakes it fiercely. "They seem to be fine," Ratho says.

"Definitely. Maybe they can sense we are not seriously hurt?"

Despite me telling him not to bother, Ratho tears a strip from the bottom of his tunic and ties it about my wound. The pressure eases the burn. "Thank you," I say.

He gives me a firm hand to help me stand. "No. Thanks go to you," he says. Mirko finally flies to my shoulder, and Thae flaps to Ratho's arms.

We examine the birds head to talon. Not one prick or bite in evidence. Both rapion nudge their faces against our necks while Mirko's hum winds down.

A pregnant silence bulges between the four of us. Finally, Ratho speaks.

"Forgive my head, which is as tough as my boots," he says. "I have shame." He blushes deeply, and Thae ducks her head beneath her wing. "Mirko is a strong rapion," Ratho says hoarsely." He is no Featherless Crow."

"It's—"

"No." He stops me. "Do you realize that if Mirko had been left on the Scree, as I spoke, I might have perished now? Who knows? He has great strength and is worthy, Tiadone."

A huge smile blooms on my face. "Yes, he is!" Mirko chortles and leaps into flight around Ratho and his rapion. Thae flaps to join him, and they begin chasing each other.

I step before Ratho and draw two fingers clear across his chest. Forgiveness. I am able to give it fully. I lean forward and press my lips to his worried forehead to prove my gesture.

"Tiadone," says Ratho, looking straight into my eyes, "Mirko is equal to all."

"As is Thae," I give the formal answer to his statement. We smile, and he grabs me in a hug that overwhelms me. His scent. His strength. Our separation has ached me more than I dared admit. He squeezes me tightly before stepping back.

I grin up at my strong rapion flapping in the open sky. Maybe other patrollers will be won just as quickly as Ratho and Thae.

"Still like the taste of winder?" I ask, sending off the last frayed tension into the air.

"Never as much as now!" Ratho laughs. The four of us turn and collect the bounty of fresh meat.

CHAPTER 25

SHUNNING

Ratho stuffs the last winder steak wrapped in rintell leaves and yucca twine into his pack. "Just in time," I whisper as the Baltang boys crest the nearby hill. It's actually good to see others. We've been jumpy around the fire, and both of us found it hard to leave the other for patrol. We're definitely shaken, as the dangers are more vivid now.

I fumble my pack closed over the skins we'll cure. We'll need to treat the meat packages during our next patrol.

The firelight glitters in the smoky edges of my obsidian knife. Plunging it clean into the sand, I motion for our rapion to take to the air. Hopefully, in flight none will notice how round they are from gorging on entrails.

Our overeager greetings aren't returned as the Baltang enter camp. In fact, they say nothing as they cautiously walk toward us. This is a different pair from the first we replaced.

Keeping an eye on Mirko, the boy with a pronounced brow moves a rock from one cairn to the other. The other skittish patroller rushes over to the hourglass and flips it quickly. They are obviously eager for us to depart.

"Goodwill," I say.

They move to the far side of the fire.

"The Four-Winged Condor protect you," Ratho calls as we step away.

With their Signicos snugged close to their legs, the boys stoke the fire. The Baltang lift burning branches and draw the smoke through the air to cleanse the site.

My face simmers. "They are saying we are evil!" I spit. Mirko rumbles and swoops around my head.

Ratho ducks under him and drags me away. He lays his arm over my shoulder and matches my stride while Thae and then Mirko rise high on a windstream above us.

He lets me walk through my anger in silence, our boots shuffling sand.

Finally I say, "I hate being shunned for Mirko."

"I can understand," Ratho says.

"I hate being shunned for being declared," I admit for the very first time to my friend.

He nods.

And because he does understand, my anger is soothed the tiniest bit. "You'd think I'd be used to it, but it's doubled now, and somehow it's worse when they react that way to Mirko."

"Yes," Ratho agrees. "It harder to look past it, right? To not react?"

"Definitely," I say, and kick a rock out of our way. It rolls and thuds to a stop.

"Well, it's not like Thae and I did any better."

"It's all right," I assure him. We continue walking, until finally my shoulders drop and I can inhale deeply.

He ruffles my hair twists. "Give them a chance. Eventually they will see Mirko's strength as Thae and I have."

"I really don't know how they can't." I glance back. The Baltang's chants for protection are barely audible now across the distance.

Ratho squeezes me close, then lets me go, and we increase our pace.

Well, even if no one else ever sees past Mirko's song and my declaration, maybe it is enough that Ratho and Thae have.

I glace at him from under my lashes. He's definitely attractive, right there at my side. I sigh. I have my best friend back. Yes, that can be enough.

I knock his pack with my javelin.

"Hey!" he laughs and chases me over the sand.

CHAPTER 26

RELEASE

Darkness settles, and we stumble into the Commons, quickly noting the empty spring and firepits. Mirko and Thae rouse on our packs. "Where is everyone?" I whisper.

Suddenly, a govern I don't recognize calls from the shadow, "Report to your division."

"But where is it?" Ratho asks.

The man rubs his plump belly with importance and points. "Follow the mesa's northern side to the first trail rising from the desert floor. Ascend and join the celebration."

"And what are we celebrating?" I call as he disappears into the Eating Cavern.

Ratho shrugs. "As if we'd really get an answer for once? Let's go." He trudges forward.

I groan. "All I wanted was to stop in the Steam Pockets and then to drop onto my shelf." Mirko chitters agreement, but I stumble after Ratho.

We skirt the edge of the stone, turn left, and meander along the northern side. A glow above encourages us forward, as well as the chant wavering in the air. Mirko drops silent when Ratho and I hurry forward.

Spotting the foot of the trail, I stop. "Here it is," I call and Ratho returns.

Beyond that narrow pillar, farther down the dark stone face, I vaguely see other upward paths. Where do they lead?

With shaking legs, Ratho and I climb this first one. From the distance we have hiked, my calf wound, our lack of good sleep, and the difficult path itself, it's unbelievable neither of us falls. In steep sections we are glad to find hand and foot holds. The occasional narrow couple of stairs are carved at just the right spots.

Finally, we crest the path, turn a corner, and emerge on a platform carved into the thick wall of stone. A small, sunken amphitheater opens around us.

All the Carterea sit on the semicircled, tiered steps with their rapion on their laps or standing by their feet. Ratho and I hurry to the closest seat. He remains beside me even when a few boys shift farther away. He doesn't shrink a bit from Mirko when others are witness.

I hardly hold back my smile as he declares we are a team. He declares it to them all. Only the pulsing fear in the air keeps my happiness from showing.

My rapion curls into my lap and shivers. "It's okay," I mouth, hoping that it is.

I smooth Mirko's wings and watch Doslump performing a complicated dance along the raised, curved stage. Lichen strands are clumped to light the area, but one misstep could tip him off the mesa edge. He twirls and leaps before a green-flamed firepit. Ancestral stones? He reminds me of Sleene at Weekly Ritual. Only his robes don't clank and jingle, and he has hair. Droslump twirls his braid until it wraps his neck several times and ends with a *thwap* on his back.

I scan the area. Jilbon is sitting on the far side, looking very nervous. And then I see Lalo poised with Els on the pillar that rose separate from the mesa. Lalo must have done a running leap to reach the platform. Els overflows in his arms. Sobs shudder Lalo's back, and his head is shaved bald.

No, no! It cannot be Els's time yet, but it is. This amph is the Edge of Release for Severation. My centerself plummets faster than Droslump would if he slipped off the stone.

I nudge Ratho, but he's already seen. He tucks Thae under the poncho he has shrugged on. I tremble despite wearing mine as well. Mirko's shivers grow stronger. My feeble whispers do not still him.

Beginning a complicated mantra, the boys sing and chant in unison. My mind can find none of the words we used to rehearse at school. The rapion rise into the air and swirl above us. Out from Ratho's poncho, Thae barges. Mirko's talons grip my trousers, but his wings betray him. Before I can hold him back, he lifts into the melee. The other birds give him space to circle and cry alone.

Flapping wings, droll notes, Droslump twirling, and then the rapion collectively screech. Not only Mirko, but every rapion here cuts the sound from deep inside their breasts. Mine is not the only Singer after all.

I clasp my ears and roll off the seat. My kneecaps bang the stone, but the pain barely registers. Huddled in a ball, I rock and pray to the Creator Spirit for the sound to stop before my eardrums burst.

I don't know how long the torture lasts. I open my eyes to find Mirko nudging his way under my elbow. He rubs his head against my wet face.

Shaking, I sit up. The seats are all empty. "Do not violate the sacred ceremony!" Droslump hisses at me from the stage. "Take your place, patroller!"

I roll my aching head to the right. Check my ears for blood. There is none, but my nose leaks a stream. I wipe it on my poncho.

The other boys stand in line to descend with their rapion. Even Ratho. He looks to me with concern while Droslump glares. Will the govern beat me with the whip he's removing from the folds of his robe?

But what about that sound? It was ultimate pain! How did everyone else bear it?

I sniff back the last bit of blood in my nose, hold Mirko close, and stagger to take part in the rest of the ceremony. My legs buckle and shake. Hopefully, all that is left is to file down the path. Droslump watches me.

Ratho reaches back and clasps my hand to keep me moving. "Come on, Tiadone." His warmth and strength vibrates from his palm into my icy one.

Mirko climbs to my shoulder, and I gently rub first one of my ears then the other while he nuzzles my neck and whimpers. I look back to Lalo for the first time since the horrible sound. Beyond a scowling Droslump, I catch a glimpse of him.

Lalo is crumpled on the pillar, holding his shaven head. He's alone. Severated.

CHAPTER 27

ONLY SILENCE

In the darkness, a chill rattles my shoulder blades against my stone shelf. All the lichen have been removed from the tunnels. We overheard two boys saying the dark is a tribute to Lalo, new apprentice for the village. On the morrow, he will receive his appointment from Sleene. His new work will make him a citizen with rights to his father's land.

Els, now her full size and strength, is returning to the Cliffs without danger from her own kind. Severation from a human bearer is a normal part of rapion maturity. The birds are ready and capable to live apart, but it's not natural that the Madronians will keep Els from Lalo forever. Aside from freedom to worship the Creator Spirit, this segregation is the greatest way we are suppressed.

Since the conquest, the few rapion who tried to return to the village were caught, caged, and tortured. Apart from mandated ceremonies, any R'tan found at the Cliffs is threatened with the box and even the stake. Like the ekthesis of firstborn girls, we live with the oppression and try to carry on. I just never knew the full pain before.

Earlier Ratho had to drag me from the Edge of Release and help me down the steep path. I was so weak-legged, he led me from there to our shelf, then to the Steam Pockets. He insisted I go in the one next to him. Mirko had little joy discovering the heat. He did string together a few low notes of mourning, which, even so, were comforting. I sweat, feebly wiped myself down, and redressed in clean clothes.

Ratho and Thae waited for us in the blackness. Together we found our niche, where we ate under-smoked winder and crawled onto our shelves. Tonight there is no racket from the other boys. No rapion are playing or causing mischief. The tunnels sound empty, like hollow, sun-dried goat bones.

"Why did you scream like that, Tiadone?" Ratho whispers.

"Scream?"

"Yes, after you fell to your knees. Don't you remember?"

"No. I only heard the rapion shriek as Els departed and his bond with Lalo was broken."

Ratho's clothes rustle when he leans over the side of his bunk. I cannot see him, but his voice is closer. "You heard a shriek from our rapion?"

"Yes. It was so painful." I sniff.

"From silent rapion?"

Mirko's tail fans across my neck. He squirms in his sleep. "Yes," I answer. "How did you bear it, Ratho?"

He pulls away. "There was no sound, Tiadone. There was only silence when Els flew from Lalo."

"What? Don't tease me, Ratho. It hurt horribly. It must have been the keen of every rapion there."

Ratho turns on his shelf. "There was no sound, Tiadone."

"But how can that be?" I yank my kidskin smooth. "I heard it so clearly, my ears are still sore. My nose bled from the pressure!"

Now the night presses against our quiet. "You must have heard every rapion's centerself, Tiadone. Maybe you heard them collectively mourn."

"What?"

He goes on enthusiastically. "My mother once told me of a R'tan with that power. An ancient one who was strongly linked to the rapion and could hear their collective pain and joy. I think that was a woman though."

My throat clenches, and I spastically cough. No! Not another sign of my amulet's weakness. Gaining control, I whisper, "How could I have done that?"

"I, I don't know. Because Mirko is a Singer?"

Yes! Maybe that is it. My amulet is not deficient. Well, aside from allowing visions to occasionally eek through. My dry tongue still sticks to the top of my mouth.

Ratho's voice quavers. "How will we stand our own Severations, Tiadone?"

"I don't know. It is horrific. And now think; Lalo and Els will never see each other again. At least meaningfully." Father's wish to be near his Nuncia haunts me. Hearing the pain of the rapion makes it easier to understand why Father wouldn't leave his land and the Cliffs. Even for me.

Ratho begins prayers to the Four-Winged Condor. I curl up and pray to the Creator Spirit for Lalo's safety. He travels alone tonight. And I pray for Els. That the rapion would welcome her at the Cliffs and comfort her. I know how greatly she mourns.

CHAPTER 28

WINTER ARRIVES

At first, the heaviness of Lalo's Severation sits on us, but eventually the days stream together like the lines of color stacked in the mesa walls, from gold and yellow to purple. Slowly autumn's chill sneaks through our uniforms. Several more patrollers cycle out, Jilbon included. We had no exchanges beyond our unfortunate first, so I managed to pity him the loss of his rapion. How couldn't I?

The pain and horror of witnessing Severations never lessens. Yet knowing what to expect and having Ratho at my side helps me to recover as soon as is possible.

And so we find a rhythm at Perimeter. Ratho and I patrol all the posts multiple times, each destination like the other with hardly a noticeable difference. There's no reason to jostle for a better position when we line up for assignments. We've seen no evidence of the Triumvirate. Only endless desert.

At the mesa we sleep, eat, and drill. Ratho and I graduated from practice with a tree to practicing along with the entire Carterea division during bola drills. Ratho has mastered the weapon better than me, but I am stronger with the javelin. We compete as usual. It is a relief to be normal again in his eyes.

It is also a relief I've had no more visions.

None of the other patrollers shows any interest in us. By accepting me and Mirko, Ratho has excluded himself from them. He says he prefers my company anyway. The nights the Carterea gather at the firepit, Ratho and I are ignored on the outskirts. At least it seems the boys have grown used to Mirko's songs; now when they quiet, I wonder if it is to only hear him better.

"I believe Patrol is manageable," I said one night while on Perimeter. Ratho had just snagged a desert hare with his bola. It was then the first snowflake fluttered past my chin, and my conclusion was challenged.

Soon we were standing in line for winter gear with the rest of the division. Now our trousers are goat hide with the fur turned inward to warm our legs. Our ponchos are thicker due to rabbit fur linings, and our boots are edged with rabbit as well. Tight leather hats squeeze our twists, secured with a chin strap to fight the winds.

Ratho and I have both grown. The round Clothier puffed and dug in the shelves for longer double-layer underclothes for us both. Ratho has passed my height. Though I believe we both must stand taller than Father now.

I step out of the mesa and her cold corridors to watch the sky lighten. The rabbit fur bulging from the neck of my poncho tickles. The early wind whips my ratty hair twists up off my back and nudges my amulet across my thigh.

Father, I call silently, *how is your health? Our home? The village goats? Frana?* Mirko flaps into the crisp air and glides above me. *Father, you are my soul's portion despite this life you've given me. I understand your choice a little more now.* I wrap my arms around myself. *And I have proven I can serve here. I wish you could see me, Father. Mirko and I are as strong as any! We belong!*

"Tiadone!" Ratho bear hugs me from behind. Thae swirls up to Mirko as I laugh and wrestle Ratho in the new snow. Flakes fluff and twirl around us. As usual, I end up straddling his waist with my knees snug against his wide chest. My stomach flutters, and my breath catches. I lurch back from his full, smiling lips. I've always longed for Ratho's touch, but this is much stronger, and much different, from any sensation before. Trembling, I hurriedly roll off of him.

"You win!" he acknowledges and knocks my upper arm. His eyes pause on mine, his dimple fades, and confusion hovers on his face. I quickly laugh again to cover my own embarrassment at the warmth spreading through my ribs.

Thae glides down to Ratho, which causes him to break his gaze from me. "Some help you were," he tells her. She shrugs her shoulders and opens her wings. Every day, our rapion act more human.

Chamber of Verities, why are these desires inside of me? Surreptitiously, I squeeze my amulet to release more power. Mirko bugles his return and alights quite heavily on my shoulder.

I force my thoughts to Mirko. "You've grown too, you know. Your rump barely fits on my shoulder." He pecks my ear.

The four of us report to bola training. It is a fresh start with our new clothes, and a new challenge to master our weapons in this colder climate. With the strength of the desert cat's heart and my father's hair coils, this strange physical attraction will certainly wither. I've heard the Carterea boys go on for a day about one female back in the village only to be moaning about another the next day. Hopefully, soon I will be moaning none.

Before me, my sigh streams out white like rapion signal smoke. I walk through it with confidence. My legs only slightly shaking, and my pelvis warm.

CHAPTER 29

COMELINESS

On patrol, the duck flails as Ratho's bola tugs the bird to the earth. "Yes!" he shouts. He and Thae run to retrieve it.

Mirko bugles and flaps on the cairn. Tiny ice shards tinkle from his feathers to the sand. Everything is glazed by crystalized dew this cold evening.

I stoke the fire and wiggle my fingers to remove the stiffness. I'll want to pluck the duck swiftly, as the cook has only been serving half portions back at the mesa. Winter hardens the governs even more.

"For you, my friend." Ratho flops the bird at my feet. The head bounces over a rock, and the empty black eyes look like cold pebbles.

I plunge my knife into the carcass and work to remove the warm entrails out the vent. "That was a great throw, Ratho."

"Thanks."

Mirko chortles his approval and Thae drops next to Ratho. Kneeling, he cuts off the duck head, hands it to her, and she voraciously bites into the flesh.

I lower the sticky heart, liver, and kidneys into the pot of boiling water hanging from the tripod I made. Mirko chirps for the remainder of the innards. I toss the glob to him and run my hands through the cold sand to cleanse them.

Ratho reaches around me and begins plucking feathers from the bird, storing them in his pack before the wind whisks them away.

Reaching again, his arm grazes my chest. Tingles travel over my torso. He moves around me and sits down opposite so we both can easily reach the carcass.

"What?" he asks. I shrug and pull at a feather that won't give way in my weakened grasp. "Here." Ratho brushes my hand, leaving hot spots on my palm, and he dislodges the feather.

"Thanks." We work silently.

This is not supposed to get more difficult, for Verities' sake! Why am I not moving past it by the strength of my amulet? I glance at Ratho. Festering fleabots! When did his shoulders broaden even further? I furtively look at my own body. My shoulders have remained narrow. His hips and backside are unchanged. As I shift and then carefully move away from the fire, the flames brighten the large cavern my rump has left in the sand. I sweep my hand through the granules as if to clean off debris. My backside has spread like Mirko's!

I look over at my rapion, who is watching. He waggles his eye-ridge at me.

I glare back. A bit of meat twirls between his beak, and he slurps it up as if in response to my fear. Certainly I am older, but is my body changing as Father warned? It can't ... it simply cannot.

Now I catch Ratho staring at me. "What?" My voice shakes.

"I was just thinking how I'm glad to be patrolling with you, Tiadone. You are a good mate."

"As are you." I give the standard reply. It is all my brain can manage.

"I need to use the trench." He rolls the goose toward me. "You can finish up while I'm gone."

"I will. I'm as hungry as you, you know."

Ratho springs to his feet. Thae nudges the duck head to me and flaps a wing in warning at Mirko, who bobs. "I'll guard your food, Thae," I say. She nods and flies to Ratho. The two drop behind the ridge.

How can I be losing my mind over his body? I shake my amulet, and then work fiercely at plucking the duck naked.

CHAPTER 30

STORM

Mirko glides before the glowing stars. I return from Perimeter and check once more over my shoulder. Except for the dull smudge on the horizon, the frigid distance is as empty as usual. A soft wind carries the scent of salt, and my nose crinkles at the strangeness. A faint light blazes in the sky to my right. Another blossoms to my left.

Mirko screeches. He dives and grasps the branch from my fist. Before I can react he plunges it into our fire, flips into the sky, and swings the flame through the air. Sandstorm!

"Ratho! Wake up! Thae! Triumverate! A sandstorm is on its way!" Running toward the sleeping pit, I snatch my goggles from my pack and tie them on my face. The dark world is divided into thin slits.

"Ratho!" I yell, slap on my hat, and knot the tie. I worm my hands into my goatskin mittens.

Ratho's shadow struggles in the sleeping pit. Sand flies and glints in the night. He's shoveling himself free and making his own sandstorm.

I smother the fire so it won't spread, then bury the torch flame that Mirko drops at my feet. We barrel toward our only shelter. Grabbing the hourglass from the tree, I roll below the rock overhang.

Ratho and Thae bundle in beside us. "Your goggles," I gasp at Ratho in the dimness, and pluck them from his bag.

"Thanks." He slips them on.

"I, I saw the sand shape, and the other rapion signals." I take a deep breath. "Then Mirko signaled." On my lap, he flutters his wings and chitters.

Thae's dark shape rocks. Brushing against me, Ratho says, "I didn't even take a second to look!" He laughs nervously. "I was too busy scrambling from the sleeping pit."

I nod and plant the hourglass into the sand beside me. "And now we wait," I whisper.

"Yes." Ratho's voice is thin.

"Not like back home," I say. "I'd be lining the doors and windows with cloth."

"I'd have to seal the barn. This is crazy, being outside!" He scoots closer.

"It is." The ground vibrates. I lean against him. "Remember old Crablon, who was caught out in the last storm?"

"Suffocated."

"And I overheard two Baltang talking about the team of patrollers who were lost in a sandstorm four years ago."

"Yes, I heard that too." Ratho rubs the grit from his clothes. "The Madronians never found their bodies. Even their rapion were lost."

The howling slams through the blackness and surrounds us. Ratho grabs my mittened hand. "Four-Winged Condor protect us!" he yells. I squeeze his grip tighter.

Beneath Thae's and Mirko's shielding wings, we hunch. The curved rock over our heads covers us as well, but the swirling sand changes directions and drives the grains around every obstacle to needle any bit of exposed skin: my wrist where the mitten has pulled back, my cheekbone below my goggles. Through the eye slits, it pebbles my clenched lids and burns.

A whimper escapes my lips, and sand drives against my teeth. I close my mouth and swallow. Daring to spit would only fill me with more grains. There is nothing to do but keep everything closed and covered as much as possible.

Long howls chase the blasts. Moans and sighs groan around us.

Driving toward the village, the currents of air whip and fall. No wonder the Madronians teach that sandstorms are angry ancestors seething at our failure to worship the Four-Winged Condor.

My spine quivers. No! The storm is not full of the spirits of our ancestors. It isn't. It is only the winds crossing the land, stopping to battle, hot and cold fighting for space. And we are the ones caught in the swirl. Father would say even this is sent by the Creator Spirit for our good. Isn't it?

I reach out and feel the sand rising slowly around us.

While the night passes, we shovel to stop from being buried. Once the sides of our pit rise and we are underground, sand only whips in occasionally from the one slivered edge we keep open for air.

We stretch our arms and legs in the tight area to avoid turning stiff as stone. Our bodies touch and shift against each other as the storm rises and falls outside. It is impossible to know if my pulse speeds from fear or from Ratho's touch. It takes everything not to roll completely up against him. I blush at the thoughts my mind entertains and pull my amulet out from under my hip so the power can flow freely.

By dawn, the swirls glitter in the softer streams of air. In the new dimness, I'm able to see enough to turn the hourglass now. My stomach grinds for food, but there is none. Ratho takes a turn watching, so I let myself drift to sleep.

Father warms his hands over the fire.
"Creator Spirit, protect Tiadone,"
he whispers.
The sandstorm
roars past the window.
"Tea?" He turns to Frana.
"Yes."
He pours the liquid
into my old cup.
Frana raises it.

His lips glide over hers instead.

"Father!" I cry and wake. Mirko raises his head. The winds are quieter, but the sand still flings past.

"Tiadone, what is it?" Ratho removes his goggles. Thae yawns and stretches. "What's the matter?" Ratho repeats.

I pull my goggles off. "Nothing. Just a dream."

"Oh." He nods and turns over. "Looks like we have awhile still to wait. Will you watch now?"

"Yes."

Mirko wedges himself closer to my thigh and bobs his head.

"It is all right," I whisper in agreement. But my centerself clenches at Father's love for Frana. What about me? I am his portion!

Anger tries to rise, but a cold finger of air tickles the back of my neck. I redirect my thoughts. Another vision. You'd think I was a visionaire! Except it's definitely the present. Father, too, is in the storm.

Mirko chitters and tilts his head.

Ratho's back rises and falls with each breath. The sand gives beneath him, and his thigh falls against mine. I clasp my hands together to keep from laying my palm on his warm leg. I try to swallow the dry grains in my throat, but they stick.

Between the visions and my desire for Ratho, I feel so lost. I lift the amulet to my nose and breathe in the musky scent. *Creator Spirit, free me from these weaknesses!*

CHAPTER 31

SURVIVING

I grip the chilled granite overhang and wiggle out through the thin space we kept clear. Mirko shoots into the blue sky where the brilliant sun blasts into my eyes.

My boots crunch in the cold sand. Amazingly, scrub brush still dot the desert. Their tenacious roots refused to let go.

Ratho slithers up and out of the hole. Thae follows with a flap. "Your face is chapped, Ratho," I say, and give him a hand up.

"So is yours."

I tap the rawness about my face. While opening my mouth, the skin stretches taut and burns. "When we hike back tonight, I'll gather some aloe."

"All I can think of is the Steam Pockets, Tiadone."

"Oh, definitely!" We walk over to the cottonwood tree and rehang the hourglass. While I gather wood, brush, and duff peeping through sand ridges, Ratho and Thae leave to scan the Perimeter. They shrink as they hike away.

Screeching, Mirko drops a limp rabbit to the ground. "With thanks," I call. He dips a wing against the bright sky and flaps away to hunt more.

Under my harsh strike, my flint rocks spark. Quickly, a small fire grasps at the dry mound of duff. The flames consume the wood bits I feed to them like my thoughts eat through my joy over surviving the sandstorm.

Father loves Frana.

I ball my hands inside my mittens. He has a love I will never have! Well, one he can act on, when I'll be alone forever.

The thought rolls, gathers weight inside me, and I hunker forward. My breath buffets the ground and ricochets back into my face. I let the reality blast through my mind with its grief. It's the truth I turned from through the storm.

"No!" I thump my fist in the hard packed sand. *Why do you get to have someone, Father, when you've chosen this for me? I'll never have a love!* "Why do you get a second?" I shout. "Why?"

To the east, the empty desert is flayed open by the sunlight. I squint at the harshness.

After Severation, why don't I just leave R'tania? Yes, why wait for a Labor Assignment, and a life alone? I could run beyond the forbidden Perimeter and never come back! Find another land. Maybe with the C'shah? I have better skills now. Maybe I could survive the journey.

There, could I begin again? Would they accept one who wears an amulet?

While cursing, my lower lip cracks. I spit blood and staunch the flow with my mitten. Mirko bugles from a distance. My father couldn't leave the Cliffs after Severation; why would I think I might?

My sobs bulge into the stillness. I coil around the pain, trying to squeeze it to silence. The state Father expects; the state I must stay in to survive.

Eventually, I sit up on my knees and gently blot my mouth and chapped face with my poncho. I can't help but think that Frana would have aloe for my sandburn.

My little fire glows and grows. I add another stick and stretch the rabbit out in the sand.

At least it's Frana that Father has chosen. Her bracelet jingles in my mind the moment a breeze nudges my twists off my tender face. It's Frana, and I have always loved her. She might become my mother, so there is some gain for me too. I wrap the thought and my poncho close.

As I tend and stoke the fire, my mind explores this crater in my centerself like Droslump's nails scamble for coins in the dark box of retribution tithes. Maybe because Father has Frana, maybe because I am nearly grown—because I feel so differently around Ratho now—it all makes me lonelier than ever.

Mirko returns with a worried cry and circles my head. Landing at my side, he nuzzles under my chin.

"Yes, I have you for now," I whisper. He brushes his head against my tears and hums. I sniff and finally say, "I am all right."

Mirko clicks his beak and takes to the air. My fingers wrap around the cooling dead rabbit. My knife slices through the soft flesh below the jaw until blood beads along my blade.

CHAPTER 32

CELEBRATION

The mood at the mesa springs out to us with cheer. Rapion dive and blast skyward into the night. Celebrations ring from the Common as Ratho and I top the last crest. Beyond the spring, the party whirls around a firepit. Spastic shadows race across the towering stone wall. Boys celebrate with dance and tumble over one another.

"Come on!" shouts Ratho. He and Thae swoop into the tumult that actually accepts them. Only because thick mash is being ladled from the urn by the Eating Cavern. Frequently served at gatherings for the new year, I've often seen how the sweet mixture intoxicates with one bowl. These boys look as if they've swallowed more than that already.

"Strange one," a handsome youth named Shiz slurs at me. His dark-lashed eyes are only open halfway. "Bring your rapion, that Singer, and have a bowl to celebrate. We survived the storm! With your return," he burps, "we've lost none." He stumbles away before I answer.

Mirko lands on my shoulder and grips tightly. "This isn't for me," I whisper. I feel the danger of someone in the flurry seeing back to my former sex.

One boy races past me and another chases after him. They collide and crash to the sand, rolling and smacking each other in jest.

I skirt the area. There's not one govern out here. Why the generosity with mash after the storm? Is it a reward? Well, I prefer a hot steam to a thudding head in the morning.

Across the crowd, Ratho lifts a bowl to me. I shrug and turn to our sleeping entrance.

Flecket, a brown-haired boy with twists to his waist, stumbles against me. Mirko shoots above, wings flapping. "Pardon me, ma'am," the boy giggles. I clutch my pack tightly to my chest. "Would you dance with me?" the boy asks and shuffles his feet. Mirko drives him back until he bumps into Dalen, who recently joined our division. "How about you. Do you want to dance?"

"Certainly," he replies in a high, giddy voice.

Inside the cavern, I flee through the passages toward my bunk. I toss my gear onto my shelf, grab my change of clothes, and rush after Mirko to the pockets.

I call out before the farthest, and when none answers we duck under the skin flaps. Mirko chortles in anticipation of the steam.

Within the total blackness, I sit on the ledge by the small pool. I'm too afraid to remove my clothes. It's exactly as I feared: Intoxicated, the boy could see my former sex. *Would you dance with me? Ma'am?*

Mirko chitters as if all is well. He brushes my trousers by flinging open his wings. The air stirs the coals in the corner, and they brighten.

"He sensed the femininity leaking past my amulet," I whisper. A slight, twisted thrill rises in me before panic annihilates it. This thing must work fully! The Madronians' threat is very real. If I ever remove my amulet, even if my remaining femininity is only a whisper, they would kill me as a firstborn female.

With the tongs, I drop the hot rocks into the water and hold my face over the steam, trying to sweat away these crazy-headed thoughts. Doubly unforgiveable would be to lure a male to me when I'm declared. Both lives would be forfeited—yearly, my Madronian teachers made that clear in my private sessions.

Mirko's eyes catch the light of the coals before steam separates us.

"It was only the mash," I say aloud to believe it. "He was just acting the fool."

I carefully remove each layer of clothing. My gritty toes grip the warm stone as I run my hands down my chest. Small breasts bulge under my palms. I have—little breasts. My waist curves in above the new hair growing at the fork of my legs. Boys have hair there as well, though, don't they?

My amulet swings against my thigh. Is it stopping my body at all from changing, like Father hoped but doubted? Why? Why can't it? A shiver tremors my chill into the steam.

One arm covering my chest, I squat and let the steam weave around me.

Mirko sings as though we have no concern. He picks at my twists in the darkness, and my body streams sweat.

After a restless sleep on my shelf, in the morning I kneel beyond the Common. Little drops of water balance on each pale green, oval leaf, making the glino plant sparkle. I hold the slim branch and run my fingers downward. The leaves are stripped into my palm. This should be enough. I pat them dry.

Mirko spirals down to my feet, and we walk back to the mesa. His head now reaches my knees, and if I am not in a hurry his gait matches mine when he chooses to walk. He rides my shoulder less and less.

The horizon lightens and tinges the spring water pink. Mirko chitters along with the splashing sounds filling the empty area. Soon the morning drum will sound, and the Madronians will have their retribution against the patrollers' headaches and nausea, all that will be left over from the party.

I duck into the Sleeping Cavern and bump into Shiz, the boy who called me to join the party. "Excuse me," I mumble.

"Shhhh." He squeezes his full lips together. His rapion, Baesa, drapes her girth across his shoulders.

"Sorry," I say, and go to step around him but get caught staring instead. His green eyes, still not fully open, are framed by brown twists that skim his shoulders. His smile snags my centerself and flips it. Definitely the most handsome boy I've ever seen.

Mirko pecks my hand. "Oh," I recover. "Um, glino leaves might settle your stomach, and silence your head." I open my trembling hand.

"Thank you," he says, and plucks a few from my moist palm.

I clamp my fist closed again. "Just suck on the leaves until you feel better." He nods, slips two into his mouth, and one into his rapion's. Did Baesa swallow mash also? She lowers her lids at Mirko, who flaps and takes a strutting step.

Shiz glances at him and steps back. "Good tidings for your day," he says as he finally heads out of the entrance.

"Returned to you." The sun outlines him until he turns out of my sight.

Mirko leans outside to watch his rapion even longer.

"You are shameless!" I roll my eyes and tug him toward our alcove. "Don't you think Baesa's wide in the hips?" I whisper. He grins up at me and winks. I huff. "So when did my rapion begin to notice others?" He chitters back as if to say: *And when did you?*

I knock my calf against his side and step to our bunk. "Ratho, wake and take some leaves." He doesn't respond. "Ratho."

Mirko warbles a song that resembles a dirge. Ratho and Thae open their eyes and groan.

"Ugh, Tiadone. Save me." He reaches out.

"Just take a few leaves." I drop two into his palm and plop flustered onto my shelf. Shiz? Now I am attracted to Shiz as well? You'd think it was rutting season or something.

Boys stumble through the hall moaning and groaning. I gather my gear. If everyone had just gone to sleep, as I did, and not swallowed mash all night, they wouldn't complain so now. Like Shiz. I pause and envision him in the sunlight.

Mirko jumps onto our bunk. He waggles his tail.

"Oh, stop!" I hiss.

"What?" asks Ratho.

"Never mind." I shove my kidskin into my pack harder than necessary.

CHAPTER 33

RETRIBUTION

The cook bangs his pots louder than necessary. "Morning slop, hot and ready," he shouts. His dark beard quivers over his supressed laughter. The boys' necks shorten with each clang. It is the first time I see bowls left behind with food stuck to the edges.

Our company reports for javelin drill wearing their slotted goggles to avoid the intense sunlight. Rapion sprawl listless in the icy, gleaming sand.

The Javelin Govern's booming voice rumbles and puffs out his moustache. "Is the morn too bright for you? Remove your eye gear, you infants, you breast-sucking babes!"

My face scorches at the words. Despite wearing my winter layers, first thing this morning I tore long sheaves from the yi plant and bound my chest. Thankfully a patch grows by the latrines, so it was easy to gather. Now the strips tighten with the govern's comment.

Groaning, everyone tosses their goggles aside. I am thankful the sun doesn't bother me. Mirko hums quietly on my shoulder.

The govern slaps his mittened hands. We begin the memorized movements, but he stops us frequently to inspect our positions. "Lift that weak arm! Shift your rapion's tail! Raise your javelin higher! Turn your face to the sun and pray to the Four-Winged Condor, because you will need divine help to endure this drill!" His wide grin shows dark pockets where several back teeth are missing. Here is the Madronian punishment: higher demands in our usually monotonous drills while the patrollers are in a weakened state.

Out of the side of my eye, I see Desl, the boy who bunks next to me and Ratho. His face pales, and he sways in the pose. "Continue!" yells the govern.

In the front line, Creo, usually with the best form in drill, heaves his breakfast. Ratho mentioned he passed out before the party ended last night.

"Hold!" The govern stalls our current position: javelin in the air, legs in a deep lunge. Creo's rapion helps him sweep sand over his slop, and they stumble back into position.

The govern whisks behind them and kicks the boy in his back. *Crack!* Creo falls into his barely covered vomit. His rapion cowers beside him. "Get up!" the govern yells. The boy is too slow and is kicked again. Whimpering, Creo stands, and I see his poncho is smeared with stomach mess. He faces the sun and takes our pose.

The govern smirks and continues to walk among us, looking for error. He flicks between our formations.

My legs begin to tremble as murmurs against Creo slip through the air. Here is another way the Madronians work to make us hate one another. This is idiocy! So they overdrank. It was a celebration. Isn't their discomfort enough?

"You swallow mash like a man," says the govern, "you work like a man the next day." He keeps us in the pose several more minutes. Shiz and Ratho hold steady on my right. The leaves must have settled their stomachs; most of the boys waver in their weakness.

Finally the govern calls, "Continue!" I move through the steps, and the shakes melt out of my legs. I wonder how many will touch the mash after the next sandstorm. Word of the glino plant may circulate, and there will be those who risk that the leaves will work. But so many Carterea look unwell. I can't believe they'll shovel into the mash as quickly. Now if it was Father's potato ale, that would be harder to refuse. My mouth waters for the taste.

FIRSTBORN

When our drill ends, Mirko joins the rapion leaping into the air. I bow to the sun, whose yellow rays warm my upturned face. I'm ready to do the work of a man today. *Thank you, Creator Spirit, for my life. Even for life as a man.* After the sandstorm, at least I am alive.

CHAPTER 34

PAINS

Our routine resumes, and everything is as before. One division replaces the other on patrol. The weather intensifies and lessens, with ice freezing and thawing and wind rising and falling. Another sandstorm follows. But this time, Ratho and I are at the mesa, safe on our shelves.

By morning it has blown itself out. Later in the day, word passes that the Madronians offered mash to the returning patrollers. Maybe mash only serves to dull the senses and memories so we are ready to face Perimeter again after a trial. At least they all returned safely as we did.

I've learned to accept my rapid pulse when Shiz walks near, or Ratho reaches out and touches me. Hiding my thoughts and desires is the only thing I really must control. None will know of the weakness of my amulet if I can help it. If I have daydreams while walking Perimeter, it hurts no one. Dreams are all I will ever have. I've decided I will have them.

Right now it is enough to reign in Mirko whenever we pass Shiz's Baesa. He swoons, making a complete fool of himself by grinning and nearly drooling. Baesa hasn't acknowledged Mirko's craziness. Either because he's a Singer, or she hasn't yet fully awakened to attraction. Most rapions don't until after release. Of course mine would be the one ready to mate.

In the midst of everything, it seems as if I find a degree of normalcy until one monotonous Perimeter Patrol. The cramping late in the afternoon is a complete surprise. "Ohhh!" I moan as I clutch my abdomen.

Ratho moves around the fire ring. "What's wrong?" he asks, kneeling beside me.

"I, I'm not sure." Another pain crunches across my hips.

"Maybe that sidewinder Mirko caught for you was sickened," says Ratho.

Mirko looks around my knees and hisses at him. My rapion would never give me unfit food. I grind my fist into my waist.

Could it be my bloodflow? The blood streams out of my face; surely it will flow straight out between my legs!

"I think I have a bit of medicinal left for stomachaches." I grab my pack and jump up. "And I, I think I need to use the trench."

"It must be that winder," Ratho calls to my back.

Mirko perches in the shrub, and I skid down the ridge, trusting he will alert me if Ratho nears. Not that patrollers don't respect privacy, but worry might inch him closer.

At the base of the slope, I straddle the ditch. With shaking hands I check and find no blood on my undergarments. "There's nothing," I hiss.

Mirko chortles encouragement.

Another cramp bites my gut. A perfect globe of blood drips out of me down into the trough. Tears float over my eyes. I tear open my pack's secret pouch and pull out the netted sponge Father showed me so long ago. Squatting deeply, I feel for the opening no other patroller has.

My hand stops. It is too unnatural to push an object into myself. The sponge dangles from my finger by the string.

"Are you okay?" Ratho sounds closer! Mirko hisses. "I'm just checking, Mirko," he chuckles.

I grip the sponge before it falls from my hand and hike up my pants. "Yes. I'll only be a bit longer."

"Well, it's time for me to patrol. Have Mirko signal me if you need help while I'm gone."

I lean against the embankment and gulp down my tears. "I will," I say, steadying my voice. "Would you bring me back some pinoni to help settle my stomach? I've run out after all."

"Sure."

"But I need the whole plant—with the root."

"All right." His footsteps retreat. He never learned medicinals, so it isn't an odd request.

I drop my trousers again. No blood stains the garments, thankfully. I fling my poncho off my head, toss it up so it catches on the bush, and resume my squat. This time I will insert this thing. I am declared male, and this will not stop me!

I get the thing placed well inside despite my roiling stomach and hesitation to touch myself. It is no different than Father sliding his fingers into a goat for a delivery, right? The tip of the inserted sponge rubs an ache all the way up against my centerself while the thick string brushes my bare thigh. I swallow and pant to ease the violation.

When Ratho returns I'll line my undergarment with a pinoni leaf. Hopefully, chewing the stems may help the fiery pain be quenched.

After swiping a hand through sand, I redress completely. Quickly, I fill in the section of the ditch I used until my blood is covered and then clean my hands thoroughly.

Climbing the slope, I free my poncho from the shrub. No wonder I've had to use a longer breast wrap. I should have faced the truth: my breasts are full now. At least it doesn't seem I will be big-bosomed like Frana. My smallness is somewhat easy to hide.

I fling my twists behind my back. Mirko walks by my side, humming a sweetness that calms me. I'll just lie in the sleeping pit until Ratho returns.

Mirko and I nest together. The sun sets and a chilled fog from beyond Perimeter billows toward us. Mirko fluffs. The warm, trapped air between his feathers slips from him to me.

"Tiadone." Ratho shakes my shoulder until I fully wake. "Here is your plant. Are you feeling better?" I nod a lie. He pulls me up and leads me to the fire. I try to stand straight but bend slightly at the waist. "I'll take your shift. You look awful, Tiadone."

"No, I'm okay." He brushes the hair from my cheek. I lean into his hand, and his forehead crinkles. Shiz is more handsome, but Ratho would make a good mate. I can't remember ever not loving him. Even when he withdrew from me, said such horrible things, my centerself couldn't fully turn from him. His dark eyes narrow, and he places his palm on my forehead.

I pull away. "I'm okay. Really. I'll just visit the latrine again. Here, I'll take the pinoni." I get up and lurch away.

"Call me if you need help walking back. Bad winder can really drain you," he says. I clutch the plant to my chest. If only it was winder.

Mirko chitters a rebuke at Ratho, swoops around my knees, and rises high into the darkness. He crows as if celebrating! Because of my sabotaging flow bursting past my amulet? What is there to celebrate?

CHAPTER 35

TRACKS

The pinoni stems work faster than I anticipate. As long as I chew a fresh bit occasionally, the cramping eases.

Firelight fans and falls. At least Ratho finally believed I'm strong enough for my shift, and he lay down in the Sleeping Pit. But now he's up again.

"Tiadone! With your illness, I forgot to tell you that I saw tracks along the line at the southern point. Beyond the distant pinyon pine."

"Tracks?" I shade my eyes from the fire.

"Definitely desert cat. Must be moving closer because of the long cold season, driven in for our village goats. The marks turned back out into the open sand, but we need to watch carefully."

"Right." A spark imbeds into my boot, glows bright, then dies.

Ratho lies down. "I don't think the cat's very large. The prints were smaller than my palm."

"That's good," I say. Mirko stretches one leg then another, and we both peer into the darkness.

No one has stood against a cat since our arrival at Perimeter. It takes all manner of skill to defeat one before it breaks through the line and attacks the village: goats or children.

I narrow my eyes to see beyond the flames. There's nothing out there now. My gaze drifts to the fire, where the glowing embers at the base look like cat eyes. I stare, mesmerized, and wiggle my fingers deep in my mittens.

The coals flicker like my thoughts do. So much has changed since I have come to Perimeter. My father loves Frana. My bleeding has begun. I have visions shared with Mirko. Unfortunately, we both feel a desire for affection.

I look over at Mirko, who whistles softly to me. "At least you will mate," I whisper, "once you return to the Cliffs." He fills his chest and flaps his wings. When I return to the village, he will mate in love. There is a hope for him after our Severation. The thought salves my centerself. Until my own future returns fully to mind.

I kick the sand with the heel of my boot. Oh, stop the self pity. What good comes of it? I have a purpose. I'm raising Mirko for safe return and contributing to the village. There's worth in that. As Father says, others may declare their firstborn females male with my success. I squeeze my knees close and watch the flames grasp at the darkness.

CHAPTER 36

THE GAME

Spring nudges closer. Mittens, fur-lined boots, and double undergarments are returned for lighter wear. Our chapped lips and cracked skin slowly heal. Most coughs and runny noses fade, except for the youngest patroller's, Devino. He coughs even now as he passes our bunk on the way to breakfast. So small and thin, it's hard to believe he is old enough to serve out here.

I lift a yawning Mirko and place him on the ground. "Come quickly," I tell him. "Ratho and Thae are already at breakfast." He nods and trails after me.

The fresh air sweeps into my lungs. The sun, rising earlier, already crouches on the horizon. I silently greet the Creator Spirit and join a couple of boys at the spring, who leave as I splash water on my face and neck. Mirko dips his beak into the burbles rushing in the trough. He gargles and spews the water skyward so that cold droplets land on my poncho. "Thanks, Mirko." He smiles, leaps down, and waddles to the Eating Cavern.

The raucous noise of the Carterea division bings off the walls. Mirko and I slide in next to Ratho. Shiz lurches into us but regains his footing quickly.

"Sorry," he says and pushes his offender, Desl, who only laughs in return. Clay bowls are tapped rhythmically against the stone ledge by each boy awaiting his meager portion. Shuffling around his pots, the cook is slow this morning. He barely stirs the slop in his kettle.

Finally, the apprentice ladles gruel into our bowls from a pot clutched in his skinny arm. The gray ooze plops into mine. A quick spoonful scalds my tongue. "Ow!"

Mirko whistles concern. I tap the burn against the roof of my mouth and find it's not bad. "I'm fine," I say.

The apprentice moves around the noisy circle, offering gruel to each boy. He looks back at the cook and receives a nod. He skips serving Devino. Bits of anger glow inside me. Why pass him when he's so sick? It's obvious the boy is gaunt, and his eyes are glazed!

The apprentice ladles food into the next boy's bowl, and Devino is too weak to challenge anyone. I let out a big sigh to cool my tongue while everyone else talks, eats, and burps. Amidst the chaos, I stand with my bowl. Ratho tugs at my arm. "Eat, Tiadone."

I shrug off his fingers despite the cook's glare. When Govern Droslump steps into the cavern, our eyes meet, but I do not stop. I take my steaming gruel to Devino and set my bowl inside his empty one. He stares down at the food.

The cacophony dies, and the only sound I register is of Mirko's wings snapping open. I climb out of the eating circle and leave the group as Mirko bugles my defiance and follows.

Play the game, Father said. Not today. I've just stepped outside of the Madronian match. No matter the consequences, I've done what is right. It is okay to play if no one is hurt, or we are just uncomfortable, or are forced to work hard. But when a life is threatened, the game has to stop. Frana would say so.

I walk outside to the north edge of the mesa and slide to the sand. Mirko dives into the lavender shrub. He will find a little breakfast. I close my eyes and let the sun warm my lids. It was the right thing to do. Devino is very ill and needs food.

Within moments, wingbeats and footsteps approach. "He didn't touch it," Ratho says.

"Devino?"

"Yes. So when Droslump left, I traded bowls with him. That one he ate."

"Hmph." I open my eyes. "Because I'm declared or because of Mirko?"

Ratho slides down next to me. "Who knows."

"Well, did you eat mine?" I ask.

"Of course." He wipes a blob off his lip. "Just as you should have."

"No." I close my eyes again.

Mirko waddles out with a mouthful of beetles and a wide grin. Legs and antennae scrabble against his beak. My stomach dips. He offers me one by laying it at my feet. It lies on its back with its legs treading furiously. I flip it over, but it's too maimed to fly away.

CHAPTER 37

DISCIPLINE

The Javelin Govern stomps through our formation. His skin rides the tendons ridging his neck. "Food received is food valued." I try not to flinch as his eyes drill into mine.

Mirko leans into my knee.

"I have been briefed concerning the extravagance shown this morning in the Eating Cavern. As a result, you will drill twice as long today." My fellow patrollers moan, silenced only when the govern raps his javelin in his calloused palm. "And you will have this extra opportunity" — he stops in front of me, inches from my nose — "by sacrificing mid-break."

I stare through the man. Now it is necessary to play the game again. He moves through the rank. To my right, Devino's rapion is pressed against the boy's leg. So Devino will miss food, regardless, if there truly was any for today. A huff escapes my lips.

"And you!" The govern backsteps to me. My mouth saps dry. "You won't participate."

"What?" say the whispers around me.

The govern lifts his javelin and strikes the back of my knees. I collapse to the sand next to Mirko, who gnashes his beak. His eyes narrow into slits as he stands on his toes. Only my grip on his left leg keeps him from attack.

"You will carry a message to the lookout and return in time for patrol, or you will receive lashes."

"Yes, Govern." My answer muffles in the sand. A sealed parchment drops next to my nose just as a final kick to my side sends the breath out of me. I curl around the burn.

"Begin!" The boys start the first drill. Their javelins and arms pulse like the Four-Winged Condor taking flight.

I grab the parchment, pull my knees to my chest, and rock onto my feet. Bent over, I scurry out of the formation. It would be easy to receive another blow by standing still during this drill. Especially when everyone seethes over the punishment I have drawn on them, which I am escaping. The Madronians stir anger like an old medicinal woman dipping her spoon in a bubbling remedy brew.

I reach the outside of the formation. Mirko nudges and nuzzles my leg once again. I look to the govern for direction. With his javelin, he points toward the north side of the mesa.

"The third trail," he says.

I tuck the parchment into my poncho belt and jog. Rounding the bend, I count the trails to the third and follow it. It's steep but eventually arches over an amph and then the Edge of Release. Mirko flies upwards and I climb higher.

Just before ascending to the top of the mesa, my calf cramps. I slump against the small landing. At least the porous, cold stone cools my moist forehead as the purple rock blurs then comes into focus. The wall curves around me like a cup. Maybe the R'tan carved it as a spot to rest, a nook protected from sudden wind?

Mirko perches above, a brown spot against a brilliant blue sky. He waits for me to recover.

I wash a gulp of water over my dry tongue. "I'm coming," I say, and cross to the final section. Mirko raises his head and bugles. I labor up, grip the handholds, and scramble onto the flat surface of the mesa. Breathing heavily, I gaze across the way. The lookout's rotunda perches, extending off the edge of rock.

Mirko sweeps open his wings.

I heave my pack straight, and tingles pull my spine vertical.

"Amazing!" The vast mesa stretches to the south. Across the flat top, red folds into orange and yellow, and, sporadically, purple shadows ring holes where tunnels have collapsed. "Imagine the villas—the R'tan that once lived in this great rock, Mirko."

Mirko sings to the beauty. The sun glints off his feathers, and sparkles of light are cast on the pink stone.

Invigorated, I limp on sore feet across the pebbled rock to the Rotunda. Mirko walks the remaining steps by my side. It has taken hours to ascend the weaving, steep trail. Midday is here; I will have to hurry down in order to meet Ratho for patrol. This retribution is worse than double javelin drills. But then I am the culprit.

At least I carry a message that may help our village. My effort has meaning.

My vision tips left, then right. I steady myself, my amulet swinging out over open space before resting again against my thigh.

Mirko whistles sharply.

"Yes, I'll focus." The edge of the mesa has no railing, and a stumble would launch me over the side. I slow my pace to walk a straight line.

The wood landing around the rotunda creaks beneath my boots. The area is empty, as no patroller serves here currently, though a thick scent of simmering meat drifts to me from under the black door. I bend over and draw in a deep breath of sweet, moist meat. Maybe goat? I haven't tasted any since I left Father.

Mirko nudges me forward at the same time the door bangs open. A grizzled, yellow-tinged Madronian crosses his arms and plants his knobby feet so wide that my entry into the rotunda is impossible. His brown robes droop, an echo of his skin on his bony frame. Mirko's warning hum draws the man's startled look, but the stranger recovers.

"Well, patroller?" His voice tumbles up his bumpy throat and out his squinched mouth.

I offer the gesture of respect, but he does not return the honor to me. I quickly remove the Javelin Govern's parchment.

He takes it without touching me and fully opens it. "Yes. Yes. I see." The spittle on his lips bounces and stretches thin with each word. "As you can see" — he flips the document for my view — "it is blank."

My mouth hangs open. "What? I have climbed—"

"You have wasted my time, patroller." He turns his hunched back away from me and slams the door shut. *Clunk.* The scent of goat meat is swept away.

I slump against the wall. "It was blank," I groan. Mirko clicks his tongue. My body trembles to contain my tears. Useless. Worthless. Another evidence of how the Madronians strip our dignity with meaningless tasks.

My hunger and thirst ache through my belly and throat. With one last swallow, my water sack is emptied. Mirko licks a droplet from the edge.

I push myself from the wall and rap the door. "Lookout," I call, quickly wiping my eyes. "Lookout, may I have some water for the descent?" I plead to the black wood. The wind whisks away my begging, and the Madronian doesn't open the door.

Mirko grasps the water sack in his talons.

"That puddle a ways down? Maybe a patch of melted snow?" He nods and flaps away.

Straight below is the Common. The boys are dots, moving about. I hate this idiocy. As if any of this turmoil makes R'tan boys stronger. The Madronians are fools.

"Thank you, Mirko," I call, weaving over to the top of the path. I sit and scoot, resting my heels in the carved holds. The winds have strengthened; a gust could fling me down the side of the rock.

I fix my gaze on the landing below and inch my way back into their stupid game.

CHAPTER 38

PIERCED

Ratho carries my pack and his own as we move in line toward Dro-slump. My head still tingles due to my labored breathing during my quick descent. Even with my full effort, I only returned just in time for patrol. I'm sure my feet are blistered and bleeding. When I climbed, I didn't take enough care not to bang my toes against the rock. Now I will pay for it.

Mirko hums beside me, and Thae smiles at me from the other side of Ratho. I manage a nod to her.

Being last in line, the four of us were ignored when we joined rank; yet the shunning felt colder than normal. My hatred for Dro-slump is enough to counter it. I'm sure he's the one who chose my punishment.

Ratho said Devino was taken to infirmary after falling uncon-scious during the second group of drills. At least maybe now the foolish Madronians will feed him.

Spinko and Fren, two patrollers who never seem to draw notice to themselves, take their portion and instructions, then jog off to the northern post. I step forward with Ratho. The apprentice darts the last map to us. Ratho takes it, but the young man won't meet our eyes. Looks like the next to the last position in the south.

"To cleanse the sin from the patrollers, Four-Winged Condor," says Droslump with tight lips. He places a wafer on Ratho's tongue.

The govern turns to me. Heat streams from his hand as his fingers extend the wafer. I hold my head steady and open my mouth wide. His bony fingers lay the bread behind my front teeth, and at the last moment, Droslump's pointed index fingernail strikes, piercing deeply into my tongue.

"Huh!" I jump back. Mirko beats his wings furiously, and my tongue throbs along with his rhythm. I spit out the wafer into my palm. It's soaked in my blood! When I look up, I see the apprentice hurrying away from us.

"Swallow the gift of the Four-Winged Condor, patroller!" Droslump hisses while tipping wine into Ratho's gaping mouth. The govern steps to me with his hand upraised. I lift the bloody bit back to my mouth. It disintegrates with a swallow of my blood.

Before I can finger my tongue to staunch the wound, Droslump holds the cup to my lips. He strikes the clay rim upward. *Creator Spirit!* My teeth ring, and I sputter flecks of wine and blood onto Droslump's embroidered condors. He smacks me across the temple and blackens everything.

"Tiadone." I open my eyes. Ratho's lips are close to my ear, and I'm suddenly alert. "Tiadone, come. We must leave quickly for patrol."

"Yeth," I mumble, my tongue a swollen mound. I try to sit up, and realize Mirko is squatting on my chest. "Go on," I say and roll him off. He chortles in concern.

With a worried Thae on his shoulder, Ratho pulls me to my feet. I take a step and soon get my legs steady beneath me. Ratho hands me his water sack, and I take a swig. I dribble the bloody stream out into the sand. The next time it runs pink.

"Droslump is gone, but I'm sure he'll be back soon to be certain we've left." Ratho brushes my twists from my eyes. He grimaces at what must be a bruise on my face. His fingertips sweep my cheek, and he makes the blessing gesture on my forehead.

I hold back my sobs. "Patrol," my throbbing tongue fumbles.

"But first, you need to change," Ratho says. I look down at my clothing. When I was knocked unconscious, I wet my trousers. Could the humiliation grow worse? "Come. It's all right. Earlier, I saw our clean clothes were already delivered." He leads me by the hand to the Sleeping Cavern. Our rapion swoop close above.

Ratho pauses. "Let me see your tongue." I stick it out past my fevered teeth, and he shivers. "Fleabots, that's bad. He must have had a poison under his nail!"

"That explains the thwelling." I feel over the lump and gouge. My head lightens.

Ratho clasps my shoulders. "Can you go change while I fill your water sacks?"

"Yeth." I wipe my damp, cold forehead.

"Let me see you walk through the opening then."

I lunge toward the entrance. "I'm fine," I mumble. Mirko lands beside me and rubs against my calf.

"Go on then." Ratho runs to the spring.

I make my way down the hallway but lean against the stone when my sight warps. The condors glare at me from their niches. "I'd like to melt every last piece in the fire pit," I slur.

Mirko hisses, and his feathered head fills my dangling palm.

"I wouldn't really do it." I sniff back my tears. "I'll play, Mirko. Nothing I did mattered today anyway. Nothing at all." I hang my mouth open for the cool air to fight the heat boiling from my tongue. My boots shlump forward in the sand.

Ratho helps me stumble out to patrol. The Baltang boys we replace hurl insults for our tardiness. Even the red seeping through the skin of my boots does not soften them.

"It's good to be rid of you! May your rapion fly low and heavy with avian worms!" Ratho curses them as they finally disappear over the knoll.

I smile. "And may you wake in the morning with bots in your nose!" I murmur, noticing my tongue feels less swollen.

"Harsh!" laughs Ratho. "Oh, your father hates the goat bots." I flop beside the fire, and Ratho flips the hourglass.

Thae assumes position on the taller cairn, and Mirko tugs at my boots. "Yes, I'll check." I pull the goatskin off one foot at a time. We all intake a big breath. My clean socks and the numbing sheathes from the ardis plant we found mid-route are blood-soaked.

I peel everything off my feet before the wounds seal further with the fibers. Tears float over my eyes. My feet are bloodied and blistered like never before. Especially the ends of my toes; one nail is already blackened.

Ratho whistles, then quickly retrieves the pot from the cottonwood and fills it with water. "We have to clean you up first."

I grimace and prop my feet on a small boulder and lie back. The twilight stars swirl. Exhaustion overtakes me.

"I'll gather aloe, and what else?"

"There's probably no ardis out here, but yucca strips for bandages will help," I say with what little energy I have. Mirko blows gently on my wounds to lessen the sting. As I pass out, I hear my stomach grumbling for food.

CHAPTER 39

A BABE

Frana washes dishes,
and Father rocks in his chair.
The room smells of sweet tuber stew.
I place my hand on Father's shoulder.
He reaches his calloused hand through mine,
and a smile flits on his lips.
He smells of goats.

"Are you sure you don't need help, Frana?"
"No. I'm nearly done," she says.
I glide my hand over the wall stones
hiding our *Oracles* and sigh.
"Do you feel a draft?" Frana asks.
She turns. Beyond her usually full frame,
her belly is rounded gently with child!
My shaking hand covers the swell.
My sibling presses back.

"Oh, the babe rolled!" Frana laughs.
She grows smaller and smaller
in a pinprick of light.

CHAPTER 40

NEVER AGAIN

I wake calling, "Frana!" The fire cracks and shows Mirko and I are alone. With glowing eyes, my Signico flaps to my side and trumpets for the babe.

"Father's bound to Frana, and she's with child!" My mind is numbed by the vision. I am to have a sibling!

What does this mean to me? I am to share my father's love with Frana and a babe? Will there be room for me when I return home? Will I belong and still be Father's portion?

Jealous fingers pinch at my centerself. The babe will not be a firstborn to Father. Already its life is better than mine.

Stop it! I fold my arms across my chest and rock, hoping to calm myself. The truth that I myself will always be alone and barren pierces deep, deep, deeply, but I cram it aside. To have a child is not the right or experience of a male. Especially, not the declared.

Anyway, what I can do is love this child, and it may love me. I vow to nurture it as I have my rapion.

Mirko nibbles my sleeve, bringing me back to my surroundings. I sit up carefully and draw my throbbing feet close to inspect them. They are clean at least.

Mirko grins and whistles. I blush at the thought of Ratho's touch: that he would look at my sores, and that I would sleep through his care. But he has done an amazing job. The open blisters don't look nearly as bad now that the blood is gone. Herbs will prevent infection, ones Ratho or I can easily find. I stretch my feet toward the fire, keeping the blanket under them.

I probe my tongue and teeth and find a pinoni leaf. Mirko waddles with satisfaction. Ratho placed it there? I sigh and smile. Certainly the swelling of my tongue has truly gone down and the ache of my teeth has lessened. The gouge still pulses, but as Father says it is good to be young. The young heal quickly. "My mouth is nearly numb, Mirko."

He fluffs on my lap; in response my stomach rolls its hunger against him. He pads his feet, talons lifted, and the cramping eases.

Soon, Ratho and Thae trot into camp. "We feast tonight!" he shouts.

At the sight of an owl and rabbit hanging from his fist, I clap and Mirko sings a celebration. "What a catch, Ratho! Bring me the bird, and I'll start plucking."

"You sound so much better, Tiadone!" He skids on his knees through the sand to my side.

"I am. Thanks to you."

Ratho shrugs. "You are my partner." I return his smile. "So, the owl had just risen with the rabbit in his grip when my bola took them both down."

"Your aim and a gift from god!"

"Yes, the Four-Winged Condor showed favor!"

I ignore his adage and set to plucking while he removes the rabbit entrails for our rapion.

Ratho glances at my feet. "I have your leaves in my pack for bandaging."

"Thanks."

"Let me see your tongue."

I stick it out carefully. Ratho bites his lip. "Really. It's better," I say.

His hand curls into a fist, but then he continues his work. As I watch the rapion tear into the innards, a quill slips and jabs into my thumb. I quickly press the wound to my trousers to stop the bleeding.

"Ratho, I won't—" He looks up. The firelight flickers across his brow. The beauty of his focus on me and his sincerity stop me. I force myself to breathe. "I won't rebel again. I ask forgiveness."

He brushes his shoulder against mine, sending tingles down my arm. "That would be good for all, Tiadone, and you would honor the Four-Winged Condor." I can't meet his eyes. "But I know you intended well," he says.

The owl's beak falls open in my lap. My mouth feels just as slack. I rush to ask what I've always wondered. "Ratho, have you"—I tumble the words out—"always believed in the Four-Winged Condor?"

"Tiadone!" He glances about us into the darkness then turns back to me. "What has happened to you? First you defy the Madronians at morning meal, and now you question my allegiance to the Condor?" He reaches over and grips my hand, stops my plucking. "It is as if you are a different person, Tiadone."

I release the feather and twine my fingers with his. I grasp him tightly. "What if the true god is the R'tan god, not a creature, Ratho, like us or the rapion? What if he's a spirit?" He locks on to my eyes. "What if God is the Creator Spirit?"

Ratho gasps and tries to wiggle his hand out of mine, but I hold tightly and rush on. "Just think. The Four-Winged Condor is not who the R'tan have worshiped from the time the first man and rapion hatched beside the sea. It has always been the Creator Spirit. Didn't your parents teach you so?"

"No!" He tugs free and slumps on his haunches. Thae and Mirko look up at our silence, their beaks rimmed with blood.

"Look at them, Ratho." I point to our rapion. "They are birds, as the condors are that fly in the southern realms. We are all created. Couldn't we have all been made by the Creator Spirit?"

"It's blasphemy worthy of the stake," Ratho whispers. He turns and fiercely peels the skin back from the rabbit carcass. "Please don't speak of this again." He reaches out and drags a bloody finger down my cheek—blood to cover my heresy.

I blink. If only I had someone besides Father and Mirko to share my beliefs.

"Never again speak of such things, my friend," Ratho begs. The fire crackles and sparks into the air, like my hope crackles out of my body with my nod.

CHAPTER 41

FAILURE

Winter completely rolls over, the weather warms, and the dina cacti burst pink flowers across the desert. Walking along Perimeter at dawn, I laugh at the newly hatched lizard scurrying from Mirko's talons. The baby snips beneath a boulder.

As soon as Mirko takes to the air, the lizard peeps out again, and I see it is a female who has survived my Signico's attack. How does the babe grow within Frana, I wonder, trying to encourage my excitement and silence my lingering jealousy.

I clamber up the boulder and run down the other side. What a relief my feet and tongue have healed over the past weeks. I've played the game completely each time we return from patrol, although my hatred for Droslump is still raw. I don't mention the Creator Spirit to Ratho again.

Arriving back at our post, I find Ratho has left a rock on the knoll to show he and Thae are off picking berries. Mirko plops down beside me when I resume work on the sandal I'm forming with strips of rintell bark. These won't be very durable, so we'll need many pairs.

"I can't believe the Madronians didn't give us leather sandals," I grumble to Mirko.

He blinks at me.

"You know, when we turned in our winter uniform for spring issue?"

He preenes his shoulder.

"Yes, well, it's not easy to make these, you know." I pull a tight weave for the soles then crisscrosses for the top of the foot. My hands do grow more nimble with each sandal I complete, as I recall little weaving tricks Frana taught me when I was younger.

That evening, when Ratho, Thae, Mirko, and I return to the mesa, we find the Carterea standing in formation in the Common. I tuck the newly finished sandal into my pack. "What could this be about?" I whisper. Ratho shrugs, and we step into line and assume position with our rapion at our feet.

When Droslump swirls out of the Eating Cavern, my centerself shrinks and flutters in the hollow. He crosses his arms and lifts his voice. "A desert cat has slipped past Perimeter and is attacking the village herds. Goats are being lost by your failure."

Groans and mumbles rumble through the patrollers. A wind whirl adds to our confusion.

"Remain in rank!" Droslump shouts.

We stand in place while the sand spins frenetically around us. I shut my eyes to the grains peppering the air until the whirl finally zips beyond the mesa. We rub our eyes and faces, then return our attention to Droslump. I listen for words that will answer my questions: Which herder has lost goats? Will the children in the village be threatened?

"For your failure, water supply will be removed until Madronian soldiers kill the cat." Suddenly my throat is lined with dust. How can they remove our water supply? That is insane!

"Dismissed, you worthless load of goat dung!" Droslump gathers his robe and stamps back into the Eating Cavern.

Everyone shifts and turns to the spring. The water gurgles to a stop, and the trough begins to drain.

"Quick!" I yell and race to it, Shiz running at my side. We scoop our water bags full before the trough empties thoroughly. He lifts his bag to me. I grin at our success, and Mirko whistles at Baesa.

"The Steam Pockets," someone yells, and Shiz, Baesa, Ratho, and Thae join the crowd.

They are willing to risk the stagnant water? I shake my head and take a sweet sip from one bag, and Mirko ducks his beak in afterward. We slide to the ground and lean against the quiet spring. With his mouth gaping wide and empty, the Four-Winged Condor looms silently above us.

"We will play their game, and pray to the Creator Spirit that the cat is found quickly," I say.

CHAPTER 42

WATER

It is Mirko who saves Ratho and me from the imposed drought. Able to part from me, he illegally crosses Perimeter and discovers a water source somewhere in the desert stretch between R'tania and C'shah. Far beyond our line.

When he first motioned to go, I refused. "No, Mirko! Absolutely not!" He took the bags and went anyway. Cursing and yelling, I ran after him until he quickly outflew me.

Ratho and Thae called me back to camp. While I suffered from separation sickness, they tried to distract me continuously until we saw Mirko slowly beating toward us, the water-filled bags looped over his neck.

Immediately regaining my strength, I berated my rapion for an entire hour. "What were you thinking? Do you know how I felt? How worried I was? It made me sick, Mirko!" That garnered a sympathetic look, but otherwise he only ruffled his feathers and waggled his eye ridge. I knew there'd be no stopping him next time either. There wasn't.

What I learned with each withdrawl was that I could never part from R'tania and leave Mirko behind. Now I fully understand why Father couldn't move away from the Cliffs. Who could? Even if separation is easier after Severation, who could ever leave?

Back at the mesa, the Carterea gather the wetness at the base of the cottonwoods when the seep springs rise. With their lips parched and peeling and their rapions' feathers raised in dehydration, they fight over the trees. Everyone is ringed with oil, sweat, and dirt. All the while, Droslump wanders through the Eating Cavern with his dew-drenched goblet in hand, and the Drill Governs guzzle from their water sacks.

"Tiadone, it could have been our error," Ratho repeatedly whispers at night before we fall asleep.

"No," I respond automatically, because what good does that worry do now? And then I pray silently. *Creator Spirit, please let this not have been our neglect. Let them find the cat, now.*

A week passes before Ratho and I stand last in line behind Shiz and Grendo for patrol. Shiz's legs tremble from lack of water. When Ratho and Thae gaze out to Perimeter, Mirko chitters and inclines his head to Baesa.

Before I can reason myself out of the action, I deftly slip Shiz's empty water sack from his belt and replace it with one of mine. He instantly feels the weight and reaches for it. Shiz drinks deeply, shares with Baesa, and then passes the sack to Grendo. Astonishment opens their faces.

Ratho looks over and raises an eyebrow at me. Finally, Shiz turns.

Unable to hide my blush, I pass my fingers over my mouth and close them into a fist. Shiz returns the motion for silence and resumes his stance. Water is sweet even from a declared male who bears a Singer.

Shiz and Grendo receive oblation and depart southeast. I tremble before Droslump for the wine and wafer, but he hasn't pierced me again, nor have I been caught outside of the game. We are assigned north.

At the top of the first knoll, Ratho and I look back. Shiz and Grendo raise fists into the air, and their rapion swirl a figure above them. Thae and Mirko imitate the pattern as Ratho and I raise our fists in return.

"That was a risk, Tiadone," Ratho says. We turn and hike through the newly sprouted shrubberies poking out of the sand. "It was a risk like you took with Devino."

I shrug and step carefully around a sidewinder in the shade of a boulder. "Everyone's near dehydration, and the cat still isn't found. If others will accept our help, I have to give it, Ratho. Even that shows how bad it is. Shiz and Grendo actually took water from me!"

Ratho's lips stretch into a laugh, and his dimple flashes as Thae ruffles her wings. "I've given my extra sack to two different boys!" Ratho exclaims.

"And you blame *me*?"

He runs ahead, daring me to chase him. Our rapion take to the air, and I take the chase. My amulet swings behind me, and I don't tug it back around.

I will catch Ratho as I always do. I smile to myself. Victory astride that boy is beyond sweet. I will snug my legs close along his torso and hold him down longer than normal. Why not? No Madronian will see. None will know what I feel. I'll enjoy what I can get, right now.

Our laughter bounces and rolls over the sand.

It is eighteen days at the mesa and on patrol before we return from Perimeter and find the spring flowing. The boys linger by its side, their bellies distended. Somone vomits over in the bushes. Too much too fast, I gather.

Ratho and I add our whoops of joy while Thae and Mirko dive about the spring's stream of water. No one even leaves.

"The desert cat was cornered in the Four-Winged Condor Garden by some surprised acolytes, and five soldiers were able to strike it to death," Shiz says to us. "No children were taken, but five goats total were lost."

"Thank the Four-Winged Condor." Ratho sighs.

Thank the Creator Spirit the children were protected, I think. My father would have confirmed the goat loss to Sleene. Is Father disappointed in me?

I linger under Shiz's friendly arm flung onto my shoulder. Even under eighteen days of dirt, his grin would stop any girl midstep. Or, I guess, catch the eye of a declared male.

I peel myself away before any sees my inkling, like his partner Grendo, who steps up and slaps Shiz on the back. There's fun and then there's danger. Especially with this many witnesses, and my amulet not as strong as it used to be — or at least what the Madronians presume. If they witness an ounce of my lust, my life ends.

I slyly tighten the sinew knot. "Well, I'm off to the Steam Pockets. Can't get there soon enough!" I hustle toward the Sleeping Cavern, tugging Mirko by the wing. He strains to keep his eye on Baesa. "Come on, lover," I whisper.

Over my shoulder, I see Grendo has wandered off to the latrine and now Ratho chats with Shiz. My centerself skips for them both. Mirko whistles at me. I really have to be more careful, but right now, I just laugh.

CHAPTER 43

SHINGKAE

Patrols continue, along with the water supply. Prayers of thanks to the Four-Winged Condor are spoken often at the spring following the return of the bubbling stream, though soon enough, we again overlook our blessings that are so constant: breath, water, our rapion. Until a Severation occurs. Regularly, rapion are returning to their Cliffs, and young men such as Flecket and Creo are traveling back for village service.

My ears never grow accustomed to the screech of despair at Severation, and my centerself is even more troubled with each departure as Mirko's grows closer. The Madronian prohibition of contact afterwards burns hot in my fear.

Added to the anxiety is the news Ratho and I hear late in the spring, when returning from patrol and joining a fire circle after evening meal. We are not welcomed, but neither do we sit on the fringe out of the circle of heat. The night air is cool, and the stars glide across the sky. Mirko and Thae are so large now they spill out of our laps.

We listen to Grendo's involved story. His thick brown twists fly about as he turns to convince each questioner of an invasion.

"Is this the truth?" Ratho breaks into the talk.

"Yes," Shiz answers.

Grendo turns to Ratho. "I heard Droslump telling the Javelin

Govern this evening," he says. "The Shingkae rose and invaded through the West Patrollers' line." Gooseflesh jumps from one boy to another. Grendo continues. "The patrollers' rapion signaled the West Lookout. Their visionaires did not see the attack beforehand, but Madronian soldiers arrived in time and held off the invasion."

Desl breaks in. "I hear Shingkae use great iron blades in their attacks."

A couple of boys nod among themselves. One speaks up and says, "Their armor rattles upon their breasts."

"But the Madronians have crossbows," Ratho says, "that can take down the metal-slowed lot, striking between the chinks."

"Yes," everyone agrees.

"There's more." Shiz pauses. "Grendo says the West Patrol Rapion made a call to the Cliffs."

Mirko trumpets. "For certain?" I ask.

"Yes!" Shiz and Grendo answer. Shiz stands, looks around, and whispers, "The Madronians were only matching the Shingkae, not winning. You can believe it was for the love of the R'tan that the Cliff Rapion responded." Baesa flaps her wings. "The birds came in force and fully drove back the Shingkae, leaving many men dead in the sand. I bet every Madronian stood in awe of the independent rapions' collected might."

Our birds rustle after his quiet comments. Mirko breaks the hush with another shrill note of pride.

"What a sight it must have been!" Ratho says.

The usually shy patroller, Tinto, stands next. "Well, the rapion aside, the Madronians are mighty. Praise the Four-Winged Condor for them. They enrich our lives and defend us well."

I throw my arm over Mirko's neck to discourage his hiss. The fire cracks and releases a blast of steam at the same moment, thankfully, and no one looks at my rapion.

Still, Tinto's tripe goes unchallenged. It is a catechism all toddlers are made to learn. How foolish can he be? It was just stated that it was the rapion who brought victory! Even Ratho does not respond, instead doodling with a twig in the dirt.

I can barely tamp down the questions wanting to blast out of my mouth. What of the way the Madronians rule us? What of religious intolerance? Contact denial after Severation? What of ekthesis, which murders our firstborn daughters? What of my life needing to be radically altered in order to live?

Tinto sits, and Grendo picks up his story. "Anyway, the attack and thwart did happen. I heard every word, as the Madronian spoke not realizing I was in the shadow of the Eating Cavern arch."

Shiz rocks a log in the fire until a yellow flame shoots loose. The color shimmers over Mirko, who seems to be settling down. His eyes are still narrowed at Tinto, but his brow isn't as angry.

A govern—I can't make out which one in the darkness—strides past our gathering. All chatter snicks to silence until his robes dragging over the sand can no longer be heard.

For everything the Madronians do to make us inferior: denying our religion, making our present intolerable, and dampening our future, it's the patrollers and rapion who help keep the village safe. It was R'tan youth and their rapion who called the soldiers for protection. I clear my throat. "What happened to the patrollers and rapion at the invasion?"

Grendo chuckles. "I didn't hear. If they are like Tinto, they hid among the boulders and wet themselves in the excitement."

Everyone laughs, except Tinto and Mirko, who rumbles. "Of course you would not hide," I tell him.

Talk of the invasion slowly dwindles and different conversations spring up. As it often does, most talk turns to girls in their villages. Who left with their eye on whom. Who has the most comely shape and what each boy will do to win affection when he returns.

I keep my blushing face down when the talk descends to female body particulars. Some strain of my former affinity bristles at their crassness. Even declared male, their disrespect cuts into my centerself.

"Two that peek out from her shirt. You know, from those open-collar tops so many choose to wear?" says Grendo. He gestures with both hands. The boys groan in agreement.

"No, it's the way her backside curves her skirts," says another.

Several chuckle. I silently beg Ratho or Shiz to rise above this. Say a woman's beauty is her centerself full of strength and care. Say breasts and backends don't matter. Did it for Father when he chose Mother or Frana? Well, maybe a little, but not in the way these drooling goons are going on about it all.

Among the group, no one does. No one speaks for the girls.

My irritation boils out. "But what of a woman's interests and passions and humor?"

Everyone stares at me, then laughter rolls through the group. "What good humor, Tiadone!" Grendo says.

I smile and chuckle to pass the joke.

The fire cracks and shimmies into the night. Sparks float down into the quiet, and I focus on the embers instead of all the boys fantasizing around me. Even Ratho is with some girl in his mind. Wait! Who is she? What does she look like? What would I look like without the amulet and my binding, and in female garb? Would I still feel as ugly as a goat who's rolled in a sticker patch and then been caught in a downpour? Would I care to be with any of these rutting rams?

I lurch to my feet and walk away, barely able to keep from running to the Sleeping Cavern.

Mirko flaps beside me and hums.

"It shouldn't matter so much how one looks!" I duck into the opening and accidently knock my forehead. I cry out and rub the tender spot.

Mirko flies before me and blinks his sympathy.

CHAPTER 44

BEYOND

Blossoms snip closed in the setting sun. I push up my tunic sleeves for the breeze to brush my wrists. A heat has crawled over the desert these past few days of patrol, and any respite must be seized.

By my sandal, a burrowing owl pops from a hole. His circle eyes inspect me, and his shoulders hump around his neck. The owl sinks below the sand as Mirko dives. "Oh, leave the little one," I say.

He chides me, flaps, and glides past.

Finally, the Perimeter stones rise in the distance. Mirko clips my hair with his talons, though he lets go before there is a tug. "What are you doing?" I ask. He flies high again.

At the edge of our assigned area, the rising moon casts a shimmering light over the sand in a faint path. Night crickets click at each other. Resting my hand on one of the stone markers, I scan the space. My ears raise a smidgen with the intense concentration.

Across the desert are the C'shah. Do they even think to attack? Probably not. They never have invaded R'tania and are rumored to be mild. I can't imagine they'd come here to challenge the Madronian Empire like the Shingkae. They are probably too focused on protecting themselves from a Madronian invasion in the future.

"Are you even patrolling?" I call into the air.

Mirko returns and plucks my watersack free. He hovers in the twilight, letting out a free, light-hearted song as if there are no worries in the world. His head gestures for me to follow beyond the cairns.

"What? Come back here, Mirko!" I stamp my foot. "What are you thinking?"

He dives at my head, circles, and shoots beyond the Perimeter. My water sack swings from his talons. This is the post where Mirko returned most quickly with water during our drought. "No! You do not mean for me to go beyond Perimeter! To the water source?" He whistles. "Despite you doing so, it's still forbidden to cross! Besides, we need no water now."

My stating the obvious doesn't deter him. He flies close, drops my watersack into my hands, and grabs a chunk of tunic in his beak. He pulls.

"Mirko!" I yell, and stumble along. He doesn't let go, instead yanks even though I try to stop. "Ow!" I shout. The tunic twists and pinches my armpit. "Mirko!"

He doesn't halt. I'm well beyond the markers now and outside of our country. Nearing where Triumvirate spring from.

I stagger forward, fear sweating out my pores. I'm beyond Perimeter!

Mirko sings that there is no danger, but I still shove my heels in the sand. "But Ratho ..."

Finally, he lets go and flaps before me. His eyes peer into mine, sending a calmness through my entire body.

"Well," I slowly admit, "I did tell Ratho we would be longer as we planned to hunt and patrol." His head tilts, and he breathes a great cinnamon waft over me.

From somewhere, bravery or rebellion pours into my centerself. A desire to be free of everything and everyone taunts me. My mind flops through the choice.

It's not as if Mirko and I are parting from each other or running away. It is only an excursion. Whatever the C'shah are truly like, they are miles and miles away. Hope and possibility snick into my blood. Mirko bugles.

"All right, you crazy talon-footed goose!"

He grins and flies behind me. Little bites from his beak nip my backside. "Stop! I'm going!" I laugh and run.

He chortles and sings now. In this undignified way, my rapion drives me beyond Perimeter.

CHAPTER 45

THE POOL

It truly isn't far to Mirko's secret location. We crest a hill, enter a forest of stacked stones, twist and wind through the pillars, and crawl the last bit through a tunnel. I smell the water before I see it.

The passageway spills into a small roofless canyon. A pool shimmies in the breeze, and the moon rides its rippled face. Rustling at the far side, a cottonwood stands with bushes crouched around its trunk. The water stretches about as wide as I can throw a stone, and the cavern walls lift like wings to the night.

I stand and sigh, not looking away from our surroundings as I swipe sand from my trousers. "It is beautiful, Mirko!" He chitters with glee.

Mirko flies above the pool, his feet clipping the water, sending droplets arching like falling stars. He sings his pleasure and calls for me to join him.

I laugh. "I can't swim! Ratho would question my wet clothes. How would I explain?"

Winging close, he plucks my tunic once again.

My laugh cuts short. "Oh, really. Take off my clothes? Madronian rules of modesty—"

He whistles. We are beyond their rule. I swallow the bulge that packs my throat.

"What if there's something in the water? A serpent or large fish or turtle that snaps?" Mirko brushes past my back and shoots across the canyon. He crows safety.

"Well, maybe I will soak my feet." He chitters and swoops overhead as I sit on a nearby boulder and peel off my boots and socks. With my trouser legs rolled up, I wade into the water. The pool is tepid and welcomes my legs, and the hike eases out of my toes into the soft sand.

Mirko wings past and flicks water at me.

Really, I scold myself. I am beyond Madronian rule and R'tania. I am in a secret place alone with my rapion. Only the Creator Spirit will see, and he knows my form. I ought to swim!

But I can't. To be naked? Outside? I tromp out of the water and flop down against a rock in the moonlight. I shove my amulet behind me.

When I end up laughing at Mirko chasing a water-glider beetle, my rigid limbs finally relax and my gumption gathers. I can swim! Why not?

Hurriedly, I shuck off my tunic and pants. My dive into the middle of the pond cuts open the water, and it envelops me. I pop up to the sweet-smelling surface; is there a hint of jasmine?

Turning onto my back, I watch the moon's reflection shimmer on my pale undergarment and breast wrap. The latter is pasted against my curves, which have certainly defied my amulet, now tethered and floating beside me.

The air chills and raises my flesh, but the water nudges warmth in reply.

While Mirko hunts along the far shore, I whisper, "Yes!" and stretch. Weaving my arms above my head and fluttering my legs, the water undulates over me.

If I weren't a declared male, would Ratho like my form? Would he fantasize about me?

Mirko sings. The notes twirl against the rock and rise into the night as my hair twists float in a dance about my head.

I flip over and swim with my wonderings.

CHAPTER 46

SMILING

Mirko forages well on our return, bringing back three winders, and since Ratho dozes in the sleeping pit he is unaware when we arrive. I remove my hat and continue to dry my twists by the fire.

The night passes smoothly, and a smile drifts onto my face frequently. If I had remained female, Ratho or Shiz likely would have noticed me.

"You seem happy," Ratho says at our shift change.

I shrug, smile wider, and climb into the sleeping pit. "Maybe the warmer weather has lifted my centerself."

"Mine too."

I lie down next to Mirko while Ratho stacks more wood on the fire. I prop my chin on my hands, watch the firelight flicker over my partner's arm muscles, highlighting each time they relax and tense. I sigh, and Mirko waggles his eyeridge.

I drop below the edge of the pit. What am I doing? Mooning like some female after Ratho more and more? Not that any are here to see, but if I continue I could slip at the mesa and someone might notice.

I duck lower. Out here, even Ratho might start to feel my attentions. It would definitely end our friendship, as well as challenge him to report me in order to protect himself. After my religious outburst, he probably would!

Chamber of Verities, what has happened? I vigorously rub my face without regard for the rough sand on my hands.

Maybe entertaining attraction dulls my amulet? Maybe giving in and enjoying wrong impulses has impaired it more and more? Or swimming in moonlight. The Madronians insist the moon is female. Oh, what have I done?

Pulling it from below my hip, I massage the damp bag, smell it, but can only note leather. It no longer carries the scent of my father tinged with a certain musky wildness. Have I drained most of its strength?

I gulp. What can I do now? For a start, not entertain thoughts of Ratho and Shiz. And no more swims under the night sky!

I burrow down in the pit, clutching the amulet to my chest. I am a declared male, I chant as I drift to sleep. However, my dream comes quickly.

Ratho's hand skims
my hair, cheek, and waist.
He lowers his lips to mine,
and I kiss him,
and kiss him,
his lips full and warm.
When he pulls back,
I groan his name.
"Ratho, Ratho."

"Tiadone?" Ratho answers from the fireside. Thae looks over as well from atop the cairn.

I sit up. Mirko nips my backside, loosening my tongue. "Oh, nothing. Never mind!" I squeak and fall backward, shame flaming my face.

Mirko chortles, and I can just make out my dream spinning darkly in his irises. "Stop it!" I shush, rolling over.

I punch my amulet. I am declared male!

CHAPTER 47

UNEXPECTED CHILL

Reported to the Madronians, the girls and their Miniata predicted a cold snap from the northern mountains, and their warning came to pass. The chill crunched down into our valley, crawled past the Rapion Cliffs, crept across our village, and sidled its way to the mesa to blast the open desert. With a bit of mercy, the governs announced the change beforehand so we could prepare.

Patrollers layer on as much spring gear as they possess. Even so, the materials are light, and the wind cuts. Nights are spent at Perimeter buried in sand, whether by the fire or in the sleeping pit. Only Ratho's and my head poke above ground when we aren't patrolling. Our rapion constantly fluff to trap and warm air between their feathers.

The only solace is that the cold will pass, and for now it helps me focus and grip my male declaration strongly. Even when we return to the mesa I don't allow my thoughts to stray to any boy, and I'm not plagued by any dreams.

"May the wind flee before you," is the greeting and departure many call to each other, and the expected jest back has become, "May your manhood outlast the blast," followed by an adjustment of undergarments. Ratho calls the taunt to me one evening at Perimeter, then stammers at his error.

I plunge forward as boldly as possible to cover it. "And may your little bit not snap off!"

Recovering immediately, he guffaws. "My manhood is as vital as my father's old Goatgrinder."

"That goat? You wish," I retort to cover our embarrassment.

Ratho laughs and moves toward Perimeter in the nightfall. "I'll find something for us to eat," he calls back over his shoulder. But I doubt he will. Creatures are scarce with the cold.

I lean against the pine trunk and heap sand onto my legs. Mirko bugles safety from the rock pile and puffs his feathers.

I stuff my hands into my armpits. This is the end of a Seventh Day. Back in the village, another Weekly Ritual has ended. Here it is strange to never stop our routine and draw our minds to the spiritual. To honor the close of a worship day, I scooch down and rehearse the Divine Beliefs from the *Oracles of the Creator*. Father is probably doing the same.

"You shall worship the Creator Spirit and no other. Offer your strength and possessions to your neighbors' needs." I drift to sleep in the quiet.

The sound is a horrific screech. I open my eyes and cram my palms to my ears. But the keen is within my mind. "Mirko, what is it?" I yell.

He dives to my side and helps claw the sand off me. The hourglass is empty, but there is no evidence Ratho has returned. Mirko flies a surveillance circle and wings back to me.

I scramble upright. He tugs a burning stick from the low fire, shoots high into the black sky, and darts an attack pattern for desert cat.

CHAPTER 48

SCREAMS

Rapion flames to the right and left carry the message along Perimeter. The Lookout will notify the village, and soldiers will form a barrier at the edge of town. The processes clog my thoughts. With my pack and javelin in hand, I hurl through the night after Mirko, who shrills above the bellows of the attacker.

We travel a fair distance at high speed until I round a huge boulder, and the horror under the full moon is before me. "Creator Spirit," I whisper.

As large as a man, the cat is a full-grown female, whose hiss and roar rumble fury. Her thick back legs are tied by Ratho's bola, keeping her from advancing far while Thae claws at the beast's furred neck. But the cat is quick to slash and shift, using the powerful forepaws that remain free to flail at the fluttering rapion and threaten Ratho, who is just beyond the feline's swipe. It's clear the cat was not always at such a distance: Ratho's leg is torn open, and his side also leaks blood into the sand. His javelin lies at the crest of a hill marked with prints from the struggle.

My fear rages into anger, and I feel the power in my amulet rush through my centerself. I whirl my bola and set it free. Screeching a war cry, Mirko zooms forward in chase. The bola collides with the cat's front legs and whips the paws together. I let out a victory scream. Mirko dives; his beak pecks at the eyes while he dodges the cat's slashing teeth. Thae rips into the neck.

Ratho spots me and yells, "Tiadone!"

I clasp my javelin tight in my fist, take three running steps, and hurl my weapon straight at the cat's breast. The pointed head strikes, and the shaft follows to deepen the wound. The cat growls, contracts, and tries to knock the weapon free.

Thae flaps out of reach as Mirko tears a furred ear in half. The cat twists its head, and Thae plunges at the neck.

I seize the distraction and run, shove my foot on the wide chest, and yank my javelin free. The cat shrieks and flips. Thae is struck hard by the open jaw and tumbles backward through the air. Her neck drives into the sand, and I shudder at the impact.

Suddenly, the beast gyrates, and before I can leap back, the cat's bound claws tear through my boot and slice my ankle. Warmth flows into my boot.

I jab but only strike air and sand about the writhing body. "Die, you dreaded beast!" I yell. The cat knocks me over with its massive shoulder, but my resolve is as strong as hers. I roll and scurry from the whiskered cheeks, pulling back from long teeth and a hot hiss.

Mirko flaps vulnerably before the cat's face. He screeches, and it is my signal to attack.

I arc around the cat, leap high, and lunge with my full weight. The shaft of my javelin burrows deep into the cat's breast, and I pound it harder and harder until only half my weapon remains in my grasp. The cat convulses, and jagged cries bubble out of its throat. Its bound paws flop to the sand, the head lolls, and blood rivulets about my javelin.

As the world engages once again around me, I notice Thae thumps her wings helplessly on the sand. Her neck has been opened. She tucks her wings to her side and rolls to reach Ratho's hand. Delicately, she nuzzles her beak into his palm, then shudders and stills.

Mirko snatches up his still-burning torch, shoots to the sky, and twirls the flame toward the Lookout. The cat is dead. The message repeats down the desert as Mirko drops the signal flame and flaps to Thae's side.

My breath fogs before me, and silence seeps through my mind. My sore ears fill with the stillness, but my body is a hollow cavern emptied by adrenaline and angst.

Ratho touches Thae's chest. The moment he wails, "No!" I fall to my knees. The Carterea rapions' mourning rings my head and blasts down to my toes.

Thae is dead.

CHAPTER 49

SKINNING

Ratho passes out while clutching Thae's body to his chest. Until the keening ends, I tremble on the sand. Soon, Mirko pulls my hair, urging me to rise. I stop the flow of blood from Ratho's leg with strips of winder skin and bandage his side as well. Then, Mirko and I quickly make a fire of shrubs. To keep the living warm is the first work. Despite our tears for Thae.

The gash in my ankle burns. I knot another winder skin tightly about it and tug my torn boot onto my sockless foot. Between my toes, blood squelches.

With his forehead pressed to hers, Ratho does not wake or release Thae's empty body. She is flopped over his arms, head twisted at an unnatural angle. I wait as Mirko sings a last song to Thae. The deep, long notes for his friend echo and reverberate for her life lost, and with each I feel his pain gush through me and pound against my centerself.

Pulling in a jagged breath, I stand and approach the cat. The one remaining eye is open and glazed, confirming death. I kick the carcass, but the body is so dense it barely moves. I kick and kick until sweat and tears race down my face.

"Where are you, Creator Spirit?" I scream. "Why did you let your creation destroy what is precious to us?" I pull at my hair and stumble. "You leave me here with a wounded partner separated from his rapion. Why? Do you even hear me?" My words strike the rocks and fling into the silent sky. "Do you even exist?"

Mirko lands heavily on my shoulder. I heave my thoughts back to what we can do. Me and Mirko.

The Madronians will send no one to our aid. A personal distress call will go unanswered. All idiocy. It is my duty to get my partner back to the mesa, despite the reality my friend is wounded and has been divided from his rapion before Severation. He may not recover from either. The blame and scorn for Thae's death alone could destroy him.

I wipe my face on my sleeve. Regardless of any god's attention or existence, I have to do what I can, right now.

I kick the cat again and roll it onto its back with my hands. Its thick, dirty fur crams between my fingers. Mirko cuts the bola ropes with his talons, and the feline's legs flop open.

I plunge my knife into the skin and saw downward, opening the belly and circling the vent. Accidentally, I rip the bag, and the entrails steam raw and pungent. Mirko leans over the guts but then turns his head from the stench.

I cough and retch. The cat was ill. I yank on my javelin until it yields from the carcass with a sucking, wet noise. Mirko stands back. I use the point to pound the rib cartilage. The thuds shake upward through my own bones, and the cage breaks in two.

Throwing my javelin aside, I grip the broken bones and pry them apart. A *crack* snaps the air. My bloody hands worm through the organs, but when I cut out the liver and tilt it to the firelight, Mirko hisses at the piece covered with diseased spots.

Everything is tainted. But, but what about the heart!

My fingers slip through the blood until I grasp it. Sliced free, it fills my palm. The heart of a desert cat I helped kill. Quickly, I wrap it in a winder skin and stuff it into my pack.

After wiping my hands in the sand, I cut around each paw, the tail, and finally the massive head. My stomach rises once more while the skin gives way beneath my knife. I lift and slice it from the carcass. Mirko helps by pulling the skin up and out for me, and soon we are both immersed in the earthy, sticky vapor from our efforts. I reach the back and roll the cat to carve away the other side, and a groan escapes my lips. Ratho still doesn't stir.

Sweat runs off my chin. My knees drive into the sand while I cut and rip the skin free, until muscle lies exposed in the moonlight. Hard, thick bands twist around the beast. Mirko chews the backstrap from the cat. The sinuous piece is good for sewing, and he lays beside me. Finished, we collapse and drink deeply from my water sack.

The cat's blood dries on my face and tightens my skin. I glance again at Ratho by the fire. He is unchanged, but his wounds do not seep. I chance a look at Thae and can see even in the faint light that Thae's lustre has dimmed with her centerself gone. "We must hurry, Mirko." He bugles and rises into the air.

CHAPTER 50

FORGIVEN

As the black night sky begins to edge in blue, I lurch forward, bouncing Ratho. Strapped in the cat skin, he rides with Thae's body on the travois I bound together using the three long cottonwood branches Mirko was able to locate. Apart from the bloody interior of the pelt facing the ground, my carrier is similar to the type Father uses to transport wounded goats.

I lean into the crossed poles at my waist and grip their further extension before me, then once again heave forward. Despite my care, the travois jostles over rocks and shrubs. Ratho is nudged and tipped, but still he does not wake from unconsciousness.

Sooner than I expect I must stop and rest and drink again. Mirko fusses over my exhaustion and ankle wound, rolling his beak against my shoulder to ease the ache. When I assure him I am fine and move to tip water into Ratho's mouth, Mirko peers down, and his mourning for Thae warbles into the air.

Finally, on the third stop, when our post is in sight, Ratho rouses. "Thae," he sobs. I lower the travois, step out, and kneel at his side with Mirko. Ratho clings to his dead rapion and whimpers.

"Ratho, Mirko and I are here," I whisper and cry.

"But not my Thae." His face is pinched.

The horizon shimmers pink with the coming dawn. Suddenly, Thae's feathers brighten, and Mirko flutters backward. The sound of heavy flapping reaches me before I see the glistening shapes rise over the nearby hill. Two Cliff Signicos dare to fly toward us!

Ratho does not see them until they hover above. His face is aghast, and the wind raised by their wings interrupts his moan. Mirko bows his beak to the sand.

Flapping in place, the two great golden-brown rapion writhe their necks and tails, mentally keening the same anguish I shared earlier with the Carterea rapion. But this quiver is deep and doesn't hurt me. Instead it echoes in my bones. Despite the gentle hum, fear holds me stiff. Will they blame Ratho for Thae's death?

As the keen ends, the rapion whip through the air around us. A wind whirl is raised, and we are its center. Mirko, Ratho, and I gaze up into the kaleidoscope of feathers and sand.

The two rapion land outside the swirl, which drifts to the ground. I squeeze one of the travois poles to keep from shrinking into a ball and covering my neck. The large birds step toward us. Wavering on my knees, I am equal in height to them. Off to the side, Mirko shivers. His stature does not yet compare to theirs.

Ratho whimpers in the cat skin when the great male bends his head. Enormous rapion tears drop from the male's eyes, roll down Thae's beak, and disappear into her neck feathers. He weeps as rapion do upon release. Of course this is graver.

The female lowers her full crest to Ratho's hair and breathes his scent. She returns hers to him, thickening the air with cloves. I look in wonder as heavy tears cluster in Ratho's hair and shine on his forehead.

They offer peace!

I wipe my face dry on my sleeve. "They know you fought well for Thae," I whisper to Ratho. "That you loved her and would never have lost her through neglect." A calm spreads over his face, and he closes his eyes, losing consciousness again.

The two rapion stand upright and stare at me. I meet their round, dark eyes but get to my feet and step back to Mirko. For Ratho, I force my words out. "My friend fought to save Thae, the village, and your Cliffs from this foul cat. Thank you for risking Madronian threats to deliver your blessing."

They hiss at the skin wrapping Ratho and then bow to me. Their wings arch behind their backs and snap open. The red dawn gleams through their pinions.

Mirko and I mimic the movement.

With a great rush, the rapion leap to the air, fly low to the earth, and burst above the rising sun. In the midst of their retreat, Mirko sings. The Signicos stall and circle.

His notes end, and they shoot into the rays of daylight. I tremble at their acknowledgment of Mirko's song and of Ratho and Thae.

Maybe they were Thae's kin? I shield my eyes and watch the horizon, but the rapion don't return.

When Mirko whistles, I focus again on our predicament. I step into the travois, lift the branches, and pull with fresh strength. Leaving our post unattended, I drag my beloved friend and the body of his rapion toward the mesa.

CHAPTER 51

SEARCHING

When I finally reach the mesa, my legs shudder and give way. Mirko flies down to me as I tumble to the sand, my body a series of jerks and my arms nothing but twitches. "I'm fine," I rasp to Mirko, now nuzzling my neck.

A Baltang boy steps out of a latrine stall and cries for help. "Tend to Ratho," I shout to him. I close my eyes to the coming chaos. Thudding feet pound the ground as I slip away from the horror of Ratho's loss.

I wake on my shelf with Mirko asleep at my neck. A moan rises from my throat. The muscles in my back and neck are knotted, and my ankle throbs. It is clear I've been drug here and left.

"Ratho?" I rasp. Mirko opens an eye and blinks at me. I nudge him off, and he curls tightly in his sleeping bowl. I sit up. Our alcove spins despite how I hold my head between my hands. "Ratho?"

I sway to my feet but find the top shelf is empty. My pack is on the hook beside Ratho's. A rank, musk scent permeates the air. My own filthy clothes or the desert cat's heart? Whichever; I will deal with both later.

I haul a waking Mirko into my arms, grab my pack, stumble into the hall, and search for my friend.

Outside, the late morning air is a bit warmer. The cold snap must be moving past us. Beyond the empty Common, the Baltang boys drill with bolas.

How can everything be so normal?

I set Mirko down and wiggle my weak arms. He flaps his wings free of kinks.

We plunge faces, hands, and talons into the condor spring. I avoid the eyes of the statue. My blasphemous questions about the Creator Spirit clunk in my mind until I swirl them away like the bloody water swirls down the trough.

I fling my hair and hands, sending out a spray of water. Mirko drinks deeply. I'll cleanse completely and change after I've found Ratho.

I scan the area. In the fire circle, the remains of the cat skin and travois smoke. Out of respect for Thae, they must be burning the pelt. At least it gave me a way to move Ratho safely. On a stray wind, the acrid stench reaches me. "Burn to ash," I hiss.

I see no sign of my patrol partner nearby.

"Let's try the Eating Cavern, Mirko." My heavy legs plod to the entrance, and Mirko beats his way inside. My eyes adjust to the dimness.

Cook is slaughtering a boar on the large table against the back wall. Blood follows the gutted channels in the wood, spills into an open clay pipe, and dumps into the rinsing area. My stomach squishes.

Standing beside me, Mirko rubs his head up into my palm. I brush his warm side. "Well met," I say to the man's curved back. He pauses with his butcher knife raised high and turns. "Can you tell me where I can find Patroller Ratho?"

Cook grunts and tilts his head at the doorway I've only ever seen governs go through. He goes back to the boar and hacks a huge piece of muscle from the rump.

"Thank you," I mutter and hurry through the entrance. Lichen piles light the hallway, revealing rooms branching off both sides. Most have doors closing off my view, yet a few are open. Comfortable beds and chairs fill the areas. Paintings of the Four-Winged Condor decorate many walls, along with weapons and robes on pegs.

I stop short. Behind a barely cracked door, Droslump kneels in what must be his private quarters. The room is large, cushioned, filled with tapestries and warmth. He sways and cries before an effigy of the Four-Winged Condor. Does he mourn Thae's passing? I hear Ratho's name and realize he's singing a canticle for my friend's recovery. I stand dumbfounded at his concern.

"Patroller!" the Javelin Govern calls from behind me. I turn and step toward him, away from Droslump's room.

"I, I was looking for Ratho, Govern." I stop before him. Mirko raises to his full height.

The govern crosses his lean arms. "Infirmary was the first door to the left."

"Thank you, Govern." I tap my fist to my chest. He nods acceptance and pushes past me to stride down the hall and around the corner. Why such help from the Madronians?

I scuttle back to the clinic door. My mind hazes over the changes around me. It's almost as if I haven't really returned to the Eastern Mesa! I look over my shoulder, but Droslump isn't bearing down on me. Madronians do believe an interrupted canticle harms the one sung for. Right now, I'm thankful for their superstitions.

Mirko and I push open the red infirmary door and enter a large, white room filled with beds. All are empty but the one in the corner. Ratho is on his side facing the wall. We are alone.

"Ratho!" I rush to him. Mirko lands on the sheets by Ratho's feet, and I kneel next to his curled form. Ratho's side is bandaged, as well as his leg, with clean strips instead of winder skins. His blood does not leak from the wraps. A pelvic undercover is his only clothing.

On impulse, I tug the twisted sheet out from under Mirko and cover Ratho's immodesty. He has the full body of a man now! Slowly, I pull the sheet to his chin. My friend grumbles and rolls onto his back. His glazed eyes stare into my own.

"Ratho," I cry, and stroke his face. He looks at me without sight.

Disregarding my filthy clothes, I sit on the bed, work my hands beneath his shoulders, and lift him to me. His head flops against my collarbone as I rock him slowly. The sheet slips away, and I clench him close; my fingers wander over his broad back.

Lips pressed into his hair, my anxiety and loss rack out of my centerself. Everything I suppressed in order to focus and bring Ratho to safety erupts. My heaving shakes him and must bring pain to his wounds, but his head only flops back, and his stare glances over me. His mouth parts. Shock from his separation?

"I love you, Ratho," I whisper and sob with abandon. My truth flows into the empty room.

I lower him to the bed. With care for his wound, I drape my arms up around his neck, my twists tumbling every which way across him. I gently rest my face against his muscled chest. The beats of our centerselves wing quietly against each other.

Mirko's humming soothes my crying. The song massages my contorted face and softens it, while Ratho's breathing becomes deep and smooth. I take a breath of cinnamon, and a wisp of peace twirls past. I turn my face, and I can't stop myself from kissing the dip in Ratho's clavicle.

Mirko sidles close, and I sit up to see my friend's eyes clear. "Ratho?" I whisper.

"The Madronians ... took Thae's body ... for a ceremony."

My joy drips away. "I supposed they would."

Ratho tears up. Mirko, who has never touched another but me, steps onto Ratho's chest. With talons retracted, he hunkers and opens his wings. His beak brushes the underside of Ratho's chin. Ratho's body stiffens, and he stutters, "Mirko?"

CHAPTER 52

THAE

Mirko's mourning keen for Thae shrieks through my head once more while he rolls his head beneath Ratho's chin. I reach under Mirko's wings, grip Ratho's waist, and look into his fearful face. He holds my gaze but covers his ears until Mirko's pain slips to a song that begins faintly and builds. Shaking, Ratho reaches down and grips my hands. His eyes focus through me. What does he see?

Transposed over Ratho's face, I watch:

Thae emerge from her egg,
a small rapion
wobbling in Ratho's hands.
Her first meal, a black-backed beetle.
Her beak crunches
the shiny shell.
She rides within Ratho's twists
and flies first
under the moon's white roundness.

Growing, she sleeps
beneath Ratho's nightshirt
as his chest broadens
and his voice deepens.

She flies and hunts
with greater skill and success.

Thae quakes at Mirko,
then loves him.
Together
they twine patterns of affection
on the wind
while Ratho has thoughts and dreams
of Jenae,
his body aroused to hers.

Thae fears the desert cat
like nothing before,
but fights with all her fierceness,
wingtip to talon.
Her last sight
is Ratho's face
shifting through her tears.

Now she fades again and disappears. My hands slip from Ratho while his fall from mine. Has he seen Mirko's life as I have seen Thae's? My rapion shoots above us.

Dazed, Ratho's hand lifts and caresses my cheek. I turn my head to the warm curve and my lips brush his open palm.

With a shock, he sits up and grasps my amulet. "You, you love me!" he gasps.

"As a brother!" I lie.

"As a female!" he condemns.

My body freezes. I can't move. Even my eyeballs are stuck between wide open lids. I know now, without any doubt, that as I saw the vision of Thae's life, Ratho witnessed Mirko's. And in that intimacy, he saw my breasts bud, my bloods flow, and my desire bloom.

But he would have guessed a declared male's body would mature a female form. Wouldn't he?

Oh, but he felt my longing for him, maybe even my lust for Shiz. He certainly saw my dream, as I saw his. I knew he was attracted to that Jenae!

Spittle collects in the corners of Ratho's mouth. "Tia." He hisses the feminine form of my name and shoves me hard. I break apart and crash off the bed. He clenches his side and groans, until curses fling from his mouth. I crouch lower.

Mirko's flapping wings still Ratho to silence. The vehemence flees from Ratho's face and fright overtakes his brow. Mirko lands in my lap, grimaces at Ratho, and clicks his beak.

I shrug Mirko off and bow my face to the floor. "Why, Mirko?" I groan. "Why did you tell my weakness, when I have the new cat heart? None of that will matter soon!" But I already know. Sharing our bond right now will heal Ratho from his separation. Mirko hops down by my side.

I grovel, knowing my rapion's generous gift may be my end. I will beg Ratho for my life. My outstretched hands quake. "Ratho, have mercy," I whisper. "I am — declared male. I strive to live so. I took the desert cat's heart to add to my amulet. It's right here in my bag. Please."

Silence beats my eardrums. Mirko's tail feathers sweep the floor.

The sheets rustle. Mutterings flash from Ratho, half sentences of disgust and fear that burst and die. "Who cares what you are going to do? Already you have ... and we played together for ... we trained ... our rapion ... we have slept ... the danger you have opened us to ..."

A long silence follows, in which my neck cramps. I look up feebly from the floor. My friend is hunched over his wounded side, weeping silently. I lay my hand on his trembling knee. When he doesn't throw me off, I look into his sobbing face. "I have lost Thae," he sobs, "and now my childhood friend, Tiadone."

I scurry onto his bed. "No, I'm here, Ratho!" But he passes out. I catch him and lay him down on his uninjured side.

My sleeve is rough against my wet face. I check Ratho's bandages. They are undisturbed, and his breath is even and slow. His skin does not burn with fever. It is only exhaustion now. I pat away his tears.

"What if he tells?" I whisper to Mirko in a panic. "Does he forgive me?" I reach out to Mirko. "Will he tell?"

My rapion blinks calmness and blows a whisper of air over my face. I nod slowly.

All right. I will wait and try not to lose my mind with worry. Aside from getting the heart into my amulet, there's nothing else to do. Nothing.

I lay myself carefully next to Ratho, cupping him close for the moment I can, and he can't resist. My friend finally knows my heart. He knows my love as I truly do.

I rest my face in his clean, soft hair twists. There's a strange weightlessness in my centerself. An open space for me to draw breath deeply. Despite what Ratho might choose to say when he wakes, someone knows my secrets now.

Mirko flaps onto the bed and assumes a pose as if he is on a cairn at Perimeter. He will watch for anyone approaching.

My anger over Mirko touching Ratho is gone. It is worth my friend's healing to take this risk. Exhaustion sweeps through me. I fall asleep holding Ratho, holding and hoping, feeling my love fully before I staunch it completely with the cat's heart.

CHAPTER 53

KINDNESS

Mirko whistles. I lurch off the bed in time to see a tall Madronian woman, who must be the Nursing Govern, sway into the cavern. Her tan robes only reach her ankles, allowing me a view of her long pointed boots as she pads across the stone. Why is her face so familiar?

She winks at me in passing, then checks Ratho: poking, prodding, and peering. He doesn't wake. She straightens his sheet and turns to us. "So, we finally meet." Her quiet voice tips like her gait. Her eyes glide over my amulet. "The cat slayer and his mighty Singer!"

I blush and Mirko hums. Praise from a Madronian is absolutely bizarre.

She steps close and clicks her tongue in admiration of Mirko. He lifts his head high. "A beauty." She turns to me. "I am Healing Govern Madgea. You are Tiadone and Mirko?"

An actual introduction? "Yes. But, Govern, is my partner going to be okay?" I blurt.

"Ratho is unconscious, but he is stable." She touches my arm. "You need to know his body is protecting his centerself from the separation. There is too much to grieve at once." With two long fingers, she lifts my chin. "But how are you, young R'tan?"

I swallow hard to keep my sorrow from bubbling up to her kindness.

"You?" she repeats.

"I am with health." I sit on a neighboring bed, and Mirko perches at my feet.

She intakes a quick breath. "You are not well!" She points at my torn boot.

"It is only a small wound, and I bound it."

She tsks. "I told Govern Stuncier I wanted to inspect you, but he said you only required rest. You were deposited straightway in the Sleeping Cavern, and now I see you are wounded!" She mutters while she gathers a wash basin, cloths, salves, and supplies. Which is Govern Stuncier?

She glides to my side and carefully draws off my boot. Fresh blood seeps up past the winder skins. Govern Madgea works at unraveling the clotted mess.

I stiffen against the pain. Mirko presses my other leg and chitters. Once the wound is finally uncovered, the govern grimaces at the slash and tenderly bathes my leg. Gently, she pats it dry. An ointment slows the seepage.

"There. Now a bit of you is clean," she smiles. "And the wound is clean as well."

"Thank you," I say.

Next, she slathers numbing salve on the curved cut. Mirko and I watch her thread a needle.

"Are you certain stitching is necessary?"

She gives no answer, only knots the thread. I grip the mattress and look away. Sharp tugs and a bit of heat remind me the govern is stitching me like a grandmum darns socks. Even Mirko's song can't distract me, though the govern smiles at his notes.

"There," she says, pleased. "Twenty-two clean stitches."

"Thank you."

The hatched line curves along my ankle bone. I shiver at the thought of the cat.

She grasps my knee. "You are safe."

I muster a weak smile. She dresses the wound. "Replace this after you cleanse, and keep the wrapping dry. I will give you plenty."

"Yes, Govern."

"I want you to return if you see infection. Otherwise, your silk plant stitches will dissolve and be absorbed. Your ankle should heal well."

I pick up my torn boot.

"Stop at the Clothiers, when you can."

"All right. We'll be back in sandals after the cold snap passes anyway."

"True." She nods.

I carefully pull on my boot and then look up at the govern. "Do you know what will become of us?" I whisper.

She stands and tucks a loose strand of gray hair back into her leather tie. "Your friend will return to the village and begin his apprentice work. Of course, the stigma held to his rapion's death will cause him to be ostracized, most likely."

"Yes," I agree. The govern washes her hands in a basin, then stacks her supplies and disinfects the needle. "Rapion death at Patrol where the twined survives happens so rarely. Generations pass without seeing an event like Ratho's."

"But how would you know R'tan history as a Madronian?" I ask.

She chuckles. "As you've seen, the governs are slow to allow any boys in the infirmary. I have much time to sit and read books from the Monast Temple." She sees the question on my face before I ask it. "My brother, High Priest Sleene, allows me access to any work he isn't currently using."

My eyes open wide. There is the familiarity in her face. "You are Sleene's sister?"

"Yes, High Priest Sleene."

"I'm sorry. Oblation for my disrespect." I bow, and she waves away my gesture.

"So, anyway, there are plenty of books my brother never touches, or intends to. I love to delve into other cultures. So many stories. So many possibilities." She laughs at me. "What? Is my interest so odd, or is it that you think Madronians are kinless?"

"No, I—" There are still books in R'tania that weren't destroyed? That aren't merely Madronian drivel?

She pulls me to my feet and hands me the package with supplies for my ankle. "I'm only teasing. Now for you. Apart from your ankle, you are truly well?" She turns me about, looking for other wounds.

"I am fine. Not wounded elsewhere. Really." She holds my gaze. "Only filthy," I say and roll my lips inward.

"I've never met a declared male before," she says.

I shrug, avoiding her eyes, and fiddle with my amulet.

"Is there anything you might need—"

"No, I'm fine. I have ... supplies."

"Good. If you have any questions, though, feel free to come to me."

"Thank you," I say, and rush on, "Govern, what's to become of me now without my partner?" Assuming Ratho keeps my secret.

My friend stirs. She walks over, picks up his hand, and massages it. "There is no other patroller without a partner now, Tiadone. Since re-partnering isn't possible, you'll be assigned to the lookout. It is your rapion that will alert the village of emergency. Maybe even those the visionaire do not see." Mirko ruffles his wings and bobs his head. "Duty on the mesa top is difficult in the elements, but the lookout will appreciate your assistance."

She prattles on, ignoring my fading color at the thought of working without Ratho. "The lookout will no longer need to light bons to communicate. Mirko will raise flares instead."

My mind is a squash left out in a summer drought. So much information is drying it thin.

"Now, Tiadone, you must go to the Eating Cavern, gather whatever weak slop Cook Antel offers tonight, and ready yourself for Thae's Ceremony of Division. It's held in a rarely used amphitheater, I believe." She tugs me by my sleeve. I strain to see past her. Ratho is lying unchanged on his bed. "My brother will be arriving, and you must be present with the Carterea. It is a beautiful ceremony, from what I've read." The woman whisks me across the room and out into the hall.

"Tiadone," she whispers, "may your god be with you. And your future days with Ratho in the village be long and sweet." My lips part without sound. She smooths my forehead. "You will see your friend again, Tiadone." She closes the door between us. Mirko and I stare at each other. "Go!" she calls through the wood.

We hurry down the hallway.

CHAPTER 54

RENEWED

My dinner roils through my stomach as I run deep into the Sleeping Cavern. Ratho and my alcove is far behind, along with the Steam Pockets where I took a quick cleanse and changed my clothes and bandage. Now I race far down the main tunnel.

Finally, I stop and gasp in breath. The darkness is rich beyond the lichen's small illumination in my palm. I slide to the rock floor, placing the glow at my feet. There's no one around. I'm in the belly of the mesa. Deep and safe.

Quickly, I pick at my amulet's tie. My thumbs and fingers feel weak against the cord that has swollen and shrunk tightly after so many years. I gnaw and tug at the bit with my front teeth as well.

There! It begins to give. The tie falls to the floor, and the amulet yawns like a flower opened by a breeze. I try to steady my hands, but they shake even more. With the amulet unfastened, all my maleness and power drain while my centerself swells behind my breastwrap in passion for Ratho.

Stop! I must stop it! If Ratho tells, and there is full inquiry, at least I will honestly be fully male with the second cat heart, and the Madronian hand might be stayed.

Hurriedly, I set the bag on the floor between my open legs. When I lift the lichen to peer inside the pouch, ashes and hair wink at me. The first heart is a powder. I've taxed it to dust and do need another!

My fingers itch to feel through the ash, to sift the core of my spirit bound with my father's hair. Instead, I yank open my pack and withdraw the new organ.

Unwound from the winder skin, the heart is tacky and firm. *Creator Spirit, make this force fill me with power to be a fully declared male, without a trace of femininity. May my dreams of Ratho end. May my lusting cease. Creator Spirit, bless this heart!*

As I press the sticky mass to my lips, my tears start. They roll down my face until I'm sobbing. For what? For ending the bit of femifnity I did have? For ending my love for Ratho?

Before I can figure it out, I hear voices. I fumble the lump into the amulet bag, where it nests in the ashes and hair. Fast, fast, fast, I gather the bag up around the heart. I squeeze the material to barely close over the top of the mound. There! Between my shaking fingers and mincing teeth, I get the cord secured and tied once again to my hips.

"Hurry," someone's voice pings down the passage. "It's time for Division."

"I'm coming," another answers. Footsteps retreat.

Grabbing my pack and lichen, I jump up and jog back the way I came. I wipe my face and hands dry on my poncho. My refreshed, plump amulet rolls and bounces against me.

CHAPTER 55

AMPH OF DIVISION

With his knuckles knobbed about Thae's belly and neck, Sleene chants among the lichen light. Breathing in the stink of his scented oils and wings, sourness fills my mouth, and anger buffets my centerself. He caresses Ratho's rapion then meets my eyes.

Instantly, I palm my amulet, full of renewed power. It's clear Ratho hasn't told my secret yet, or I wouldn't still be here. For now, I'll relish my strength in Sleene's presence!

Emboldened, I glare back at him and stroke Mirko. How can this be Govern Madgea's brother?

The only witnesses to the Division this dark night are Sleene and the silent Carterea. Rapion huddle at their feet in this amph to the west of the Edge of Release. Despite my new power, my hand trembles on Mirko's back. He catches me looking toward the Edge and rests his head against my knee.

Thae's head flops and her narrow tongue slips from her mouth as Sleene's chant ends. He lifts Thae's body high so her wings open and cascade down his fleshy, pale arms. "Four-Winged Condor, grant remission for the loss of this rapion. Curb your condemnation and prevent your fire from striking your servant, who stands to humbly return this body to you." Sleene's little steps gyrate the bones, bells, and jars dangling from his waist. His black wings sway. The priest hazes in my burning tears.

There is no need for remission. Ratho did well to defend our village. It was Thae's offering of herself that kept the cat from encroaching until Mirko and I arrived. Sleene's putrid hands full of falsehood have no right to touch Thae!

Mirko hunches closer to me. I slide my hand down his wing, and a tear slips over my cheek. At least Thae's centerself has flown already.

Spittle sprays from Sleene's thick, blue-lined lips. The droplets glob on Thae's back as he lowers her to his feet. His sleeves slide and meet Thae's crumpled neck on the rock.

I grip the stone to keep from running to her. To caress her wings into place. To straighten her body.

Narrowing his black eyes to dark slits, Sleene holds out his hands in Madronian blessing. "I journey now to return this body to the Four-Winged Condor. I will continue to plead for remission for your failure to raise and protect this honored beast, created in the near image of the Four-Winged Condor."

My hands ache.

"Return to Patrol," he spits.

Cowed, the boys get up and make their way down the faint path. The rapion take wing and descend from the mesa through the air. Each dips a farewell to Thae's body before soaring below the cliff face.

Sleene watches me follow the other patrollers then plucks the lichen strands and drops them into his burlap bag. The glow seeps through the spaces and lights the glee in his face. The look is exactly what would come to him when a boy failed his reading in catechism class. That sick thrill sat comfortably on his forehead before he struck a child, or before a R'tan was whipped by an acolyte and put in the box for mentioning the Creator. I huff. Govern Droslump has some concern for Ratho. In Sleene, I see only evil.

I walk behind Tinto, and Mirko flies high. He flaps his good-bye to Thae then loops back to me. With a heavy weight, he lands on my shoulder, hardly fitting any longer, and chitters uneasily.

"Yes," I whisper. Descending the rocky slope in the dark mist, we drop from Sleene's sight.

Mirko weaves a song that I have come to know means I must hesitate. Reaching one carved stair, I sit on the edge. To stall, I remove my boot and check my bandage. The numbing ointment is weak, and the cut pulses, but my wound doesn't appear to seep though it's hard to see for certain in the darkness.

I pull my boot back on. A gust blasts down the pathway and shifts my hair and Mirko's feathers. The last boy, Dalen, walks by me, continuing to the desert floor. His rapion glides below view.

Mirko chortles. I stand and shift the bola looped through my belt.

My rapion leaps off of me, his form joining the blackness of the clouded night. Only an occasional ruffle of feathers betrays his ascent.

A nerve twitches in my thumb tucked into my fist, matching the thick pulse in my ankle. Against my back, the mesa swoops another draft over me.

Mirko calls from above as he circles the emptiness.

I wipe my wet upper lip on my shoulder and climb back to the Amph of Division. One of Sleene's garment bells shines on the stone next to the only remaining, fading lichen. I stomp on the accent bell, crushing the weak metal and killing the tinkle that tries to escape.

With the lichen's faint glow, I follow Mirko to the Amph's western edge. There! Another pathway leaves the performance platform on the opposite side from where the patrollers descended. In the distance over my shoulder, the freestanding pillar by the Edge of Release is a haunting shape. I jerk my eyes from it.

Mirko flaps before me. "What?" I ask.

He whistles once and flaps left. Twice, and he moves to the right. He releases descending notes and drops, and ascending ones and rises. Instructions. "I understand!"

He sings his joy then drops the notes. I hurry down the trail, skidding and sliding, before I can get my feet under me. Mirko whistles caution, and I slow, making my feet find purchase before taking the next step.

Just before reaching the sand, I slip once more and somersault onto the desert. *Oof.* I stop with a thud. "I'm all right," I whisper.

Mirko whistles once. I climb to my feet, shaking the grit from my twists, and follow his lead away from the mesa. Soon, I find him perched between two boulders. He looks at the cleft between them.

"In there?"

He bobs his head. I shimmy down through the opening and discover a tight, sandstone canyon. Above, Mirko wings back and forth over the crack. He whistles for me to follow, and I do, with the lichen held out before me.

My rapion leads me into the darkness. From the sky, I'm guessing he's tracked Sleene, and returns to quietly relay where I should go. With the canyon's twisting branches and jutting corners, there's no way I could find the priest on my own.

There are times the stone arches over me, and I feel desperately alone, but as soon as I emerge below an opening, Mirko is there to direct me farther, sometimes flapping at my side before returning to the sky. He keeps me moving, climbing up and down.

My legs begin to shudder; my ankle wound burns. I'm still weak from dragging Ratho back to the mesa. With the thought of his name my centerself once again worries over whether he will keep my secret. Yet, right now, I know there's a more urgent danger from Sleene. All inside and out of me quivers like the legs of an early born goat.

Mirko's soft whistle conveys greater urgency as I stumble into a covered passage. Smoke weights the air. Ahead there is light and sound; maybe just around the corner? It must be Sleene. I creep forward to look, but instead, Mirko swoops out of an adjacent passage. He chitters for me to follow him and slips out of sight, his feathers rustling against stone.

I crawl up into the little tunnel and worm higher. Dust tickles my nose, while my poncho, trousers, and fat amulet scruff against the rock. It is like a hiding hole I once had back home. When we were little, playing together, Ratho never found me snaked inside the tunnel.

I reach forward one more arm's length and brush against Mirko's tail. After scrunching into a small hollow that opens wide to the starry sky, I sit up and dust off my hands.

Mirko points with his beak to a jagged crack. The fissure opens to a large cavern, likely near where I was standing a moment ago. Inside the room, the red walls waver, and the stone curves and shrinks up the winding shaft. I shake my head; it is only the play of firelight that causes the room to ripple.

Mirko tugs the neck of my poncho closer. I stretch to see what he has. Beyond the roaring fire pit, over to the side, is a jutting slate where Thae is splayed. Sleene sways before her.

CHAPTER 56

ABOMINATION

Sleene's whispery dirge and bells echo around the chamber like the hisses in a den of sidewinders. I gnaw a chunk of flesh open inside my cheek.

"Thae's body needs to be respected," I whisper. "She must be flamed to rejoin creation."

Sleene turns, setting off a chorus of clinks and rattles. His eyes pierce the shadowed edges of the cavern. Quickly, I stuff the lichen under my tunic to cover the glow and draw back from the crack. While I hold completely still, the priest stalks the circumference of the cave, drawing nearer. A blade winks in his hand.

I count the pulses in my ear. Mirko clings inside the shaft above. *Creator Spirit, protect us!* I cry from habit.

Sleene's bells stop tinkling on the other side of the wall. He sniffs, then thrusts his knife into the opening. I hold my knees close, and the cold metal sweeps under my feet and just misses my thigh. Sleene reaches the knife as high as his arm allows and thwacks the sides of the shaft. *Clang, cling, clang.*

One of Mirko's feathers drops from his tail and twirls down through the air. I gently blow it toward the wall, and it catches in the shadow on the rough rock. It teeters toward the light.

As Sleene withdraws, the feather twirls down and lands in the opening. I remain perched stiff on my tailbone. Cutting grooves,

Mirko's talons begin to slip down the stone. We eye the gleaming feather in full view.

Finally, Sleene's chant resumes from a distance. I roll to the opening and nab the feather, shoving it into my pocket with the same deft movement.

Sleene is back with Thae's body. He lifts the knife high, then draws it down. He slices into her belly and pries apart her flesh with the blade and his fingers. I muffle the scream trying to worm from my lips.

From a black vial strung on his belt, he pinches out a powder and sprinkles the mixture into the cut. Thae's coagulated blood begins to bubble up and out.

Sleene drops to his knees. "Four-Winged Condor, give me the power of the rapion!" he yells and lies down below the shelf atop his own stiff wings. With arms and legs spread, robes thrown out to his sides, he looks like his god!

My ability to stay quiet is further tested as his open mouth receives the bloody cascade. Sleene spasms. More blood drips from Thae into the priest's dark mouth, and his body jerks in ecstasy.

My vision fades in and out. Sleene, the cavern, the shadows ... Ratho!

Ratho gasps.
The blood draining from Thae
drains Ratho of his centerself!
Govern Madgea hovers over him.
Her long hands flap like moths seeking light.
She searches Ratho for what ails him.
His body arches in a seizure.
His lips drain of color.
"Tiadone," he gasps.

"Mirko," I rasp. "Stop Sleene." My rapion beats up and out of the shaft.

I reach for Ratho but only grapple loose stone. His face is superimposed on Sleene. Thae's blood, in an unnatural amount, streams into and bubbles within the High Priest's mouth. It spills out and down his jaw, pooling around his bald head. Sleene convulses, flails, and falls inert. His fists open.

"Mirko! Sleene is unconscious!" I screech, hoping it is true. I press my face into the fissure. Thae's blood still boils from her body and splatters the priest.

Mirko descends into the cavern from the wide opening above and sharply backwings. Sleene lifts his blood-spattered head then drops it. *Clunk.* His eyes roll backward.

Mirko grips a flaming branch from the fire pit, and bits of glowing embers scatter over the floor. He flaps to the ledge and gently touches the torch to Thae. Her body incinerates in green flame.

The obscene blood-letting violation is over. I lean my sweaty cheek on the rough stone.

Sparks float to the floor, and three burn holes in Sleene's robe. Motionless, his mouth still drools Thae's blood. His feet are flopped outward, and a sandal is flipped across the floor. A meaty, pale leg lies exposed, as does his netting. Sleene is a eunuch, like one of Father's gelded sheep. He is nearly female himself! Swallowing bile, I dart my eyes from the sight.

Mirko bugles triumph and flaps his wings fiercely. The beat whirls Thae's sparkling ashes through the cavern. The dust swirls upward and drifts down into the cave crannies and floor. None lands on Sleene.

Thae is returned to creation at last.

I close my eyes and see Ratho breathes easily. Govern Madgea wipes the blood from the corner of his lip.

Up and out of the cavern, Mirko's feathers nip from sight, though his victory bugles echo. I let out my breath, pull the lichen from under my tunic, and with quivering arms and legs scooch out of the tunnel.

CHAPTER 57

QUESTIONS

Mirko leads me out of the canyon and back to the mesa. I hardly track where I am going. Sleene is a cannibal to drink Thae's blood! I howl out my anger and punch my fist in the air.

Sleene has tried to make himself equal to his Four-Winged Condor by drinking the blood of a winged creature that twines with man. The priest wants to be his own god.

My chest heaves as the cook's dinner slops in my belly. A big gulp of air quiets the tumult but does not still it completely. I lean against a pine tree and adjust my amulet, the very thing that gave me the power to follow Sleene. Mirko flaps beside me and nuzzles my hand.

Who has ever dared drink the blood of a rapion? "I wonder if the Cliff Rapion could sense the violation."

Mirko bobs his head. I shiver over the thought of Thae's kin attacking the mesa. "It is good you stopped the abomination before they retaliated." He whistles agreement, and I lumber after him.

Who else knows of that canyon? Anyone besides Sleene? Maybe not, since he believed he could get away with his vile act there. My limbs are heavy, and my mind slugs up further thoughts with my steps. All questions return to the Creator Spirit, the supposed one who makes and sustains all creatures.

There was no sense in Ratho being attacked. Why did Thae have to die and her body experience desecration?

My boot stubs a rock; I stumble, and graze my palm on the mesa. I pat the scrape on my poncho and blow the heat from my hand. "Why would a creator allow Sleene to disrespect a creature's lifeblood?"

Mirko rumbles at my impertinence.

I trudge on but eventually break our brooding silence. "Mirko, what if there really is no god?"

His intense hiss startles me. I sweep my forehead with my arm and turn the corner to the Common.

I wake again in our empty sleeping nook. After the climb out of the canyon and a long sit in a Steam Pocket, Mirko and I fell onto our shelf just before dawn. I thought to only close my eyes a moment and then join the Carterea for morning meal and drills, ready to face my upcoming consequence, but we slept through everything. Why are we left alone?

Oh, my muscles have shrunk! I stretch and groan through the tight pain. Beneath the fresh bandage my ankle is less red, and the stitches have held. At least the cut is not festering.

Mirko rouses and yawns. My wish is to hide here forever and never face Sleene or Ratho's possible confession. The weight of future ill presses hard on my breastbone. If only my friend will show mercy.

I squeeze my amulet and notice blood soaking through the red leather. There is even an odor. Certainly it is decay, since I wasn't able to dry the heart first. Well, a little odor and oozing is worth the gain. None will likely notice.

I roll up and push all thoughts aside. After readying myself, I jog out to the Common. This morn, I do not even bother to pray, and I sense no retribution.

There's not a Madronian near to instruct me, so I take my time at the spring. I hurl a handful of water into the face of the Four-Winged Condor before going to the latrine.

Mirko scavenges beetles for himself and cactus fruit for me. Returning, I drain my water sack and refill it. After replacing my boots at the Clothiers, assuring the woman that I'm fine and accepting her condolences for Thae and Ratho, I wander back into the Commons to decide what to do next. The way everyone is leaving me alone makes no sense. I'm skittish as a desert hummingbird, darting back and forth, up and down.

"There you are." Govern Madgea strides to me. I stand straight and salute, trying to believe I am ready for the ultimate consequences of my previously unsuppressed femininity. My only defense is that I've corrected the weakness. Maybe my effort will arouse this woman's sympathy.

The muscles in my legs seize. If I have the chance, I will beg to live for Mirko's sake. He sits up and covers the last beetle with his foot.

"There, there," the govern tsks at my salute. "No need to be formal. I'm only seeking you to let you know your friend has regained his presence."

Mirko trumpets. My smile stretches wide, and then the joy is snuffed and my centerself quakes. "And, and what are his concerns?"

"The usual." She pulls me to have a seat beside her on the edge of the spring. "He worries if he has failed. If you, his brother, are disappointed in him. If his family will receive him. And last night he was in a fit over whether Thae's body would be returned. He had quite a spell that truly unnerved me, but he came through it."

"Well, she was returned!" I exclaim.

She glances at me. "Yes. According to the boys' chatter, the ceremony went well." She pats my leg. "But I'm sure my brother is happy to be back in the village today. He dislikes the open desert so much."

I nod and sip from my water sack to wet my cracked throat. Is Sleene still unconscious in the canyon? Or does he sit in the Monast wondering what happened? Did he see Mirko when he raised his head? Or were his eyes clouded or filled with blood? Will he return here full of suspicions?

Govern Madgea cuts through my raging questions. "He did look quite green when he left this morning. But in full character, he refused any medicinals."

So he recovered! I gulp another swallow of water. He left and does not seek me. He must not have seen Mirko.

What Govern Madgea said of Ratho finds meaning in my head. He called me his brother. His brother!

I sputter water, and the govern pats my back. He has kept my secret! Ratho cares for me at some level. Tears fill my eyes, and joy and relief plunge through my body.

"Are you all right?" she asks.

"Yes," I answer, sputtering to control my glee. "Yes, I am!"

Her hand pauses on my back before pointing at my ankle.

"Oh, it's healing well. Thank you, again. I checked it this morn-ing." I slip off my boot. She kneels before me and carefully unwinds the bandage.

"Well, this is good. I thought I smelled infection."

I cover my leeching amulet with my pack.

"So, yes, very good. Or as good as can be expected." Wrapping it again, she goes on to chat about the weather, the breakfast Cook offered, and my new station.

I interject. "Govern, why haven't I been instructed about my new work?"

"Oh, it's foolery." She shakes her head. The rings pinched to her earlobes tinkle. "They think you cursed, Tiadone."

"What?"

She stands and places her fingers on my shoulder. "It's lunacy, to be sure. But they wait to see if your Singer will join Thae in grief or disaster."

Mirko rises to his toes and flaps a great gust that raises dust over our feet.

"I said it was craziness." The govern laughs and pats the debris from her robes. "Mirko is obviously well. I believe you'll receive orders any moment."

I nod and get to my feet.

"Well then. Govern Droslump should be prowling over soon." My eyes widen at her disrespect. "Oh, pishah," she blows out. "He was a bully in school and still is one. I see more students in the infirmary due to his hand than accidents on patrol. Although he's careful enough with his discipline to be able to keep his report to my brother positive."

What she speaks rings true; he inflicts just enough to damage without completely incapacitating patrollers. Like what he did to my tongue.

She continues. "But I bet you didn't know the harsh fellow has a fondness for puffed desert mice."

"He eats them?"

"No!" She giggles. "He keeps them as pets. He has a cage in his quarters and cares for several at once. I hear him crooning to the little rodents every now and then." Now we are laughing together. "Don't you pass that on!" Madgea says.

"It's a secret," I agree. Droslump's so brutal that the thought of his caring for mice is bizarre. As strange as his prayers for Ratho and Thae. But then maybe those were only for his self interest, as Madgea's hinted. He wants to keep a reputation of success at the mesa. No boys or rapion lost, no Triumvirate dangers slipping by him. I wonder what penalty he received for the goats lost to the cat before. Or if now he'll be charged with Thae's death in some way?

"Anyway," Madgea says, "for today, we can rest, as this horrific incident seems to be behind us. May another not occur for a decade."

The saying tickles my mind. Is that a R'tan injunction? "Thank you, Healing Govern."

She smiles and turns. "There's our great Govern Droslump now with your gear for Lookout." She faces me and moves her hands in the pattern for good health and safety. I return the broad gesture to her.

"Oh." She grips my arm. "I almost forgot Ratho's message." She tuts and releases me. "Early this morning he begged me to send you thanks for returning Thae to the soil." My centerself plummets. She continues. "Rathos's still not completely lucid. I'm sure he meant thanks for returning them both to the mesa so Thae's body could be honored."

"Of course." Ratho saw what we did, as I saw him in that moment!

Madgea pats my cheek then hurriedly circles the spring and avoids Droslump.

"Patroller," he calls.

I assume the position of lower rank: feet widely planted, open palms by my hips. Mirko lowers his head in deference. I have to push aside the thought of puffed mice so as not to laugh.

Droslump halts in front of us and drops a parcel at my feet. "By your failure you have lost your partner." I'm surprised the sand is not red from the anger gushing off of me. All temptation to even grin is gone. "You will report to Lookout and assist in relay." I knock my fist to my chest to show acceptance. He turns without acknowledgment. "Bewitched Singer," he mutters.

I grip Mirko's crawling neck feathers. We remain motionless until the govern disappears into the Eating Cavern.

"Fool!" I growl. Mirko crunches the beetle in his talons and gulps it down.

I push my twists back from my face. "Let's forget him, Mirko. Sleene is gone, and Ratho called me his brother." I splash my hand through the spring. Mirko bugles and flaps through the spray.

CHAPTER 58

LOOKOUT

The hike to Lookout is not so endless this time. My stomach is full, my feet are toughened, and I'm careful not to bang my toes against the mesa. Because of the distance and my ankle, I pace myself.

Droslump's extra parcel is awkward, but inside we found extra water skins, which we filled and laced onto my pack. I carry more but know how and where this trail will end. The handholds and occasional stair are expected. The main difficulty today is the ache still in my limbs from returning Ratho and then from tracking Sleene. His filthy name burbles my gut.

Mirko returns above me. "Is Sleene truly gone?"

He bobs his head.

"Good. The incineration's a mystery then, an intervention of the Four-Winged Condor." I wink, and Mirko chirps. "And if he does wonder if another took part, the shame will keep him from inquiry. I can't imagine the other Madronian priests supporting his vileness."

Mirko whistles for me to keep climbing.

Finally, we reach the mesa top and cross to the wooden platform. Mirko leans close to support my weak legs.

At the rotunda, I squat to gather my breath and still my nerves before knocking at the door. It bangs open, pushing me off my haunches. I tumble backward and nearly fall to the Common below, stopped only by Mirko, who snatches my sleeve with his talons and rights me. My chest thuds as pebbles clink down the stone face and then silence in their great drop.

"Nearly got you!" The lookout's wheezy breath whistles in his teeth. The jaundiced skin puckers below his cheekbones with each inhale. It is the same man I saw before.

I scramble to my feet and jump away from the cliff's edge. With crown feathers bristled, Mirko chitters anxiety.

The lookout rolls his head dramatically on his stick neck. His eyes are enlarged today by thick goggles perched on his bony nose. "That Singer again," he snarls. I lower my hand to Mirko's head.

The lookout moves his lips wordlessly. His eyes slide across my amulet, and his nose wrinkles. He snaps his focus back up to my face. "Your position is there, at the back of the rotunda. Erect your camp and await notification of flame necessity. A wait and a wait and a wait!" His laughter turns into coughing. He wipes his mouth on the back of his spotted hand. "That is all you will do the majority of time! Wait!" The door slams shut behind him. "Six days and then one day below," his muffled voice carries through the black door.

Sand grits beneath my shifting feet. I follow the rotunda wall to the backside and see a small space for me to make camp on the platform. Despite my jumpy nerves, I drag my supplies to set up. Can the waiting be so bad? Mirko shadows me.

Yes, the waiting is tedious. Monotony drains, and the heat zaps. Mirko and I dip into the slow rhythm of Lookout. We eat the dry wafers that are our only ration and sip water to pass the time.

What would it be like to have books as Govern Madgea does? R'tan works that were not burned, and books from other lands? I imagine time would run quickly with such stories, while I could gain strength from the knowledge. No wonder the Madronians pretended to destroy all of our books and yet kept a collection for themselves. Anger heats in my belly like the sun heats black rock.

I do not see the lookout again until the dawn of the fifth day.

He bangs out of his chamber and announces, "Your partner has departed!"

In front of my shocked face, he dances gleefully around the platform. His rheumy joints allow a hobbled jig. Mirko hisses at his lunacy, but I only keep my head down as he sings, "You failed him! He failed his rapion!"

Who cares what this fool thinks? Sleene already spewed this idiocy. It changes nothing, and I know the truth.

My only care is that Ratho is leaving the mesa. Thankfully, my heart only lurches to lose my friend, not my lover. Abiding the stench of the decaying cat heart was worth the power. Now the odor is gone, and the bag is smaller. It just would have been nice to show Ratho and assure him of my declared state.

Without my visible anger to play against, the lookout mutters a curse. He goes to close my wafer bin, and that is when I realize he's hard of hearing.

"I'll get it," I say. Oblivious, he fiddles with the lid.

I grin at Mirko. "I'd say we have our privacy." My rapion chirps, and the man doesn't hear a thing.

"There." The lookout wheezes after successfully shutting it. "Keep it closed, fool." He scowls and hobbles back inside.

It's a relief to know we are truly secluded on the platform. However, the revelation pales as I refocus on the fact that Ratho has left.

My disappointment oozes up. I am a fool. Why did I expect I'd have the chance to say good-bye to Ratho? An opportunity to ease his mind? To say I do love him again as a brother. Only. And that I'll miss my partner greatly.

Now he is gone. I curl around the loneliness like a snail sucking back into its shell. The fact that I will see him once I return to the village does not comfort me. How many walls might he build before I can connect with him? Plus, it is so far away and only brings Severation to mind.

Below our thin linen awning, Mirko and I mourn on the platform and watch the shadows and light play over the riddled mesa top.

Finally, the long day passes. The sun melts and an orange moon rises. In lazy circles, Mirko flies against the darkening sky. I toss my hair twists out of my face and scuff my sandals over the wood.

Wait. Was that a call?

Mirko dives to the right and flies below the side of the mesa. He's gone moments and then bursts straight up into the air. He twirls and sings and skids to a stop beside my hunched shoulders.

"What is it?" He pulls my tunic in his beak. "What?" I ask, fear and excitement whirling through me.

Mirko nips my backside. I jump to my feet, and he drives me toward the trail. "What are you doing?" I say. "I can't leave yet! We have another day before return."

He butts his head against me. "Mirko!"

My rapion wings the direction he obviously wants me to go and returns to the platform behind me. "So you want me to go down, and you will wait here?" I whisper. "What if the lookout appears?"

He raises his eyeridge. True. It's not likely. And he hears almost nothing.

"Fine!" I squirm down the holds and maneuver to the carved cup to appease him. I spin around. "Ratho!"

He stands waiting for me. His dark eyes reflect the light of the lichen in his hand, and his brows slope upward in anticipation. My feet are heavy stone like the mesa.

Ratho steps to me. His boots nudge against the tips of my sandals. As I peer down he drops the lichen, and with two fingers lifts my chin.

I lower my eyes in submission. "Ratho, my friend," I stammer. "I am so sorry. I can assure you now, my affection is that of a brother. My amulet is renewed and—"

He lifts my face. Our breath mixes in the slender space until he presses through it, and his lips touch mine, softly then fiercely. My mouth parts, and I kiss him fully. Not like a brother.

"Tia," he whispers.

CHAPTER 59

ALWAYS LOVED

*S*itting close, Ratho holds me tenderly. He assures me his wounds are healing, even shows them to me, then pulls me close while shoving my amulet out of my hands.

"You've told me of your empowered amulet, Tia, of your renewed declaration, but can you still deny our attraction?"

I hide my face against his chest, which somehow still smells of lavender.

"You freed it in me in the infirmary. After you left, I knew of my love, how I had suppressed it for so long. No amulet is going to stop this. Stop who you are." He leans forward and kisses me. "I am not a brother to you."

"Why?" I whisper. "Why would you risk everything and come to me, Ratho?" He strokes my arm. "Why draw up my femininity?"

He places his finger over my lips. "You are my life friend, Tia. My partner. The one who saved Thae." His lips brush my smile, and I return his kiss. "It's you I have always loved without even realizing it. Even when I was frightened by Mirko, I loved you."

"Even when you dreamt of Jenae?" I tease.

He blushes. "Now I will dream of you."

"But the Madronians—"

"The Madronians need never know. The Madronians who

would defile Thae? They deserve nothing from me. I question everything from them now."

He caresseses my twists, and I lay my head back again, still in
shock that our love is stronger than my amulet. And that he returns
my affection.

Next, he whispers his fears of return. I promise that he will do
well. His arms tighten around my waist, and I stroke his cheek.

Together we mourn Thae. I kiss his tears and praise her sacrifice.
Neither of us mentions further the abomination Sleene performed.

"And what of us now, Tia?" he asks me, and brushes my hair
from my brow.

I turn and straddle his lap. He intakes a sharp breath. "What, I
ask?" A sly smile sneaks onto my face. "This is no different than the
millions of times I pinned you in play."

He laces his fingers below my backside and tugs me closer. "This
is much different," he claims with a husky voice.

I grin and circle my arms around his neck. Our kiss is long as
his hands rove over my back and to my breasts, but they are bound
tight. The yucca knot only tightens in his tug. I pull him to my
chest and hold his head close. A sob catches in my throat.

"What, Tia?" He looks up at me, his eyes round with inquiry.

I scoot back. "I would bind myself to you and be with you
entirely but for the risk."

He unlaces my tunic fully and rests his head against my breast
wrap. "And I swear by whichever god is true, I will bind and be
with you."

I stiffen, slide off his lap, and lace my tunic closed. "You asked
what we will do now, Ratho." He reaches for my hand and holds it.
"What's next is that you'll return and begin your life."

He kisses the back of my wrist. "Until you join me," he declares.

I gaze past him. "First, I'll finish my work, endure Severation,
and return to the village." My tears burn the back of my throat.
"Then, for a time, I'll live with Father and find satisfaction in my
labor."

He shakes his head and runs his thumb down my jaw. "How will

I live without all R'tania knowing of my love? How will I wait for us to secretly bind?"

I pull my hand from his and press my fingers to my eyes. "You won't. You'll find another, Ratho."

"What?"

"You'll find a woman to wife. One who can love you and give you children."

"No!" He grips my shoulders and shakes me. "You are my love, Tia. You! I've just discovered this, and I won't lose you!"

I jerk from his hands and get to my feet. In the moonlight, Mirko still sits at the top of the mesa. He hums sympathy. I rest my head on the warm stone wall. "Because of my declaration, you must find another, Ratho. Protect us both."

"No, Tia, we could live together as best mates. Within our home, we could set your declaration aside. We could live as husband and wife!"

"And what would everyone say when my belly rounds with child? There would be no explanation for a declared male with pregnancy. I won't risk your life, Ratho." I turn to him. The lichen glows softly against his sadness. "You've given me more than I ever hoped. I've given all I can, but you deserve more."

He gets to his feet and clenches me to his chest again. "No," he moans. "No! There must be a way."

I force the words out. "You must go, Ratho, before I endanger us further." I press my cheek into his shoulder, relish his soft twists brushing my face. I breathe deeply to hold this moment in my centerself for life, then I step back from him.

"You are my portion, Ratho." I kiss his palm.

"And you are mine, Tia." His lips walk from the heel of my hand to my fingertips. "Only for your safety do I leave. Only for yours." He glances up toward the top of the rock.

I wipe my face across my sleeve. "Go." My voice cracks.

He takes a step away, then lunges back to me. Our embrace is full and long. Every part of me presses against him. He strains to be with me fully.

Mirko's whistle is the only thing that breaks us apart. Ratho traces my tear down my cheek then mingles it with his own.

He moves away, still mouthing, "No, no, no," and turns.

I stand in the grotto and listen to his steps sliding down the path. He leaves me far behind, holding my amulet.

CHAPTER 60

MONOTONY

The days and nights circle above the mesa. My centerself cracks and crumbles over Ratho's departure. Mirko sings for healing, but even his notes hardly bring peace. I have lost my friend and my love. My declaration has been turned on its head once again, although I yearn after none but Ratho. My amulet feels weightless on my hip.

For six days Mirko and I wait, and then we descend to the Common, cleanse, sleep on our bunk, find food and water, only to return to the platform and wait some more.

It is hard when there is no labor to distract the mind from its endless circling: denying myself Ratho, him binding to another, Severation, the absence of a god, my emptiness.

A rock spider darts over my hand. I don't even raise my head when Mirko plucks it up and swallows it. I almost wish someone would end my misery the same way.

CHAPTER 61

SIXTH DAY

Lookout service during the summer is brutal. Blossoms that stretched across the desert floor are withered now, as brown as I feel. Deep breaths fry my lungs. Shallow breaths are better.

One afternoon, I rake my knife over the ruffled lizard skin and wipe the muck off on a rock. Mirko helps pull the skin taut. *Scrape, scrape, scrape.* My hands mimic what has been done to my centerself.

A couple of clouds whisk above the heat shimmying off the mesa. I tug the lizard skin straight under my sandal. Stray sharp scales stick to my sweaty ankle, where the healing scar glints red. I sigh and shove everything aside.

Mirko sips from the water sack, then I rinse my hands and ankle. My matted hair rests heavy on my shoulders, so I twirl the mess up and tie it into a head wrap.

"At least it's the sixth day, Mirko. Despite the heat, I long for the Steam Pockets." He bobs his head. "The full moon will help me descend the path. And you know, the Carterea will return as well. Which means Baesa will be in sight."

Mirko whistles. I still tease him about the one he desires, but Shiz holds nothing for my eyes now. For that I can thank my amulet. Otherwise, all I can do is curl around my pain for Ratho until a shell hardens over the hole in my centerself.

I get up and adjust the awning pole so that the shade is cast over

Mirko again. After using the latrine stall connected to the Tower exterior, I lie down next to Mirko. His body shimmies heat, and his outstretched wings ruffle in the occasional hot breeze.

I really should do my javelin patterns. But it's broiling. A nap is better until the sun drops lower. I drift to sleep.

Ratho bends over the goat
and holds it steady.
Father removes bots from the animal's nostrils;
Ratho's grimace makes me chuckle.
He looks up, and a smile touches
the corners of his lips.
His dimple sinks deeply.
There are the lips I have kissed.
I twirl close to his neck,
rub my forehead in his twists.
I soar deep into his dark eyes.
Ratho! Are you well?
As well as one separated.
As well as I can be
away from you.
How is Mirko?
A bugle answers, and peace fills my centerself.
Your wounds have completely healed? I ask.
I am whole of body, but my centerself aches.
I am the same. I try to smile.
And you apprentice under my father?
Yes, he answers proudly.
My vision pulls backward
and Ratho grows small. Smaller.
My love, he calls.
He grows faint.
My father asks, "Are you well, Ratho?"
"Yes," he answers. "I am fairly well."

The two faces I love most disappear. Awake now, I refuse to open my eyes. I pinch them closed more tightly to return to the vision, but it doesn't resurface.

Ratho continues life without Thae or me. Eventually, I'll see him again, but our relationship will be small, and I won't have Mirko.

I turn over and press my sweaty back to my rapion's. For now I will rest in amazement that I have spoken with my friend through vision. None can take that from me. But it's not nearly enough.

CHAPTER 62

FULL MOON

That evening, I snap the second to the last wafer in two and give one piece to Mirko. He crunches it and pecks the crumbs from the platform, while I place the last one in my bag for later.

I reposition my feet in my sandals, and my poncho flaps in the night breeze. I check and recheck that everything is stowed from lizards' reach, since we will be gone for the sixth night and seventh day. My awning is down. Only one lichen strand glows on the platform. I stash it in my bag as well.

The vision of Ratho returns to my mind, and I feel a grin widen. Thoughts of him will keep me buoyed during the descent tonight.

I hang my remaining full water sack on my pack and see the platform is bare. I'm ready. "All right, Mirko."

He digs his talons into the wood and stretches. I hitch my pack between my shoulder blades and swing my arms to get the blood flowing. The rock still radiates heat, but the night is quickly tugging it away. "Mirko?"

He sits staring at the rising moon. The light skims the immense mesa, collapsed tunnels looking like dark blood spatters on the gray surface. Mirko cocks his head. "What? What do you hear?"

He lets out a low whistle.

"Well, it's not the lookout. We haven't seen him for weeks." I sigh. "Will there ever be an alert for you to signal?"

Mirko doesn't answer, but moans rise from his belly. He shoots straight up into the air, snaps his wings open, and hovers. His screech sirens through my skull. A shaft of lightning cracks near him, burning into a distant spot on the mesa. The hot light sizzles and glimmers float up from the hole.

"Mirko!"

CHAPTER 63

THE CALLING

Tumbling from the air, Mirko backwings in time to stop from crashing into me. I catch him around the waist, and his wings droop over my hands; his talons curl closed against my belly. The cinnamon scent is overpowering, steaming from his beak.

I unhook my water sack and quickly tip it over his face. The rivulets hiss and cool.

"Mirko! Mirko! Are you all right?

His head lolls then lifts. With heavy lids, he blinks, and I am able to breathe once more. He gestures to the mesa surface with his beak.

"I know," I whisper. Everything inside of me yearns toward the spot that was lit.

Mirko drops from my arms and drinks deeply from the sack. He sways, rights himself, ruffles and flaps. "Are you certain you are okay?"

He trumpets. Renewed strength seems to vibrate each feather. He chortles for me to follow.

"Yes, I'm coming!" I pull out the lichen and hold it before me. Instead of going down the path, back to the Common, I step off the wood platform and follow Mirko across the broad expanse ahead.

Darkness broods in a crumbled section ahead of me, like the space left in a crone's missing tooth. I give a wide berth to the weakened area, which reaks of decay, likely the fetid standing water trapped below. My ankles don't wobble, and my centerself doesn't quake. My amulet hangs quietly at my side, finally pumping me with power. I'm crossing the top of the mesa to whichever chasm the lightning cleansed. The calling pimples my skin.

We work our way across the rock. The journey is farther than we traveled for Sleene. What is it that compels us?

The moon sweeps up the sky as I weave carefully forward. The tugging in my breastbone doesn't wain despite my body tiring.

Finally, Mirko backwings above a narrow hole. Wearily, I stop beside the opening. "Is this it?" I whisper. "Are you sure?"

My rapion crows and darts into the space without hesitation. His wings knock rocks free, and they clatter below. It sounds dry down there, at least.

Gingerly, I sit on the lip which holds me, for the moment. Lowering my lichen, little shows but a curve of stone leading downward. I stash my light and shove aside loose rocks rimming the edge until I find a firm hold. I look up at the moon watching me, down at the yawning hole, already swallowing my legs. To the right and left, I can't see either end of the mesa. Who knows exactly where this is?

"Go, go, go," I chant, and with a great breath I swing off the edge, into the heart of the mesa.

Mirko chitters from somewhere in the blackness. My feet kick against stone, so I let go, only to fall and skid. It is a slanted tunnel going down! Desperate, I shove my hands and feet against the walls and stop my slide.

Crash!

"No!" I shout, ducking as rocks tumble from above. A large one cracks against my shoulder before rolling past. The opening has collapsed!

"Mirko!"

He chirps below, sounding all right, maybe even flying ahead to scout.

I hang in the tunnel, my pack pressed between the wall and my back. I wait for the dust to settle, wait to draw a breath and steady my centerself. Tearing up, I slip before pressing harder with my feet. My palms burn from rock abrasions. My shoulder aches.

What, what am I doing? Why did I climb inside? Of course the opening could have collapsed. Before my panic completely eats free, Mirko wings into my lap. I slide farther, but wedge myself to a stop once again. Wait. Is that a dim light glowing under us?

My rapion sings and sings, the sound ringing in the tiny space, knocking free tiny pebbles that bounce off my headwrap. Mirko tumbles off and calls for me to follow. As if I have a choice? To climb back up would be extremely difficult, even dangerous if larger rocks tumbled free while I tried to dig my way out. It's impossible. And what of that light? It's definitely light.

I scoot down the winding tunnel after my rapion, who now sings with a thrill. Suddenly, my compulsion returns. I can't move as quickly as my centerself demands.

CHAPTER 64

TRUTH

The moment I drop from the passage and my feet slam onto a flat surface, Mirko buzzes ecstatically. With my head wrap slipped over my eyes, I crawl forward and sit on the smooth floor. Shoving the material back, my blood stops pumping. We are in a round room with carvings covering the wall. They must be the work of early R'tan as I can't decipher all in the old script.

I spin on my knees. Clumped along the floor's curve, lichen illuminate the room, except for one dark hole. Like a gullet at the base of the wall, it's positioned directly across from the tunnel we fell down from.

Mirko bugles. Stillness descends on, in, and through me. I shrug off my pack, gaping at the imagery around me. Nestled in a myriad of others are a few pictographs I recognize from our *Oracles*. Ones I studied year after year as Father read the greater passages to me.

Wait. All the images and truths are here, the ancient marks and scenes collected in one round room exactly as Father described. "The Chamber of Verities?" I whisper into the holiness.

Mirko rings the circle with great wing beats. The light shimmers across his feathers, and he bugles louder. The sound thrums the stone as well as my bones. He confirms my guess.

I slowly get to my feet and stand before the wall carved with pictures of rapion, fish, animals, plants, and people. "Look, Mirko!"

He flaps beside me as I try to read. "'The Creator Spirit moved … through the empty. His breath turned—no, twirled into being desert, waters, and sky.' It is the beginning of the *Oracles of the Creator*!"

My rapion lowers to the floor and hums. Each Oracle of Life is glowing, every Divine Instruction is illustrated.

I breathe as quietly as possible. The Creator Spirit himself is said to have whispered the carvings into the stone in the presence of his prophets. The broken history of my people pieces together as I explore.

One wall depicts the R'tan formed by the sea along with the rapion. Both hatched from great eggs buried in large sand mounds, and their descendants were our ancients who moved to the mesas and the cliffs.

There are three panels showing the Triumvirate, but the swirling symbol of the Creator Spirit glides below the cat, the enemy, and the storm. Even in difficulty, the god is there.

My fingertips trace the spirals. Faith sparks and consumes my dry doubt as I'm infused and able to believe to see the truth. The Creator Spirit is God!

I run around the room fluttering my hand over the holy words Father taught me. *Creator Spirit, forgive my unbelief! You are the God of my people!*

I twirl and dance until I'm breathless, panting, bent at the waist to recover. How could I have doubted? How? My breath slows, and I shake my head at my former foolishness.

The dark hole beside me draws me closer. I kneel and peer into it. Is it another tunnel? Possibly a way to leave?

"Is that water down there?"

Mirko doesn't answer, as he's transfixed before one of the panels showing rapion. I sniff. If it is water, it isn't putrid.

I stand and turn to the handprints that cover a portion of wall exactly as Father told me. They reach from the floor to nearly the top of the room's arch. I reverently place my palms on each one I can reach.

"These are the prophets of old who testified to the truth of the *Oracles*!" Mirko joins me and bows.

I step back to the middle of the Chamber of Verities. Twittering, Mirko flies spirals up my body as he used to when a hatchling. The air lifts my hair and garments. I raise my face in holy reverence.

Righteous laughter bubbles out of my centerself. "The Creator Spirit is my God!"

CHAPTER 65

THE CHAMBER

We remain in the Chamber, mesmerized. Concern for how we might leave barely touches my thoughts. Instead, I read the carvings, truths, and histories as much as I am able. The joining of rapion and R'tan is shown in a large panel. Both step from their eggshells and reach to touch.

One image depicts large eggs wrapped to boys and small eggs dangling in netting from girls' necks. A portion is given to visionaires with eyes staring forward, birdlets perched in their hair. One girl even reminds me of Jenae. Before them, patrollers stand ready with javelin, bola, and large rapion on their shoulders.

A dark section describes the afterdeath Place of Passing for those who violate the *Oracles* and the Creator. Worms twist in the bodies of the screaming, while rapion and men feed on each other. Above is the carving of the Place of Rest, where men and women and rapion twine in peace. Mother and Thae are there now. "How beautiful is it?" I ask them.

Another immense scene shows everyone standing before a person who casts a rapion-shaped shadow. A prophet!

A thought niggles me until I face it: There are none portrayed with an amulet. I scan all the images of people several more times to confirm, and not one has the declaration hanging from their hip.

Of course. It is a Madronian vestige. I reach down and squash the bag, moving it behind me.

Mirko rubs my neck with his beak. When he climbs onto my lap, I share my last wafer in the silence. I yawn, and Mirko stretches his beak wide with a great breath.

Suddenly, a mighty rumble vibrates through us. Reaching for the floor, my hand slaps water.

"Rain, Mirko? Is it rain?"

He trumpets.

We jump up as a trickle of water tips from the tunnel we entered from. My skin pimpling, I turn. With a roar, water belches from the low, dark hole and sloshes around the room. It has been so many months since rain fell that my cover is unused, sitting back in my cupboard. Not that it matters now. The water swirls about my ankles. From somewhere, rain is pounding into the mesa, filling whatever is behind that hole and overflowing into here. I lift my pack from the wetness and swing it on.

The rumble grows louder, and alarm wrinkles Mirko's brow. "What?" I raise my voice. "What should we do?"

Mirko wings the room. He darts up the high tunnel but returns. More water pulses in from the floor hole, and my rapion flies out through the narrow space left.

"Mirko!" I cry as the water gushes again, filling the opening completely. The pool rises to my knees, the torrent spinning like a whirlpool.

"I, I could drown," I whisper.

I wipe at my face, but the water splashes up again. I blow it off my lips. "There has to be an escape!"

The pool deepens. "Mirko!" I yell, even though he's out of hearing, hopefully safe, ahead of the flood.

Suddenly, my feet are swept from the floor, and I'm thrown to the wall, dragged with the flow around the chamber. Water burns up my nose. Tethered, my amulet floats and jerks about me as my head submerges. I push it away from my paddling arms and slash about for air. Gasping, my head breaks the surface, and I tread. The water bulges higher, sinking more of the holy carvings beneath the flood.

My tears of panic are swept into the pool, and I gulp mouthfuls of water. Choking and sputtering, I'm slammed against the wall of handprints. I reach out to the stone to steady myself, and with the motion a light flashes and a burn sears my palms. My body becomes a stiff plank I cannot control, and even my wet hair sizzles. I jerk my hands from the wall and gape at the black-shadowed imprint my palms left behind. Water douses over my head, but I bob up again.

Popping to the ceiling, I gasp. The water is high enough to reach the other tunnel now. It's gone from sight.

Creator Spirit, save me!

Pressed against the dome of the chamber, I take the biggest breath I can and dive. I kick and swim hard. The shimmering light of the lichen twirls like fingers pointing the way out. The hole! There it is! I fight my way into it, my feet now kicking the top and bottom of a tunnel, my fingers clawing, pulling me forward. My breath bangs inside me, trying to burst out.

Keep going, I beg myself. The second I can't, can't fight against the sweeping pull, can't push with my feet or burned hands any more, I rise the smallest bit.

Flailing, I discover the tunnel is open above me. I kick with the last of my centerself. I swim to live, and my head breaks through the surface. It's the top of the mesa. While I sputter and gasp, Mirko nuzzles his wet face against mine. "I'm, I'm so glad you are safe," I cry and he hums the same in return.

I grip the stone ledge with my burned hands and pull through the pain, pull myself out and collapse on the rock. The early morning's gray veils of rain brush over me.

My flesh trembles in the air. Mirko nips at my headwrap, twisted around my neck, until the material falls free. He tears strips with his talons and beak, and I wrap my hands, barely able to look at the horrible bubbling burns. The wet knots tighten when Mirko pulls a strand, and I tug the other with my teeth.

My breath jerks and heaves.

Unbelievably, Mirko whistles for me to stand and follow, and he's right. This edge might collapse just as easily as the last hole did. I lumber up, my pack streaming water, and follow. Like a second skin, my cold clothes are pasted to me. Even my amulet is weighty and tacky.

I glance back at the tunnel, to the Chamber of Verities. The edges of the hole cave, rocks shift, and the opening is quickly covered by a wide pool. Frantic, I look about for a landmark, something to show me where I might return, but everything is a haze in the rain.

Mirko whistles and I reluctantly follow, no longer feeling my numb feet. My hands bleed through the wraps and curl like claws to ease the pain.

We must trudge nearly all the way back to the Lookout. By the time the rain lessens, we reach a solid section of the mesa surface not dotted with holes. I can't pull my heavy body any farther. Whimpering, I collapse, and the last bit of energy shakes out of my bones.

Mirko helps pull my pack off and nudges it beneath my head. Tucking himself close to my belly, he chortles as I curl around him.

Between half-open eyes, the desert horizon wavers beyond the mesa. I sleep.

CHAPTER 66

IN THE MIST

In a grove of steam, I blink. The evaporating water sways and swirls above the mesa. I sit up carefully. Every piece of me hurts, and I'm alone.

"Mirko?"

There's no answer, but a breeze parts the mist and sweeps trails over the edge of the rock. I hold my hands before my face and tug the wraps off with my teeth. Between gasps, one strip then another flaps to the stone. My palms are blistered and ragged; my fingertips are bloody from dropping into the chamber and then clawing out of it. I wince. "This is too much to understand." I roll my lips. "Too much!"

Mirko flaps to my side, with full water sacks, and my centerself calms. Fresh steam swirls back from us. He crouches by my legs.

I hug him and hiccup. We are encased again in the warm mist. I meditate a moment on the Chamber of Verities, what I have seen, what no other in my generation has.

The power of the Creator Spirit quickly pours strength into my centerself. Maybe more than my amulet ever did before. I take a great breath and let it out slowly. "We are well," I say to convince myself, to grasp the possibility. I wobble upright and look for the sun. We have time to return to Lookout. We will not have been missed.

Mirko twitters agreement.

Suddenly, the sun burns through the vapor and penetrates the clothes on my back. Its warmth bakes my skin. I hiccup again, while hanging the water sacks on my pack. "Thank you, Mirko." He only shrugs.

The mesa belches steam and swallows shadows. "Mirko, do you think the Chamber was damaged by the waters?"

He whistles doubt.

"Right. It has stood for centuries, and now it is hidden again."

Mirko bobs his head and takes to the air above me. Across the remaining distance I see the rotunda and hobble carefully toward it. The creaks click out of my body, and I return in Mirko's winged shadow.

CHAPTER 67

WONDERING

*S*essions later at Lookout, Mirko has to flame alert to the village, but the sandstorm turns at the last, thankfully. If another does strike, our plan is to offer the signal then I'll race down the path to the Common. Hopefully I can make it down in time. Mirko can, but I know he won't leave my side unless I'm safe. It's not as if the crazy lookout will offer us protection in the rotunda.

Now, in the pink, early evening, I carefully slice through the lizard meat Mirko caught while he tears at the entrails. Tender, my hands are healing due to careful wrapping and aloe treatments. Maybe because I didn't visit Madgea to avoid giving her an explanation, the wounds will scar worse than the mark the cat left on my ankle. I brush a twist from my eye with the back of my bandaged hand. Still, I'll almost cherish the scars as a reminder of what I saw. I set the knife down and wipe my fingertips clean on my trouser legs.

"I can't believe we lost the Chamber, Mirko."

He whistles. "I know you've looked." He's repeatedly flown over the area but hasn't found it again.

"Maybe it is as the Creator Spirit wishes," I admit, and he bobs his head.

What would Ratho say of my discovery and experience? Would it rouse faith in the Creator Spirit, now that he questions the Madronians?

"So you really think it was lightning, Mirko?"

He sighs and nods once again.

I shake the pain from my palms. "Why would the Creator Spirit mark my prints on the same wall as the prophets?" I whisper.

Mirko nibbles the lizard heart and doesn't look up at me.

"The Creator Spirit has preserved me twice." My rapion chortles agreement around the food in his beak. "The desert cat and the flash flood. Maybe that is the reason. One marked hand for each trial." I snort. "It's not as if there are any more prophets in R'tania." Besides, I am a declared male, a Madronian creation. I lift my amulet and twist it round on the sinew strap. As I let go, it spins in a race to unwind.

As it dangles on the strap, I poke it. What is its true power? With the second heart, it still couldn't withstand Ratho, but with only the first I was able to perform fully as a male patroller. With two, I followed Sleene and found the Chamber. The stained leather bag swings from my fingers. It's so confusing. I can't imagine who I'd be without the amulet.

I drop it from my fingers and rest my lizard meat strips on the hot rocks nesting in our little fire beyond the platform. The sizzle tickles my nose. Waiting for the meat to cook, I move through my javelin patterns without the shaft in my grip. But it isn't long before I pause and stare into the red sun slipping to the horizon.

What I do know is that I've found much here: the Creator Spirit, the power of being male, and a lingering strand of femininity that nests deep inside me. And I'm not afraid of it. It only belongs to Ratho. All of that discovery has worth, doesn't it?

I turn my meat over. "I've found much, but I'm so tired of being alone," I whisper.

Mirko bugles a rebuke. "I know I have you," I say, and sit beside him. His long tail flicks irritation, but he continues to eat. *I have you—for now.* The poisonous thought oozes through my mind. I shove it away and inhale the good scent of cooked lizard.

"How do other boys survive at Lookout without their rapion able to leave their sides and hunt?"

Mirko licks his beak and strikes a pose.

"I know your strength and worth." I laugh and nudge his flank until he leans into my wrist.

I retrieve my meat from the rocks. It is perfectly done. Mirko and I eat side by side.

CHAPTER 68

HERESY

In time, my hands heal completely, and Mirko and I adjust, finding a simple satisfaction at Lookout. So, it's a surprise when, late one night, I keep waking from sleep. I shrug up my poncho against the nippy air. The stars journey in an arc above me, taking the brightest a bit farther each time I open my eyes.

Something nudges worry inside me. I turn over, and Mirko grumbles softly. My arm stiffens across his back as I fall asleep once again.

Flames strike blackness.
Village faces gleam and fade.
Sleene drags his wings through the dust
and lifts
The Oracles of the Creator.
"Heresy!"
He holds the book
over the heads of the hunched villagers.
"Forgiveness, Four-Winged Condor!" he snarls.
He drops to his knees, and the black wings
curve behind him.
"Forgiveness through flame!"
The people murmur,
but none dare raise their voice in true protest.

Sleene rises,
and the villagers part
like sand driven by wind.
Visionaires ring the Monast roof;
their pale dresses glow.
Acolytes march a man forward.
His hands are held behind him,
and his head is covered with a sack.
"Blasphemer!" Sleene shouts.
"Here is he
who draws blight and disease.
Here is he
who brings death to sons!"
A woman howls.
"Recant or burn!" Sleene spits.

The book drops to the dirt.
The acolytes release the man's hands.
Sleene jerks the sack off his head.
Father!

CHAPTER 69

RECANT

No!" screams Frana.
She bustles through the crowd.
Fear-stricken, Ratho holds her shoulders.
"No," Frana begs, and coddles her rounded belly.

"Recant or burn," Sleene hisses.
Father cowers.
Sleene shoves him to the ground.
Father's hands give way, and his face
grinds against the book's cover.
Heaving sobs rock his body.

Slowly, Father stands, book in both hands.
Acolytes thrust him to the bonfire.
Sweat beads faster than his tears.

Sleene lifts his arms to the sky
and closes his eyes.
"Four-Winged Condor,
here is your offering!"
The fire cracks.

Father lifts the book
and throws it into the flames.

The pages crisp and curl.
He crumples.
Sleene kicks him in the side.
"To the box!" the priest shouts.

Acolytes haul my father
to the edge of the village.
He's shoved into a wooden box
more suited for a goat.
The door clumps closed.
A huge lock clanks shut.

Frana breaks from Ratho.
He drops to his knees by the fire
while she flees to Father.
Weeping, she kneels
and presses her cheek to the rough wood.
My sight is swept back to the Monast.
Jenae stands on the roof with Zoae.
I'm drawn into her brown eyes.
I'll see to his care, Tiadone.
Please, I cry.
She disappears
in a spot of glowing light.

I wake screaming. Mirko pulls me from the mesa edge, where my arm and leg already dangle in empty space. I shrink into a ball and crawl on all fours back onto the platform. Mirko keens into the black night; the note, higher than my ears can hear, twangs my nerves.

My father has recanted what I finally and truly know. I have seen the Chamber of Verities. The Creator Spirit is our god. And now — *now* — my father has burned our *Oracles*. "Creator Spirit, have mercy," I gag between my tears. "Mercy." I sit up, and my thoughts teeter. We will never again hold the sacred book or read its holy words.

But it is my father. Would I not rather he recant than have him burn? *Creator Spirit, have mercy on me!*

Mirko leaps from the ledge and spirals high to the stars. I watch, frozen, as he dives in a death dance and pulls up just in time to avoid crashing into the top of the mesa. He wooshes past, and my tunic, amulet, and twists tug to follow.

I curl up tightly. Has my father lost his spiritual centerself just as I found my own?

CHAPTER 70

MOURNING

As the sun rises, Mirko and I keep our heads lowered. Dust shadows his feathers and my skin; we have rubbed the dirt we found beneath the platform onto ourselves. It shows the Creator Spirit we beg for forgiveness for Father.

The sun slides up the sky, yet we do not put up the linen covering but stay kneeling or squatting. Mirko's wings are close to his sides. He chirrups his own prayers while I meditate on the vision. Father's pain. His loss. Frana's great belly and fear. Ratho's care. My connection with Jenae.

How did that happen? Could it happen again? If it does, will she believe the vision comes from Mirko's ability to sing? Not my lingering femininity? Through another vision right now, I could give Jenae my explanation and see if Father is all right.

None comes.

We fast, and the sun passes until our shadows stretch to the east. Sweat pools in my chest wrap and adheres my arms to my sides. My prayers tumble out one after another. *Allow Jenae to send help for Father. Make Frana and the babe strong. Force Sleene to release Father. Show mercy, Creator Spirit, even to those who don't know you or who deny you, as I once did though you were merciful to me.*

Finally, the sun sizzles down. Mirko and I turn to each other.

"It is the end of another sixth day." The words scratch from my dry throat.

He ruffles his feathers, and dust puffs into the dusk. Slowly I move my stiffened joints.

Groaning, I get to my shaky feet, straighten my belongings. With my pack on my shoulder and Mirko before me, we inch down to the desert floor. We have mourned our fullest; it is time to cleanse and rest in the Sleeping Cavern.

We descend below the shard of moon snagged in the night sky. Tonight, there is no call to the Chamber of Verities. None at all.

CHAPTER 71

CONFRONTATION

While Mirko and I trudge through the cavern, boys whisper and
shrink from sight. None could already know what Father has
been accused of. Could they?

"Spawn of a heretic," someone whispers from a tunnel. I glare
down the passage but see no one. So much for hope. My stomach
rolls like a windweed.

Mirko and I hurry to the Steam Pockets. Inside an empty one, I
disrobe and plop the hot rocks into the puddle of water. Mist rises,
but my body cannot relax. What now?

The night on my shelf flows past quietly. It is the morning that
snaps forth in chaos.

At the spring, Droslump intercepts me. I raise my dripping face,
though before I can wipe my eyes the govern strikes me across the
cheek. His skeletal hand smacks a sting so hard that I stumble backward. Mirko launches to the air, but I grab his tail and stop his
attack. With talons open wide, and keening, he flaps furiously.

Droslump doesn't take even one step away; his breath is weighted
and fierce. "Your possessions will be searched. You will turn out all
you own. Even now your lookout post is being inspected."

I shrug and get to my feet. Mirko settles at my side, but his feathers remain bristled. "You will find nothing," I say.

Behind two desert cat hearts and my father's hair coils, you cannot see my hidden femininity, Govern, and you cannot see my prayers! You cannot see I worship the Creator Spirit, and you'll never see my palm prints charred onto the wall of the Chamber of Verities. I have hidden the *Oracles* in my centerself where you cannot reach!

My eyes narrow, and I refuse to look away.

Droslump spits onto my sandal, leaving a glob that slips between my toes. He snaps up my pack and begins to search.

The Eating Cavern empties, and the Baltang boys linger around the spring. Most sneer. A few rapion bristle at Mirko. I know the birds may worship as their boys do, if at all, until they return to the Cliffs. However, Father says Cliff Rapion worship the Creator Spirit. At release these will learn from their clan and know the truth. Shame will fill them for mocking me now.

Glaring at my amulet, Droslump discards my belongings into the dust. He kicks my water sacks, herb packets, and dried lizard meat. My mouth is drier than the sand and a tic jerks my eyelid.

The govern's clawed fingers bump over my pack's outer, now empty compartments. He feels along the inside as well. His hand moves over the hidden pouch for my flow sponge. Not that the discovery would endanger me, but it would make everything more complicated. The Madronians wouldn't want all to know my body defies their amulet.

Playing indifferent, I brush my matted twists off my neck. Droslump throws my pack at my feet, never finding my sponge. He swirls his robes about his ankles. "I will inspect every crevice of your shelf." Before I answer, he's gone.

Mirko helps me gather my possessions. We dust them off and place each in my pack. I take off my sandal and splash water over my foot to cleanse it. I keep my head down to avoid the boys.

Until everyone reports for drill, I stay busy at the spring, filling my sacks and washing my tender face again. As well as tightening my amulet sinew. Finally, I slide to the ground. What has my father done? First allowing the Madronians to find the *Oracles* and then recanting? Was it right for him to do so?

I kick a dead shrub loose with my heel, and with my toes fling it high into the air. Mirko echoes my anger and catches the plant. He makes drastic turns and spins and tears the branches to pieces. They flutter down onto me.

"Wasn't everything hard enough already?"

CHAPTER 72

NO ORNAMENTATION

In preparation to return to Lookout, I pick berries from the squat fracksaw cactus. The purple globes will soften when I boil them and make a sweet paste for our dry wafers.

Above, Mirko whistles a warning. With a *thwimp*, my javelin strikes the soil at my ankle. I had left it in my alcove, as I was only collecting berries. I spin around.

Droslump drags his robe across the sand while advancing with speed toward me. I'm far from the mesa, so this must be important. My muscles tighten, and Mirko circles to my side. Beyond Droslump, the Baltang are departing for patrol.

I tug my javelin from the ground to see the handle carving has been struck through. The pictures Father made, the intricate wool curls and the smoke rising from our house, are marred with black lines of soot and deep hashes. I cover the damage with my hand. Mirko burbles empathy and lowers himself on his haunches. Droslump approaches, presenting another javelin.

"Standard Madronian javelins have no ornamentation!" Droslump thrusts it into my free fist. Mirko growls, forcing me to block him from Droslump's path. I have seen other boys with images on their weapons. The govern merely looked for anything that could hurt me.

"My father—"

Droslump squints, and my words are sliced off behind my tongue. He snatches my javelin from my hand and cracks it over his knee. The sound jars my teeth. He throws the pieces to the dirt, raises a whip from his robe, and lashes before I can fully turn my back. The slash curls over my backbone and licks my side. I duck and roll, expecting more strikes.

Instead, Droslump sputters and curses. I peek under my arm and see Mirko flapping violently, finally ripping the whip from the Madronian's hands. With a bugle, my rapion flings the weapon and flares each pinion above the govern, whose face blanches. My rapion, now nearly full size, is ferocious.

Droslump steps away mumbling what I know are empty threats. He bends and retrieves his whip while keeping Mirko in sight. Hatred is carved on his face as he looks at me a last time.

Mirko advances, screeching and swooping. Droslump cowers and ducks, then jogs to the mesa.

"Mirko!" I shout. He turns and flies to me. I run my fingers across my back. There is no blood drawn, because my breastwrap cut the whip sting. But even if it had cut deeply, my own hatred is hotter than the lash. I slide the Madronian javelin into my hip holder.

Mirko lands at my side, chittering. "I'm fine, but that was dangerous, my friend."

He tosses his head at Droslump receding. When the govern is out of sight, Mirko nudges through my broken javelin pieces.

"That javelin bested the cat and came from Father's hand," I say. Mirko nudges a piece toward me until I pick it up. "Yes, I'll save this."

With my knife, I cut away an undamaged chunk and bore a hole through the end. Tugging a leather strip from my pack, I lace it through the wood and dangle it around my neck.

Mirko kicks dirt over the rest of the pieces. He whistles at me and flaps toward Lookout. Stuffing the fracksaw berries deep into my pockets, I follow.

I finger the bit of wood dangling from my neck. It's engraved with an image made to look like a rapion flapping on the horizon, but I know it is Father's image of an open book: *The Oracles of the Creator.*

CHAPTER 73

SOUGHT

I gently swipe the berry paste from Mirko's beak. His tongue follows my finger and nips back into his mouth. It is enough to make me smile.

With another weekly Lookout session ending soon and the clear night moving about us, I bank our fire on the rock and lie next to Mirko below our awning. Surprisingly, sleep comes easily tonight on the warm wood despite my worry for Father, and my upcoming blood time. The stars blur as my lids close. Images spin in my dream.

I am little,
twirling in the kitchen
with a dishrag about my waist.
Father jerks me to a halt
for acting like a girl.

I am curled on his lap
as he reads the *Oracles*
and rehearses that I am male.
I repeat it over and over.
"I am a boy. I am a boy."

I pull on one tunic,
another, and another,

until I'm wrapped and bound
in a cocoon of male clothing.
My breath strains
against the gauze covering my face.

"Tiadone," Jenae calls.
Her pale brows raise.
The Monast fades,
and Zoae flits around her head.
"Tiadone, I have reached you!"
"Jenae?" I stretch my hand
to her soft cheek,
but my fingers slip through air.
She smiles.
"I speak to you and Mirko through vision,
as visionaires speak to each other."
Mirko's wings open next to me.
"It must be possible because my rapion
is a Singer!" I eagerly say.
She nods.
"That was my thought!
I knew I felt your presence, Tiadone,
when your father was boxed.
But I want you to know
he's released now
and recovering at home."
"Father is well?" My voice quivers.
Jenae lowers her eyes.
"He is released, Tiadone.
He will recover. But he is not well.
There was the confinement,
lashings,
and withholdings of food and water."
I bite my lower lip.
"He is weak and frail

but has held to his recant.
There will be no further punishment."

I blink and nod slowly.

"Tiadone, it is good to see you!
Even if
your twists are horrid." She laughs.
A grin tugs at my lips.
"And you are as clean and prissy
as any girl."
"Well, I deserved that, I suppose."

Moments pass.
I have ached for a friend
since Ratho left.
Only Jenae would be brave enough
to reach me.
I turn from thoughts of Ratho's dream
of Jenae.
Mirko lifts upward.
Zoae joins him.
Warm drafts tumble down.
The rapion touch.

"I must go, Tiadone.
I have risked another visionaire joining us."
I gesture thanks.
She begins to fade.
"I feel an approach!"
And she is gone.

CHAPTER 74

PLANS

With Jenae's comfort, I'm able to commit my full attention to Lookout, as needed. Like now. Mirko twirls the warning flame for invasion! The strand of flame stretches across the sky before he spirals down to me and drops the branch into the fire pit. I jump back from the popping sparks.

"Well done!" I rub Mirko's head.

The lookout flings open the door. "Resend the flame," he growls. "It was only a sand whirl. Idiot patrollers." His rheumy bones clack back inside the tower.

At least the threat was false. My centerself starts to unwind. "Mirko, isn't it better to be cautious then overlook a danger?" I ask.

He whistles, seizes the flaming wood, and shoots high again. He signals to the village and visionaires that there is no attack. "Stand down to the military," his fire strikes. He drops the torch into the fire pit and comes to a skid on our platform.

I toss him a lizard strip. "That was the most excitement we've had for a while," I say. The patrollers' rapion flares across the desert were impressive. I could see all the positions along our Perimeter.

Of course that's the most hubbub not counting Father's recant and my visions. Sitting down beside Mirko, I wonder, how has my father healed? How is he now without his *Oracles*? How is his centerself? And Frana? I wish I could know more through Jenae. We have not reached each other again.

Mirko swallows his lizard. He picks the sand from between his toes with his tongue.

"I don't count Severations as excitement," I add. Mirko stops and shivers. I rub my ear, remembering the keen of the last one.

Working Lookout, we did not attend release for Shiz or for Grendo, but we still heard the grieving rapion. Poor Mirko. His Baesa is released, and he will not catch sight of her again until he returns to the Cliffs. Although his own return is not far away.

I smooth my fingers over Mirko's shoulder blades and down his back. His tail wiggles. I laugh and scratch his neck. Glittery, minute feathers puff into the air around my fingernails. He lets out a long, relaxed whistle.

"I better stop or you'll be drooling soon!" I say. He grins, shakes, and settles on his haunches.

I wrap my poncho about my knees. Autumn is slipping into our summer, proven by how the mesa shimmers pink in the late light. I nudge my hair from my face, and Severation wisps back into mind. Maybe if I speak of it, it won't haunt us so. "What, what will happen when we severate, Mirko?"

He nibbles a ratty hair twist lying on my shoulder and coos sympathy.

"Apart from Droslump shaving my head!" I nudge him, and he chortles.

A silence waits between us. Mirko's eyeridge lowers in worry.

I keep trying. "I'll return for apprenticeship and live on my ancestor's land. I will be able to visit Ratho. Carefully, at least. And what about you, Mirko?"

He tucks his head beneath his wing. I reach in and pull his face free, forcing myself to smile. "You will have joy, and that will comfort me," I say.

He warbles a soft song and snuggles his head beneath my arm until I encircle him with a hug. "You never know. Maybe I will find a little happiness myself." I shrug.

I've lived with these oppressive Madronians. I've found truth and faith, and accepted the limits of my amulet. I've served the R'tan by patrolling. Whatever my Village Assignment, I might be content. There is a life of sorts for me ahead. Maybe others will declare their firstborn daughters because of my success. Just maybe.

"I know." I grasp at a joke to lighten the mood. "You'll wing straight for Baesa!"

Mirko whistles and waggles his eyeridge. "Mirko!" My laughter bubbles up as he leaves my side and mimics the mating dance of the rapion. "Oh, please. Stop!"

I reach out to him. My palms are scarred as I expected, yet it is my finger that stops me. It is without ornament and will never flash the ring of commitment females wear. I hide my hands in my lap.

Jenae will marry. Maybe even Ratho, despite his Patrol experience. She is bold enough to not let it matter. There's a chance Ratho will not remain lonely for life. I hug my knees as the thought of him with Jenae hardens inside me.

Mirko stops his dance and hops to me. His tongue tickles my ear. A little giggle escapes from my tight throat. "Hey. You were just cleaning between your toes with that tongue!"

He wiggles it at me like a sidewinder.

I tug him close. We have a few more weeks together. At least we have a few.

CHAPTER 75

GOOD NEWS

I exit the latrines and wander the empty Common. Mirko's rump protrudes from under a lavender bush, and my stomach growls in anticipation of his catch. I could use a rabbit pelt once my head is shaved. I have to focus on the practical; it's the only way to get through the coming days.

"I'll wait for you at the far fire pit, Mirko." His tail flicks. I hitch my pack and stroll to the ring. It seems like yesterday I was greeted by Lalo, and Mirko and Els twirled together. I squat by the remaining coals and move a few twigs until little flames spring up among the windweeds.

"Might I join you?" Govern Madgea surprises me. She sits before I can answer, nudging my amulet aside. With patrols changing, I didn't expect any company. My mind finds no small talk to share. I worry a twist.

"Ah, the warm fire oils the aching joints."

"That is what my father would say," I blurt.

She smiles, but I look away, ashamed I mentioned him. Surely she's heard of his punishment and recant.

"Your Singer?" the govern asks.

"Oh!" I startle. "He's under that shrub trying to snare a rabbit."

She draws her skirts over her skinny ankles and shades her eyes to see the lavender.

"Um … He is able to roam farther than most rapion," I say.

"Curious," she says, and turns to me. "So I understand your Severation is only days away."

I will my blood to pound slower.

"You will be fine," she says. I force a nod. "As you said, your Singer is special. I doubt you will lose complete contact after Return."

"Oh, we will. Rapion do not come to the village, and R'tan are not permitted to visit the Cliffs."

She straightens her apron. "Yes. That is an unfortunate injunction. But don't lose hope."

I resist huffing at the impossible.

Madgea taps her front teeth. "I still haven't found any Singer information in my readings."

"R'tan writings?" I whisper.

"Tut, tut. Me and books, Tiadone." I stare at her. She whispers now. "I can't be separated, you know. My brother kept many volumes from your library when it appeared he destroyed everything." She winks. "I entertain myself with reading of your culture in particular." I will my mouth to close. She pats her hair as if we were simply discussing the clouds. "I find the R'tan — intriguing." I glow from the praise for my people. If only we had access to those works! We could know our history and so much more. And the R'tan would gain power.

"Oh." She touches my leg, "I have news."

"Yes?"

"Two boys reported for Patrol just days ago, from your village. Both took a stomach strain and were sent to me for recovery. My occasional questions received good responses for you."

"Me?"

"Yes." She grins. "Ratho is doing well. He is reunited with his family and has been assigned work with the flock keeper." I attempt surprise. She continues. "And your father — let's say he's well again and teaching Ratho."

I lay my cool hand to my hot forehead. "This is good," I say. I raise my eyes and look into her open face. "Thank you for thinking of me."

She smiles and holds her hands to the fire. Mirko's victory cry pierces the quiet. With two rabbits gripped in his talons, he swoops overhead. "Ha!" the Healing Govern laughs. "You will not be hungry tonight!"

Mirko flaps downward. Emboldened by her kindness, I ask in a rush, "Would you eat with me, Govern, before I return to Lookout for my last week of service?"

She winks. "I'd love to, Tiadone."

CHAPTER 76

SHAVING

The week disappears. I can't stop the sun from chasing the moon, and now the time is here. Mirko follows close beside me as I return my weapons to the Armory. "Go through that door there." The Armorer adjusts his eye patch, then points with a javelin shaft he's shaving.

I part a curtain and pass through an arch. Mirko's tail swishes on the rock floor, and I attempt to capture the sound in my memory. We stop in a circular room with a stool in the middle and a fire pit roaring in the wall.

Droslump and a frigid draft enter behind me. "Sit."

I do. Mirko squirms close to my leg; his shoulder feathers hackle in warning. I release a deep, slow breath to still the jangles threatening to drive me from my mind. I don't even know how I am functioning. My body continues to move apart from my shrieking fears. Father's words lilt through my thoughts: *The Creator Spirit gives grace at the time it is needed.*

Droslump flips his braid behind him and pulls a long knife from his sleeve. The firelight flickers on the metal as he approaches with the point aimed toward me. Mirko hisses, but Droslump sidesteps him. I refuse to shrink away. What could be worse than Severation from Mirko? My death would hold less pain.

Droslump yanks matted twists from my head and hacks them away. I flinch and jerk at the tugs, nicks, and gouges.

Mirko hums encouragement, growls at Droslump, and worries the hair twists about his feet. More knotted clumps drop to the stone.

The last yank makes me gasp, and the last scrape is a puncture that brings out a yelp. Droslump dances back from Mirko's talons while a warm trickle of blood winds down my forehead.

Droslump stoops and gathers the mess. Unnoticed, Mirko slides a hank of hair beneath his foot. The rest is thrown into the fire by the govern. The reek is overpowering.

"When the strands are fully received by the Four-Winged Condor, cleanse and report for Severation." He slips the knife back up his sleeve and shakes his fingers clean. Glowering, he backs from the room. His braid swings like a sidewinder over his chest.

My hair incinerates. I breathe through my mouth, and with my sleeve I wipe the blood off my face. My scalp feels prickly, tender, and sticky. Pressed into the burning cut, my sleeve staunches the blood.

Using his beak and talons, Mirko weaves the piece of hair he kept. Spittle lines the lock until a coil is formed. He raises his foot to me, gestures, and I wrap it several times at the base of his leg. My knot holds it firmly.

A part of me will stay with Mirko. It is the only thought that keeps me from insanity.

CHAPTER 77

MEMORIES

Mirko and I step into a Steam Pocket one last time. The open wounds on my head burn as I grimace and sweat away Droslump's touch. Toweled clean, I dress in my last set of issued clothes. It's true that what I wore on arrival would no longer fit, just as we were told by the Clothier.

I straighten the poncho and cinch my trousers while Mirko flaps beside me. We push aside the skin covers and return to our shelf. I pause at the empty cupboard to slide the key inside for the next patroller. Not that it will protect anything.

Holding the kidskin to my nose, I think of home. I'm actually going home! It's hard to see past Severation, but home will ease some aches. To Father, and Frana, and soon—her baby! Ratho will be there. And Jenae.

Mirko walks on Ratho's shelf and rubs his beak in Thae's sleeping bowl.

I swallow, tuck my kidskin into my pack, and shrug my arms through the straps. Mirko flaps down and sits in his own sleeping bowl one last time. I run my hand over my shelf. The rough stone was always welcome after patrol. Ratho's and my laughter bounced off these red and golden walls many nights before we fell asleep. My silent sobs burst out, and I drop to the floor.

Nothing matters, because Mirko is severating from me. I can't, I can't live through this!

A warm breath of cinnamon brushes my cheek. Mirko climbs onto my lap, and we cry together. *Grace, Creator Spirit. I beg. Grace and strength for us both.*

My legs wobble but amazingly still climb. The dim path rises in the evening's softness. Making the ascent harder, Mirko walks nearly underfoot; I welcome the difficulty.

My nose runs, and I wipe it dry on my forearm. I don't want to weep before the Carterea. Shiz is gone. No one else has ever spoken to me save a few words. What do they care beyond worry over their own future Severations? Madgea will not be here, and her well wishes from last week fade with each step.

I reach the top, and the Amph of Return swallows me into the side of the mesa. Every youth and Signico of the Carterea stare at us.

Around Droslump's feet, lichen spill their glow. He gestures for me to leap to the dark pillar. Blackness meets the edges of the circular top, and my fingers glisten with sweat. I wipe them down my trousers, but they only grow damper. Mirko springs from my side, flies above, and hums as he has done hundreds of times before when my heart needed encouragement.

I gauge my position. In my running start, my joints threaten to lock up, but I vault from the mesa and soar through the empty space. My amulet, arms, and legs flail. I hit the pillar, my knees collapse, and I'm hurled forward by the weight of my pack. My face skids and burns against the rock, but I stay hunched a moment, trying to get the raging panic to subside.

The rake across my cheek burns. I sit up and stifle the screams threatening to burst out of me. Mirko lands in my lap and rubs his head against my shoulder.

Next, Droslump leads the boys in a chant; my mind can't even hold the words. I know it is some Madronian prayer for blessing.

Mirko climbs onto my back, and I kneel with my forehead to the stone. His wings open, and the cinnamon scent cascades over me.

Mirko's hums transition into an aria I've never heard. The notes rise and soar and tumble like a rapion in flight. Mirko holds the final measure; the sound streams over my neck into my centerself.

My tears spill onto the pillar. "I love you, Mirko."

I raise my head and look into his wide eyes, which peer over my shoulder. He presses his head to my cheek until our tears mingle. His cold beak brushes the outer corner of my lips.

Droslump's rumbled commands break us apart. "Return, rapion! Return to your clan and honor the Four-Winged Condor. Return!" he yells. As if it is he who causes the Severation!

Mirko rubs his cheek once more on mine, and his wing caresses my bald head. He flaps before me. Our eyes engage. In his pupil, rapion rise from the Cliffs.

He howls, falls backward, slips onto an air shaft, and spins into the darkness. His feathers wink away; his keen tears open my centerself. No other rapion join us.

Face down, I collapse on the stone and wail for Mirko.

Eventually, I lift my face and crawl upright. In the darkness, the Amph is empty. From now on, Droslump's only a bad memory to vex my sleep. Sleene will become my living nightmare once more.

Bawling, I tenderly touch the cuts on my head and my cheek, and clutch my aching belly. *Creator Spirit, compel the Cliff to welcome the one you gave me to tend, the Singer you created.*

I suck in a broken breath through swollen, cracked lips and creep along the edge of the pillar, feeling for handholds. There; to the west. I sit up and lower myself over the edge, my hands and feet finding indentations until a path emerges down the slope. The emptiness swells behind my ribs.

At the desert floor, the sand gives beneath my boots, and my ankles roll. I lean against the mesa and rest my wet forehead on the cool rock. My lips press the surface and cling. The amulet is a lump between my thigh and the stone.

Creator Spirit, here I regained Ratho. I saw Thae sacrifice herself, and entered the Chamber of Verities, where I discovered the palms of your prophets. Here I loved my rapion and returned him to the Cliffs. Make swift his flight and fill my lonesome steps with comfort.

I peel my dry mouth from the rock. Above, the stars point home. I take a hesitant step away from the mesa and begin my trek.

STOPPING

Water spills from my sack, cascading down the front of my poncho. I swallow the bit remaining in my mouth and fall to my knees. The Severation weighs like four rapion on my back when there are none at all. The angst heaves the water I swallowed up out of my mouth until I gag and sputter.

Dropping to the dirt, I slip off my pack and roll onto my back. The night oozes past. Maybe if I wait till morning, the severing will not weigh so, and daylight will speed me home.

I lay my head on my pack, crimp like a hatchling around my amulet, and shiver. Sidewinders, owl burrows, and lizards could be beneath or beside my body, and I wouldn't know or care. I am without Mirko. How will I bear it?

CHAPTER 79

DELIVERY

hills prickle my back. I toss. My eyes squinch tightly. "No, no,"
I pant, but the cold vision opens nonetheless.

Frana braces herself in the birthing chair
and adjusts her grip in the handholds.
A great cry flings from her wide, open mouth.
Her skirts ride high
above her red-lined belly.
Her thick thighs tremble
as she grunts loudly,
screams,
and bears down.
Father stands at her back,
his hands fastened to her shoulders.
Sleene squats beside her,
his wings an arching black omen.
Frana's fleshy knee smacks
against the priest's concave cheek,
but his eyes remain locked on her sacred place.

A midwife pries a babe
from Frana's squelching womb
making her cries peter into weeping joy.

Sleene licks his lips,
and he grasps the babe.
The infant is swallowed in his palms.
It gurgles, cries,
and squirms facedown in Sleene's clutch.
Father kisses the top of Frana's head.
Wet strands of hair cling to her face
and her eyes snap wide.
Puffing, she leans forward, which
flops the afterbirth
into the birthing bucket.
The midwife lifts and cuts the cord.
She presses a cloth to Frana
while tugging her skirts
past the priest's sharp shoulder.

The baby screams.
Sleene flips it over in his bloody hands.
"A girl," he spits, and stands quickly.
"But she is not my firstborn," Father proclaims.
Sleene raises his eyes.
"But she is the woman's."
Frana gasps.
"It is Madronian law as of last spring,
to limit these worthless additions."
He hangs the shrill baby by her foot,
dangling her before his disgusted face.
"This is the first from a second binding
for me to declare or dispose of."

"But the law was not
announced to the R'tan!" Father shouts.
Impervious, Sleene shrugs;
his wings echo the dismissal.
"And that thwarted the complaints
for me to bear.

The law will touch few, and now it is known further."
He cups the shrieking babe in his hands once more.

The newborn's cry is joined
by Father's and Frana's,
like the keen of mourning rapion.
The babe
is Frana's firstborn girl,
my sister.

CHAPTER 80

TAKEN

My body stiffens on the sand. My teeth grind.

As Sleene tugs a strip of brown linen from his belt,
the midwife manages to knot the cord
against my sister's belly.
Sleene shrouds the babe.
He pauses.
"Or did you wish to declare her male?"
His eyes wait on Father.
Frana mouths, Yes, please, yes!

"No. No, not again," Father whispers
into Frana's ear.
"I can't do that
to another.
No matter the *Oracles*
or what other R'tans
might or might not choose.
The life I've given Tiadone,
the falsehood she must live,
it eats at me.
I can't face another questioning me,
why, why, why?"

He looks up to Sleene.
"No. I'll make
no declaration."
He turns his head
from my sister.

"Please! My child," Frana begs,
and tries to get to her feet
but falls back into the chair.
"We will declare her male!"
Sleene ignores her wishes.

The midwife clings
to her birthing bag and bucket
and cowers against the wall while
Sleene dangles the babe
knotted in cloth.
She swings and wails at his side.
Father frantically turns back.
"Please, just let her live," he sobs,
falling down on his knees.
"Heretic, mark your words,"
Sleene growls,
"or it will be two lives lost this morning."

Frana grasps Father's shoulder.
"Please!" she screams.
In the tumult,
Sleene gestures peace and goodwill
from the Four-Winged Condor.
He flings open the door.
Dawn floods into the room
and then is cut off
until his wings clear the threshold.
The babe is gone.

The midwife scurries out,
stopping to empty the birthing bucket
on the refuse heap.
Father cries,
"When was this new law enacted?
When?" he babbles.

Frana lurches upright in the birthing chair,
squeezing the handholds.
"We should have declared her male!"
"I can't!" Father shouts back.
"Look at Tiadone, Frana. Look at her!
In constant danger of a slip,
believing there is some power
in a worthless amulet?
Performing work maybe not even
suited for her sex?
She lives the lie I chose.
She is forced to live
as if she is not
the woman she is!
You don't know
the burden I carry
for what I have given to my daughter.
You just don't know
what it is like to try to explain
and fail,
both of you knowing
the farce
picked for my frailty."

"Well, then, let's retrieve my baby
and leave the land, husband!"
Father's face slackens like melting wax,
and he pulls from her grip,

rocking on his knees.
"I
can't.
No.
I can't!
Tiadone will return.
I must at least be here for her — him.
And there's
my land.
My land holds
my centerself.
And don't you have your own rapion
still at the Cliffs, Frana?" His voice warbles.
"I do." She answers. "But I have strength to leave!"
She wipes her upper lip on her sleeve.
"I have not glimpsed my Miniata
since Severation.
And our child has not yet received a rapion.
Listen to me!
I understand you do not
want to declare the babe a male.
But Tiadone already is.
She needs no oversight now," Frana begs,
"and we need no land
if we are together!
Leave Tiadone the land."

"No!" Father hunches and curls
his empty arms around himself.
"It is me or the child, Frana," he whispers.
"I cannot leave."

He looks up to her teetering on the chair.
Blood rings the floor about her pale feet.
"Do not leave me, love!" he begs,
and grasps her ankle.

"Please,
do not mark me with abandonment
when I am already
marked for heresy!
You have forgiven me once.
Please forgive my weakness now,
and I will be the man I promised.
None would ever accept my company
if you left me, Frana.
And remember!
Remember that our next child will be accepted
no matter the sex!
Have mercy, woman."

He curls more tightly and covers his head
with his free hand.

She pulls her ankle free from him,
slides from her perch,
and tumbles into the wetness on the floor.

She weeps and shakes
while he lies huddled alone.
"What of your belief in life ..." she begs.
He only sobs in return.

Finally,
Frana lifts her weary head
and gathers her skirts
in her trembling fists.
"For you, I will remain," she rasps.
"For you only.
Oh, my daughter,
forgive me!"

CHAPTER 81

DECISION

Huhh, aughghgh!" I roll to my knees and hack the bile from my mouth. The morning sun shines in the spittle dangling from my chin. I wipe it on my shoulder and lurch to my feet.

"No!" I yell, pace, drag my hands over my bald head, kick stones, and punch the air. I stop and plant my feet wide. "Why the new Madronian law and a girl, Creator Spirit?" I shriek.

I drop to my stomach and stretch out prone. "Why?" I bellow.

A morning dove hoots in the distance. Something scuttles over my outstretched arm.

The full truth of what I have heard bombards me like a flash flood. My father called my life a lie! A lie he would not want to tell his second daughter.

I am female. Truly female!

I scream and kick the dirt, thrash my arms. My entire life I have denied my feelings. No wonder I love Ratho! And now I learn this, after I've given him up forever?

Life has greater value than obedience to a ruler, whispers in my mind. It is the *Oracle* Father's openly rejecting.

The thought gains momentum as it runs and catches more and more truth. My sister has worth as a female. My centerself rises above the waves, refusing to be drowned.

I shove myself up. "My father loves his land more than me or my sister!" My voice strikes out in all directions. "He loves his own back more than the Creator Spirit!"

Spitting, I yell, "I hate you, Father!"

I drop to my knees and hands. I hate him for declaring me male and making me live a lie. I hate that he wouldn't leave R'tania for me. I hate that I can't have Ratho, even though I love him. I hate that this amulet is utterly powerless. It is a sack of stink and disappointment, a sack of nothing. After I've succeeded in every way. After others in the village might be encouraged to save their own babes, he kills my sister!

Sweat scorches my cuts. I curl my fists and toes and strike the sand. "I hate that you are weak, Father! I am worth more than this false life." I howl long and deep. "And my sister is worthy just like I am!"

Perspiration beads on my back, my fiery scalp, and behind my knees. The landscape stills, waiting, waiting for me.

I sit up on my haunches and yank at the sinew on my hips until it snaps. The belt falls free. My amulet lies detatched from me in my fist; the long cords dangle like veins.

With my teeth, I tear open the pouch, spitting the tie away. I scream out my own power and overturn the sack. The second heart lands with a thud as ashes and hair puff up into the air.

My fingers grasp the organ, then fling it as far as I can throw. It smacks sand and rolls out of sight. I scramble the rest of the sinew cords, pouch, ash, and hair into the dirt, mixing it with my tears. Mixing and mixing it, choking and mixing.

Finally, the rage gives, and I fall like I've stepped off a cliff. I drop over in the dirt and let my tears stream unhindered. Let them tumble over every lie and every loss.

As the sun rises higher, stretching rays of warmth out to me, I'm finally able to slowly sit up. A gulp of water from my sack flutters over my quivering centerself. I douse my hands and face and rub dry on my poncho.

I wait silently with my truth. My shadow stretches behind me while songbirds flit, lizards creep, and spiders scurry.

When I am strong enough to stand, I project my new course on the horizon. I head for the Scree.

CHAPTER 82

SEARCHING

"Where are you?" My heart beats erratically before the sinking sun. My fingers thrust between the flat stones left by the ancient glacier, clawing through silt and overturning small boulders.

My thick tongue fills my dusty mouth. "Creator Spirit, help me find her!" I cough.

My boots slip on a patch of dry, flaky lichen, and I thud onto my tailbone. Nothing's in sight but scrub brush, rocks, and dirt.

I lurch up and run. Frantic, I search among the shale, trip, and stumble over a knoll. Sliding on the rocks that clatter like broken dishes, my hands scuttle for a hold, and my trousers tear at the knee.

I finally slow to a stop and sit up. The Scree is enormous. How can I find one babe? The reality smacks my hope to pieces like the shale jumbled around me. I crawl forward and get to my feet one more time.

"Where are you?" I yell. Silence fills this dead place. I must try another way. Taking small steps, I begin to circle around this particular spot. My circles widen, and I cover more and more distance knowing I haven't missed her within the area.

I turn wider, and a strip of cloth waves to me. I scramble to the material. Little bones are left meshed in blue linen. A small finger, perhaps. The rest of the body has been eaten by predators.

I turn and vomit. The watery slosh runs between the stones. The bones are not my sister, because Sleene wrapped her in brown linen. I rinse my mouth with water and spit.

I kneel by the remains of the little girl. Carefully, I cover her with smooth stones. The last bit of blue material rests under a white rock. I place my palms on the pile and quickly pray for the parents. *Creator Spirit, maybe you can forgive them.*

Stumbling upright, I begin my march again. I walk and scan until my knees pop trying to be rid of my body's weight.

"Help me," I beg. I drop to all fours in the shifting rocks.

"Creator Spirit, help me; help your creation," I pray. I keep my head down and sway. I remain void, cannot even lift my head with the weight of my failure.

Screeeeeee rips apart the air. I lift my eyes to a rapion twirling above me, watch as it swoops low and rises. "Mirko?"

It is impossible!

I rub my eyes to clear my vision. The rapion flies past again, and this time, it bursts with song. "Praise the Creator Spirit!" It is my rapion!

Crying, I leap and shout, and wave and laugh. Mirko wings to the right and whistles for me to follow.

My centerself flies equally high as I chase after him for an explanation and a touch to know he is real. I gain knolls and dash through ditches until Mirko twirls upward and floats on an airstream.

"Waaa, waaaa, waaaa!"

"My sister!" I hustle up a high ridge. There! At the base! She raises her fist and waves it furiously.

Far to the side, I stumble down the slope to avoid triggering rocks that would crash over her. I run across the base to the tiny bundle and fold my hands around her. I lift her close.

Little beads of sweat shine across her sticky, angered brow. She cries more fiercely, and punches the air. I thrill at her fight for life.

"Mirko, my sister!" I yell and raise her to the sky.

Mirko bugles, dives, and circles both of us. My sister hiccups, quiets, and gazes at the sparkling brown feathers drifting down on us.

CHAPTER 83

VINTI

*S*till flying high, Mirko leads me to the far, far edge of the Scree, to an overhanging rock beside a meandering stream. Beyond the sweet-smelling water, the vast desert stretches. The nearest Patrol post would be a bit to the south and few miles out. Across the desert are the C'shah. I turn the thought in my mind like a pebble tumbles along a river bed.

Despite my overwhelming joy and the demands I shout to know how Mirko has left the Cliffs, he wings away without a touch. My fingers ache as he diminishes in the distance.

Was that all we might have? Did he leave the Cliffs only to help find my sister, and now he returns because of Madronian fear? Like the two Cliff rapion did at Thae's death? Or as the league that battled the Shingkae in the border skirmish? Each retreated to their home again.

My breath enters with a jerk; what I received is more than I could expect. Mirko is well, and I now hold a child. So, I try to turn from the thought that I have again lost my rapion.

Heading to the flowing water bordered by clumps of short yellow irises, I soothe my whimpering sister. "Shhh," I say. "I will wash you while I think of what we must do next. Like find food."

I unwind Sleene's shroud and lift handfuls of tepid water over my sister's skin. Her body curls to receive them. The dried birth fluids rinse away, and her cries quiet as the droplets glisten on her beautiful body.

I've just finished wrapping the babe in my poncho and nestling her in warm rocks when Mirko's *screeeee* returns again.

I stand slack-jawed, staring at the stolen sack of goat's milk he drops into my hands. He lands at my feet and rubs against my leg. My fingers nestle in his crown, and the cinnamon scent puffs around me.

"You, you —" I stammer. He shifts in my tears as I drop to my knees and nuzzle my face to his. He hums and rubs his eyeridge against my forehead. "You returned!" I bawl. "But will you, will you leave again? Will you return to the Cliffs to live?"

He whistles and shakes his head no. There is nothing to do but hold on to my rapion and weep. We will not be kept apart!

Following Severation, Mirko has somehow been allowed to return to me. Is it because I have not returned to the village? Or that he is a Singer? Whatever the reason, thank the Creator Spirit. *Oh, thank you, my God!*

Mirko nudges my arm. "The baby! Yes!"

I dry my eyes and scan the bits of vegetation until I spot a tuber cactus, and rush to it. "How did you ever manage the theft?" I blurt. Mirko struts with bravado around my whining sister.

I peel the skin from the cactus and prick a hole in the end after pouring in Mirko's gift. Greedily, my sister latches onto the nipple. I gather her close and watch the milk disappear from the case into her puckered mouth. Before today, I'd never held or been so close to an infant. Her smallness is enormous.

Captivated, Mirko snuggles close and sings a soft lullaby. The three of us sit in a tight circle below the great blue sky.

When the tuber is nearly empty, my sister's little eyelids flutter. I remove the suck, and a milk droplet escapes the edge of her puckered lips. I brush her cheek dry with my thumb.

Mirko and I gaze at her beauty. Each sweet, warm breath from her pursed mouth fills the space around us.

Yet, it's time to face my new reality. "I've torn away my amulet, Mirko."

He lifts his head.

"There's no place for me in the village without it. Nor if I take my sister from the Scree." I whisper the obvious. Mirko blinks, and I rip my thoughts from Ratho.

"And I won't leave my sister to perish, Mirko." He adds a hum to my declaration. "I'll traverse the desert and find a new home. On my own or even with the C'shah. Maybe they would welcome us. An outlying village? My survival skills are honed, thanks to the Madronians. And I have my own strength and yours!" Mirko fluffs his feathers.

"We can break through the patrol without notice. It will only take perfect timing and then a blessing for protection from the Triumverate." Mirko chortles encouragement as my voice wavers.

My centerself leaps as hope tries to bloom inside me. "Maybe the place will offer new friendships—and books even! A copy of the *Oracles*, possibly. You never know, right? Maybe we will ... find acceptance, dignity, and respect among strangers, Mirko. Each of us!" He nods firmly.

The babe stares up at me. In her fist, she clutches one of Mirko's fallen feathers. I lift her to my shoulder and pat her back.

"Tell me now, Mirko," I demand. "What has happened? Were you welcomed at the Cliffs?"

He tweets. "And you found your clan?"

He whistles and ends with his special notes for Baesa. "Please," I laugh. "No details!" Mirko bobs his head and grins.

"But how have you left them? How have you left the other rapion?"

He sings a tender string of notes. "Because you are a Singer?" He grins and moves close, resting his head upon my shoulder.

"And you truly will not leave me again?"

He sits back and shakes his head. My huge inhale cleanses everything inside of me. With my sister in one arm, I envelop Mirko with my other and hold him tight. It is more than I ever even thought to hope; we are united for life.

The babe releases a little sigh, and I curl her in my lap. Mirko and I watch her drift to sleep.

"Vinti is your name," I sniffle. "Ancient R'tan for girl."

CHAPTER 84

THE BEGINNING

Despite my protests and concerns, Mirko scavenges items Vinti needs from farms throughout the night and very early morning. While my sister sleeps in the dawn, and Mirko flaps off one more time, I hunt to distract myself from lingering worry.

Before long, I've speared a lone winder, but I will have to cook it later as the smoke might draw attention. I fill my water sacks. Standing at the water's edge, the rippling coolness calls to me.

I strip off my clothes. Forget these tight knots on my breast wrap! I slice through them with my knife. The long sheaths flap in my hand with the breeze. Opening my fingers, they flutter into the stream and twirl away.

I turn to the rising sun and roll my head. The warmth curves over my nakedness as I raise my arms high. My necklace — the carved piece of my javelin strung on my leather tie — rests between my breasts.

I slowly enter the clear water. Dunking and resurfacing, it is strange to not feel the weight of wet twists on my shoulders and to see my bald head in the reflection. The stream's flow tugs and pulls. My open sores ease as I soak in the river.

Finally cleansed, I walk from the water with the sun sparkling in the droplets on my skin. In my created glory as a woman, I clasp my hands and chant praises to the Creator Spirit for my life.

My notes drift to silence as the stream continues the song. I add prayers for Mirko's safety and quick return.

Dry, I shrug on my trousers and tunic, but my breath continues to rush freely into my unbound chest. I climb the nearby boulder and scan the distance. I don't see Mirko yet, but far on the horizon is a smudge. My father's home. A trail of smoke rises in the autumn air.

My throat closes back my tears of confusion. Hatred. Love. Longing. Pain.

All will believe I perished on the return from the mesa. Maybe my amulet will be found. Winder, desert cat, loss of my way, or depression over Severation could have claimed me. They will believe I am dead, as Tiadone truly is. Will others not declare daughters now? I grieve if that is so, but right now I have to care for Vinti and myself.

"Good-bye, Frana. Good-bye — Father," I choke out.

"Jenae, may love and health find you. The best possible," I relent. It is sad our visions will likely fade with her Severation.

"Ratho, my portion, I will miss you so much." I look to the sky, but my tears rush down my face anyway. "I will miss you most, my love. As a woman, I will always love you."

In my mind, he laughs under my straddle. He walks before me, looking back over his shoulder with his brows raised in cheerful challenge. His fingers touch my cheek, and his head rests on my breast wrap.

I crouch down and weep for our loss. My tears speckle the rock. One droplet falls next to another. It is a long time before I can lift my head.

Ratho will find another to love sooner with my absence. There will be no pining or arguments between us of what we can't have. He will think I have perished, and ultimately it will free him. My chest constricts to think of him loving another, especially Jenae. But it is my dearest wish for him.

I groan and get to my feet. "Move on, my friend. Move on. Find love," I whisper, and clench my arms around myself, squeezing the pain I'll always carry for Ratho.

I turn my back on my home and skid to the rocks below. Vinti still sleeps, so I slice up the winder I caught.

Finally, Mirko back wings down to me with more supplies in someone's burlap sack. "Praise the Creator Spirit! You are safe!"

He raises his eyeridge at me and snorts.

"Well, the sun was up. You were moving around the village in full daylight. Don't you think that causes me worry?" He chitters. I smile at his skill and bravery, seeing he has brought all we need and extra.

We feast on dried goat meat, and I pack the rest he has scavenged along with the winder I killed. Someone has lost their long undergarments from their drying line, another has lost a baby bunting. There are rags we might use for baby wraps, while some wife won't find her biscuits cooling on the window frame.

"You are incorrigible, Mirko!" He licks the last of the meat from his talons.

An idea tosses back and forth in my head. With Mirko's savvy, I believe it is the right choice.

"There is one more thing, Mirko." He flutters to my feet, eager to do my bidding. "My centerself struggles over sending you once more, except it is for a kindness."

He bobs his head and sits up taller.

I pull my necklace off and place the leather in his talon. "If we delay our leaving until tomorrow, tonight you might fly this to my home and hang it from the withered pine."

Mirko nods.

"And this." I go and scoop up the shroud from the river's edge. Mirko takes it from me.

"I have found pity in my centerself. I want my father to know that Tia lives, and both Frana and Father to have comfort that their infant daughter survives. If either chooses to tell Ratho, it is their choice. Maybe in this, they might know best."

Mirko chortles, and before I can stop him, he rushes up and across the sky.

"No, wait!" I cry. "I meant tonight under darkness!" He doesn't stop. That prideful bird! The bit of my javelin swings freely below his pumping body while the linen clenched in his talons streams behind him. His scree calls back to me that this is a good act, and he is brave.

Now I must pray for his safety again! Why couldn't he wait until tonight? Ugh! I should have known. He is nearly out of sight already. My centerself crashes with worry.

May the Creator Spirit have mercy on Mirko. I have brought this danger on him. I must be more careful with my wishes!

Though it is true that this is a good act. If I am prone to pray for mercy, I can at least try to give it to my father and Frana.

I smother my fears with work. I rearrange our supplies for the best fit in the bag. When Vinti awakens and cries, I rinse her and my poncho in the stream, then bundle one of the rags around her little backside. Cozy in the bunting, she eagerly takes a feeding. Her round eyes watch me intensely, until she finishes and snuggles down for another nap.

The milk sack is still quite full, but we will have to find the cactus that bleeds when you pierce its wide lobes. The white juice is a good substitute for milk. I do not want to endanger Mirko again, and we have a desert to cross. They are common enough plants. We will find them.

Right now, there are no more preparations to make. It's only a matter of waiting for Mirko's return. I lie down, curl around Vinti, and pray.

CHAPTER 85

LIFE

I wake to Mirko tickling my cheek with his beak. His smile stretches as wide as is possible. I sit up. "Mirko!" I launch my arms around him. "You are safe, you wicked bird. Please don't worry me like that again!"

He shrugs and winks. "Well, did you hang them in the tree?" Vinti stirs, so I lower my voice. "Did you?"

Mirko whistles.

"Thank you! You always amaze me!" I pet his head and ruffle his crown.

He ducks out from under me and raises his foot, still ringed by my hair.

I try not to grin, and fail. "What more have you stolen?"

He opens his talons. A small red-shelled egg drops into my hand, and I gasp.

"What? No! Did you?" He bobs on his toes. "You took Vinti's placenta from Father's compost and presented it to the rapion?"

Mirko clicks his beak and raises his head.

"And that is why you wouldn't wait. You knew this egg would be available soon?" He hums and smiles.

My eyes fill with tears one more time. Newly laid, the warm, Miniata egg smells of anise. The red glows in my palm.

I press it gently to Vinti's lips, then tuck it safely against her belly behind the wrap rag. Soon I will weave a net so that she can wear it around her neck. Vinti has her own rapion!

"But can we leave the Cliffs now that Vinti has a charge?"

Mirko thrums, and the answer springs to mind. "For years we can, right?" He nods. "We can leave, eventually returning the shell to the secluded Stone of Offering! Later, we might release the Miniata from the desert edge. You are magnificent, Mirko!" I bend and kiss his head, before he lifts into the air with a song.

As I gather up our supplies, his whistle rises on the wind, and it sounds so like my name. "Tiaaaaaaaa!"

I laugh outright with a joy like never before welling from my centerself.

Vinti wakes and coos. She reaches up and clasps my finger. I pick her up and hold her close to my chest.

"We are worthy, Vinti. This is life!" I follow my soaring friend out into the open desert.

Aquifer

Jonathan Friesen

Only he can bring what they need to survive.

In the year 2250, water is scarce, and those who control it control everything. Sixteen-year-old Luca has struggled with this truth, and what it means, his entire life. As the son of the Deliverer, he will one day have to descend to the underground Aquifer each year and negotiate with the reportedly ratlike miners who harvest the world's fresh water. But he has learned the true control rests with the Council aboveground, a group that has people following without hesitation, and which has forbidden all emotion and art in the name of keeping the peace. And this Council has broken his father's spirit, while also forcing Luca to hide every feeling that rules his heart.

But when Luca's father goes missing, everything shifts. Luca is forced underground, and discovers secrets, lies, and mysteries that cause him to reevaluate who he is and the world he serves. Together with his friends and a very alluring girl, Luca seeks to free his people and the Rats from the Council's control. But Luca's mission is not without struggle and loss, as his desire to uncover the truth could have greater consequences than he ever imagined.

Available in stores and online!

BLINK

Remnants: Season of Wonder

Lisa T. Bergren

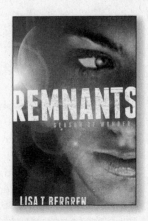

Their coming was foretold for years.

Andriana is a Remnant, one of several gifted teens born on the seventh day of the seventh month, of the seventy-seventh year, and destined since birth to act as humanity's last hope against the horrors that now plague everyday life.

After years of training in stealth and warfare, Andriana and her Knight protector, Ronan, are finally ready to follow the Call and begin the life they were designed for. But as they embark with the other Remnant on the first of their assignments to course-correct humanity, they quickly discover that the world beyond their protected homes is more dangerous than they imagined.

The Sons of Sheol will stop at nothing to prevent Dri and Ronan from rescuing any individuals sympathetic to the Remnant's cause. As the Remnants attempt to battle the demonic forces, their enemies close in on them, placing all of humanity in peril. Dangers intensify, but so do Dri's feelings for Ronan—the one emotion she is not meant to feel. In the midst of their mission, Andriana must find a way to master her feelings or risk compromising everything.

Available in stores and online!

BLINK

Doon

Carey Corp & Lorie Langdon

Veronica doesn't think she's going crazy. But why can't anyone else see the mysterious blond boy who keeps popping up wherever she goes?

When her best friend, Mackenna, invites her to spend the summer in Scotland, Veronica jumps at the opportunity to leave her complicated life behind for a few months. But the Scottish countryside holds other plans. Not only has the imaginary kilted boy followed her to Alloway, she and Mackenna uncover a strange set of rings and a very unnerving letter from Mackenna's great aunt—and when the girls test the instructions Aunt Gracie left behind, they find themselves transported to a land that defies explanation.

Doon seems like a real-life fairy tale, complete with one prince who has eyes for Mackenna and another who looks suspiciously like the boy from Veronica's daydreams. But Doon has a dark underbelly as well. The two girls could have everything they've longed for … or they could end up breaking an enchantment and find themselves trapped in a world that has become a nightmare.

Captives

Jill Williamson

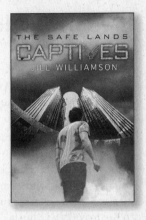

One choice could destroy them all.

When eighteen-year-old Levi returned from Denver City with his latest scavenged finds, he never imagined he'd find his village of Glenrock decimated, loved ones killed, and many—including his fiancée, Jem—taken captive. Now alone, Levi is determined to rescue what remains of his people, even if it means entering the Safe Lands, a walled city that seems anything but safe.

Omar knows he betrayed his brother by sending him away, but helping the enforcers was necessary. Living off the land and clinging to an outdated religion holds his village back. The Safe Lands has protected people since the plague decimated the world generations ago ... and its rulers have promised power and wealth beyond Omar's dreams.

Meanwhile, their brother Mason has been granted a position inside the Safe Lands, and may be able to use his captivity to save not only the people of his village, but also possibly find a cure for the virus that threatens everyone within the Safe Lands' walls.

Will Mason uncover the truth hidden behind the Safe Lands' façade before it's too late?

Available in stores and online!

BLINK

Merlin's Blade

Robert Treskillard

Merlin's greatest weakness could become his greatest strength.

When a meteorite crashes near a small village in fifth-century Britain, it brings with it a mysterious black stone that bewitches anyone who comes in contact with its glow—a power the druids hope to use to destroy King Uthur's kingdom, as well as the new Christian faith. The only person who seems immune is a young, shy, half-blind swordsmith's son named Merlin.

As his family, village, and even the young Arthur, are placed in danger, Merlin must face his fears and his blindness to take hold of the role God ordained for him. But when he is surrounded by adversaries, armed only by a sword he's named Excalibur, how will he save the girl he cherishes and rid Britain of this deadly evil ... without losing his life?

Book includes location map and detailed character index.

Available in stores and online!

BLINK